Praise for Sky of I

"For many years I have had the privilege of publishing Ghahremani's charming, nostalgia-laced words of wisdom on the pages of iranian.com. Now it's time for a broader audience to enjoy a heartfelt journey into a fascinating life."

—Jahanshah Javid, *iranian.com*

"Ghahremani is that wonderful kind of writer who tells compelling stories in rich and lyrical language. ***Sky of Red Poppies*** is an illustration of her mastery of both."

—Judy Reeves, author of *A Writer's Book of Days*

"Ghahremani understands the many conditions of the human heart... ***Sky of Red Poppies*** is a compassionate story of universal truths."

—Yvonne Nelson Perry, author of *The Other Side of the Island*

"Sky of Red Poppies is the moving story of relationships tested under the most stressful of human conditions, that of a repressive government. Ghahremani writes with warmth, humanity and a poet's vision."

—Claire Accomando, author of *Love and Rutabaga*

"Set against the backdrop of a pre-revolution Iran, ***Sky of Red Poppies*** is a poetic epic and a powerful read."

—Jonathan Yang, author of *Exclusively Chloe*

With best wishes,

[illegible signature]
2012

Other books by Zohreh Ghahremani

SHAREEK-E GHAM (PERSIAN, 2000)
THE MOON DAUGHTER, AVAILABLE 2011

Zohreh Ghahremani

Sky of Red Poppies

A NOVEL

Author's Note: Although parts of the story were inspired by the recent history of my homeland, this is a work of fiction. Any resemblance to actual persons, living or dead, or locales, is entirely coincidental.

First trade paperback published in the United States of America
by Turquoise Books.
Turquoise Books and the "t" logo are trademarks of Turquoise Books.

For inquiries, please contact:
Turquoise Books
P.O. Box 178664
San Diego, CA 92177
Please visit our Web site at www.turquoisebooks.org

Cover painting, *Sky of Red Poppies* © 2004 Zohreh Ghahremani.
Book layout designed by Anton Khodakovsky
Cover designed by Susie Ghahremani
Author photograph © Elvee Froehlich

Grateful acknowledgment is made for permission to reprint "The Poppies" from translation of Coins in a Fountain © Manouchehr Neyestani.
Translated from Persian to English by Zohreh Ghahremani.

Library of Congress Control Number: 2010932442

ISBN-13: 978-0-984-57160-4 (pbk.)

10 9 8 7 6 5 4 3 2 1

Printed in the United States of America.

To my dear friend Shahin,
who taught me the true meaning of devotion…

ACKNOWLEDGEMENTS

DEEP GRATITUDE WOULD REQUIRE ME TO THANK EVERYONE who has helped me along the way. However, this book evolved over a span of a quarter century, which in turn makes it impossible to name everyone who has contributed.

First, and foremost, I am grateful to my sister, Ladan Khazai, my very first reader, whose encouragement turned me into a writer at a very young age. Also, I might not write if it weren't for the lessons of Mrs. Pouyan and Mrs. Mahmoudi, my schoolteachers, who put me under the class spotlight. Wherever they may be today, I hope they'll see this long overdue product of their hard work.

Thanks to my husband Gary, for giving me the chance to pursue my lifelong passion. His subtle presence has been my column of strength.

My children, Lilly, Susie and Cyrus, used their immense talents to help Mom in every way they could. They have been my inspiration and, in a role reversal, it was their 'pep talks' that at times gave me the strength to go on. Each day they continue to teach me something new and for that, I love them even more.

I am indebted to Yvonne Nelson Perry for teaching me the "craft" of writing, to Shelly Lowenkopf for telling me I was born a writer, Sid Stebel for showing me where the story begins, and to John Daniel and other Santa Barbara friends and conference leaders for believing in me.

≈

I AM GRATEFUL to Jahanshah Javid for publishing my articles only hours after they reached him. Deep gratitude goes to Judy Reeves and the entire crew at the SDWI for catching me each time I was about to fall and to Dr. Ali Gheissari for walking me through the corners of history that seemed otherwise obscure.

I deeply appreciate friends and colleagues who took the time to read the entire manuscript and share their reflections: Rebecca Sloan, Barbara Sack, Bryna Kranzler, Michele Yeppiz, K. Ryan, Mike Sirota and my own Lilly and Susie. Thank you all for helping me to clarify those otherwise vague passages.

Finally, I say to Anne, Claire, David, Katherine, Nirmala, Michele, Patrick, Pennie, Lita, Bill and many more writer friends: Thank you for being the best co-travelers on this journey and for your guidance while understanding my accent!

My Iranian-American friends throughout the country, specifically those in Chicago and San Diego, you have been my sanctuary and have provided me a venue for my work long before this book. You are my family away from home.

If I have not mentioned your name, it is simply to limit the length of this page. Please know that by holding this book in your hands, you are showing your lasting support and for that I will forever remain grateful.

No one ever told me I would remember the hands that sculpted me or that words could be carved into my soul. Now, decades later, I reminisce, sometimes with affection but often not. It is the flexibility that I miss the most about my childhood. It is the remembrance of that innocence which helps me to forgive myself for who I have become.

PART I

The Clay

One

AT SIXTEEN, I WAS CURIOUS about many things, but the activities of the Shah's secret police weren't among them.

Mashad, my hometown in northeastern Iran, had awakened to a rainy day in the spring of 1968. Taking hurried steps, my ponytail bouncing, I skipped over the puddles along the sidewalk. There were no students on the street, which could only mean I had already missed the first bell. Just as I was about to cross the street, a car sped past me, splashing rainwater over my clean shoes. I looked up and saw a black Mercedes making a u-turn. It parked in front of my school. Two men got out, wearing huge sunglasses that covered half their faces – the kind that had become a trademark of the secret police. The mere sight of them was alarming, though I had no reason to think their presence had anything to do with me. Instinctively, I ducked into the small bookstore across from the school.

Warm air and the smell of a kerosene heater filled the shop. As I barged in, the old clerk rose halfway from his chair.

Trying to catch my breath, I forced a smile despite the pump, pump of blood rushing to my ears. I turned to the display window and picked up a book of calligraphy. I was familiar with those books and their curved letters, for I had stopped by many times to admire their colors, ornate frames, and miniature designs. But on that day, I looked beyond the case and watched those men across the street. They passed under the blue and white sign, *Shahdokht High School For Girls,* hanging over the tall wooden doors that led to the walled-in schoolyard. One of them pushed the heavy door, and they both disappeared behind it.

"Don't be scared, Miss Roya." The clerk's voice gave me a jolt and I dropped the heavy book.

A bookworm by reputation and a frequent visitor to his shop, I was no stranger to the old clerk. "They're not looking for *you*, are they?" he asked, his calm tone indicating he already knew the answer.

I shook my head and wondered if he could hear the crazy beat of my heart.

The headline I had seen the previous week in the paper flashed before my eyes, "Following Tehran University's riots, SAVAK arrested two students." The acronym SAVAK referred to a security establishment, but to me it had a frightening resonance. They seemed to have nothing better to do than put students in jail. That morning, while my father listened to the news on the radio, I had overheard something about a possible execution sentence for the arrested students, calling them "the enemies of the crown and throne." I did not dare ask Pedar any questions as he had strictly forbidden such discussions, but now wondered if there could be a connection. Lately, university students had organized too many demonstrations, and I'd heard the demonstrators distributed pamphlets insulting the Shah. But that was in Tehran. What could SAVAK possibly want in my school?

"These days they are everywhere." The clerk said. "It's enough to horrify even an old timer like me."

I studied him with caution. This was the first time someone outside school had talked to me about the secret police. Unsure if I could trust the man, I turned my attention back to the window. My father had cautioned, "Never discuss such matters in public, especially not with strangers." One never knew who might be a secret agent. "It could be a cab driver, a relative, even someone at your school," he had said.

The shopkeeper took a step closer. "Don't worry, Miss Roya," he said, as if reading my mind, "I'm not one of *them*."

I shot him an embarrassed glance.

The second bell rang. The man picked up the book I had dropped and put it back in the window. Then he went to his chair behind the counter and said, "You better run along now."

Outside, heavy rain had turned into drizzle, and a crisp morning breeze crept inside my overcoat. I clutched my books tighter and hurried past the back of the Mercedes. Its engine was idling and, for just a second, I saw the silhouette of the driver beyond the steamed-up rear window. I looked away before he could notice me and scurried in.

No one was in the schoolyard, but I peeked through the glass doors to make sure the men weren't in the hallway. Once inside, I took the stairs two at a time and ran to my class.

In the murmur of our classroom, other students didn't seem to notice my tardiness. It surprised me to see that our teacher was not yet present. Mr. Elmi always arrived a few minutes before the bell to write on the blackboard. In his curved calligraphy, he would inscribe a verse, a quotation or a topic to be discussed during his lessons of literature. Defying school's petty rules had gained our favorite teacher the nickname *Jenab* – His Excellency. Not only did he design his own curriculum, but he also didn't hesitate to break any rules he disagreed with. He even rebelled against the teacher's dress code by wearing a sweater, and he rolled his tie into a ball, which he stuffed into his pocket. Unpredictable as he might have seemed, he was never late to class.

Small groups gathered in different corners of our classroom, chatting in hushed voices, even whispering. The acronym, SAVAK, mentioned here and there, created a frightening hiss. Before I had a chance to join in, someone shouted, "Jenab's coming!"

We all shuffled to our seats and a charged silence filled the classroom.

The door opened and there came Mr. Elmi, hauling his overstuffed briefcase and taking long, heavy steps. He did not bother to greet us and his face was tightened into a somber expression. I could not tell if he was anxious or just angry. He dropped his case on the desk and went straight to the blackboard and wrote in large letters: *I think, therefore I am.*

Twenty-eight teenage girls stared back in silence. I counted on him to be bold enough to discuss what was going on downstairs. Coming directly from the office, he had to know. But as he continued to stare at the class without offering any information, I thought that perhaps he, too, had decided to be cautious.

Gentle rain rapped on the window, and the smell of burning coal wafted from the corner fireplace. Our classroom rarely had enough heat and now the thought of secret agents being in the building made it impossible to feel warm. Jenab ran his fingers through what was left of his graying hair. With half-opened lids of droopy eyes, his expression held a permanent gloom, but now his eyes seemed darker than ever.

"*Some* days do not begin on the best note," he said. "But I ask each one of you to remain in the present. Here and now. Because despite what's pouring out there," he nodded to the outside, "our jobs are within this classroom." He turned to the window, as if to mask his apprehension.

I couldn't decide if his words were just a reference to the rain or if he had hinted at what went on in the office. Fierce wind outside pushed the raindrops in different directions and the little squares of glass created a jigsaw puzzle of a gray, rainy day.

Jenab was the only teacher who spoke his mind and earlier, I had feared it might be him that those men had come for. I ran a list of other teachers in my mind, but none stood out. It was no secret that any negative comments about the Shah or the slightest hint of sympathy for the oppositionists could bring in the SAVAK. But no one else at our school discussed such matters, nor had I heard of any demonstrations in our town.

Someone coughed and, as if the sound had pulled Jenab out of deep thought, he shook his head and went back to the blackboard. Reading the phrase he had written, he tapped a finger under each word, leaving a clean dot with each tap. "If what Descartes said is true, then your existence began here." He smiled his crooked smile. "With me."

I believed that, and took the deep silence of my classmates to mean they did too. Jenab thrived on his aptitude to mesmerize an audience and at sixteen, I adored those who could mesmerize me.

"There's a unique substance in each one of us," my favorite teacher finally began. "A raw matter known as the child, pure and impressionable, flexible enough to be molded. Like clay." His hands slid around an imaginary mound in the air. "Unfortunately, in the heat of the kiln we call life, that clay hardens and before we know it we've become the unchangeable adult." He went back to the window and stared out at the sky hanging there like a wet sheet. "If an adult is dissatisfied with the outcome, he can take on a variety of colors to disguise his true identity. But deep down, the hardened clay maintains its true form."

Jenab went back to his desk and extracted a book from his briefcase. I studied him amid the shuffling sounds of notebooks and pens as my peers prepared for a lesson in literature. Jenab opened his book, cleared his throat and began to read in his slow, deliberate manner. He may have distracted the rest of the class, but I felt let down. On any other day I would have considered his monologue a true lesson. His philosophical approach to literature gave flavor to the monotony of textbooks, but this time he wasn't persuasive enough. I didn't grasp his clay metaphor. Too young to fathom the end, I could not believe my free spirit would ever be caged.

"Think about that," he concluded, tapping on the side of his head with an index finger. "*Think!*"

"Isn't thinking forbidden?" A husky voice rose from the back of the classroom.

I turned to find Shireen Payan, one of the two girls who shared my bench, had just arrived. Seeming to be in no rush to take her seat, she leaned against the wall with her arms folded across her chest. Her question, and especially the sarcastic tone, sounded like a hint at our social restrictions, perhaps even a bold reference to that morning's incident. With the secret police entering the fortress of our school, her remark had a chilling resonance.

"Miss Payan, please take your seat," Jenab said. "There will be plenty of time for discussion." And he turned his attention to the roll call.

Shireen wove her way through the desks and sat on the edge of her seat.

Our classrooms had rows of old wooden benches fixed to the floor. Each bench would seat three and seats were designated based on the height of students. Consequently, my small size had placed me in the first row, next to Shireen Payan. On my left side sat Tahereh Ahmadi, a shy and quiet girl, who most of the time seemed almost invisible. I only heard her speak when a teacher called on her, and even then she sounded as if she had to will her voice to come forth. Shireen was also the quiet type, but she showed confidence and was great with words, as if saving her gift of speech for serious matters. She often arrived late, and was one of the first to leave, so we seldom spoke. Sometimes I wished they had paired me with a fun student, someone with whom I had more in common.

Impressed by Shireen's courage, I studied her with newfound interest. Her headscarf had slipped back, revealing silky, shining brown hair. I had seen her coming to school wrapped in her *chador,* the dark cloth that covered her head to toe. In Mashad, many girls from fundamentalist families observed their *hejab,* wearing a similar wrap in public. But chadors were not allowed inside the walled-in school, so most of them exchanged their chador for a headscarf, while a few didn't bother to cover their hair at all.

As if sensing the weight of my stare, Shireen looked up. Her defiant question had sparked a connection, and as our eyes met, the clarity in her brown eyes reminded me of pure water that allows one to see all the way through.

"Miss Roya Afshar," Jenab called on me. "Would you take this down to the office?" He signed the attendance form and tossed it on my desk.

Normally, the vice-principal wanted that form on her desk no later than fifteen minutes after the bell. This had been my job every morning, but on that particular day the office was the last place I wanted to be. I hesitated and, when Jenab did not return my worried gaze, I rose, took the form and left.

Shireen's words echoed in my mind. For nearly a year, this girl had shared my desk like a stranger. How bizarre it was to hear my own thoughts in someone else's voice. Halfway down the hallway, I could hear other teachers from behind the doors, and the knowledge that school was in order gave me a semblance of security.

As I reached the staircase, I heard strange hushed noises downstairs. The sound of hurried, small footsteps in the hallway below, a screech as something was dragged, followed by a hushed cry. A voice rose above it all, "Shush, you!"

I tiptoed down a few steps, but it wasn't until I had turned around the landing that I could see feet on the mosaic floor below: Two pairs of men's shoes, clean and polished, and a pair of muddy sneakers crisscrossed between them. I took a few more hurried steps to see more, but as soon as I recognized the men I had seen outside, I froze in place.

Each man held onto one of the girl's arms and they pulled her while she tried to resist by pressing her feet on the tiles and struggled to free her arms. When I spotted Mrs. Saberi, the vice-principal, trailing behind them I thought my heart would jump out of my chest.

With no trace of compassion on her dark face, I knew she wasn't about to help that poor girl.

As the girl continued to kick the air, her skirt was jammed against one of the men, exposing her thighs and underwear. Her face was still hidden under a mound of unkempt hair. Why wasn't anyone stopping them? I wished I could leave, run, or hide, but my knees shook so violently I could not take another step. Pressing my body against the wall, I prayed no one would see me.

Mrs. Saberi held the door for the men while they lifted the girl and carried her outside. Just before the doors closed, the girl turned her head and looked behind as if to beg Mrs. Saberi for help and for an instant, I had a glimpse of her face. I recognized a senior from my sister's class, one whose name I did not know. Outside, the sun had just emerged and its glare on the wet asphalt was blinding. The last thing I saw was the light reflecting off one of the men's bald heads and soon they were gone.

Mrs. Saberi turned on her heels, looked up and her fiery eyes found me halfway down the stairs.

"Afshar?" she said in a surprised tone, but hostile enough to make me shudder. Unable to find my voice, I waved the attendance sheet in the air.

She motioned me forward and as soon as I came within reach, she snatched the paper from me with one hand and grabbed my ear painfully with the other.

"You saw nothing," she hissed. "Not a thing!"

I nodded hard and the tears that had pooled in my eyes found their way out.

"As far as any of you lot are concerned, that girl walked out of here of her own free will, and she was accompanied by her father." She shook me as if to make sure I understood. "One single word about *this* and you'll be next." When she finally let go, my ear was on fire. She gave my shoulder a nasty shove and nodded to the stairs. "Now, back to your own business."

Feeling her burning eyes on my back, I ran up the stairs and only stopped to catch my breath in the upper hallway, where I could not be seen.

Inside the classroom, Jenab was writing something on the blackboard. When I entered, he turned around, studied me, and briefly glanced out of the side window into the yard. When he faced me again, he had a compassionate expression, as if he knew what he had put me through. Then again, maybe he had known all along, maybe that was precisely why he sent me, to spy, bring him news.

I waited for his permission to sit down and he nodded to my seat without a word.

Had Jenab been by the window moments before? And if so, had he seen anything? I wondered if he could sense my deep fear, or if he'd ask me about it later. For the rest of the hour, I did not understand a word he spoke and was grateful for not being called on.

As soon as the recess bell rang, I ran out and looked for my sister, Mitra. I found her near the outdoor basketball court among her classmates. Though only a year older, compared to me Mitra looked like a grown woman. Tall, elegant, her wavy brown hair fanning down to her shoulders, she had none of my mousiness.

"Maybe it was only for questioning," the girl standing next to Mitra was saying.

Mitra didn't seem pleased to see me there. "What is it, Roya?" she asked coldly.

"Can I talk to you?" I said.

Annoyed, she whispered something to her friends and walked over to me.

"What?" she said.

"Was the girl... er... the one who left... a friend of yours?" I tried to work my way around the question without mentioning SAVAK.

"Alieh?" Mitra chuckled. "What in the world would I have in common with her?" She looked as if the thought had given her a bad taste. "What is it to you, anyway?"

"Why did she go with *them*?" I asked, making her departure sound voluntary.

"Shhhh!" Mitra glared at me and, without another word, she turned around and walked back to her friends.

For the rest of that morning, we had free sessions while teachers gathered in the office. A few parents also came in. Students speculated, but none of us had an idea what went on in those meetings, and teachers who came out of the office acted as if nothing unusual had happened.

At noon, I saw Mitra leave with her friends as she often did. Usually my father's driver, Akbar, would be waiting for me, but that day Pedar needed the car to attend an important meeting with the Mayor. Any other time I would have welcomed the stroll home, but now the mere thought of leaving the walled-in school and walking alone gave me the creeps.

In the heat of an unseasonably warm sun, steam rose from the damp sidewalk, extracting its earthy scent. In the distance, a melancholic *Azan* invited the pious to noon prayer. Mashad, our town of a half a million, was named for the martyrdom of the eighth Shiat Imam, and it also housed his shrine. Its two contrasting groups of residents formed a unique society: worldly city folks outnumbered by devout Muslims. I was neither.

With short distances, little traffic, and a two-hour break at midday, most people went home for their biggest meal of the day. The noon traffic seemed to be at its peak. Students from the boys' high school around the corner were participating in their usual girl watching, and a few drove back and forth in their father's cars, making noise. Each time a horn sounded, it made me jump. I looked over my shoulder and was relieved to see most cars in colors other than black.

Delicious aromas filtered out of windows: sautéed onions, seared lamb with turmeric, saffron rice. I wondered if Alieh would be home for lunch.

We lived in the northern part of Mashad, the more modern section of the city and away from the Shrine in its south. Most people I knew defied religious rules; faith seemed to matter to them only in times of need. Here, houses were taller and brick walls isolated their vast gardens. With a population of only a few thousand, my neighborhood became its own small town. Did the people behind those walls have any idea what had happened earlier? Did anyone hear Alieh scream, or were SAVAK's cars soundproof?

Halfway home, I had talked myself into a calmer state. After all, in a society as harmless as ours, such incidents were uncommon. That girl must have done something dreadful. I wondered if Pedar would hear about this, and if so, would he ask me about it? I wasn't sure if my promise to Mrs. Saberi included keeping it secret from even my father. I had never lied to him before.

Golestan Avenue was quiet and I could hear a water fountain gurgling behind a wall. As a child, I used to picture my mother in one such mysterious garden, alive, strolling among flowers.

Now I knew better.

A *joob* ran along the trees that lined both sides of the street and, although one couldn't tell if its murky water were irrigation or waste, it provided room for tiny floods of rain. The breeze swept a piece of paper over the sidewalk and dumped it into the current. As it sailed by, I saw words scribbled on it. A note?

While the crumpled paper made its way downstream, I imagined it taking a coded message across town to someone on the south side, the way secrets were passed in the movies. I had no idea where Shireen Payan lived, but judging by her dark *chador* I pictured her living close to the shrine and among the pious. On my occasional visits to the Holy Shrine, where my mother's tomb lay, I had passed through those neighborhoods. This *joob* may eventually join the bigger one that ran through Bala Khiaban, where pilgrims used the foul smelling water to do their wash. That piece of paper could be my note to Shireen, a message from a free girl to one incarcerated in *hejab*. But what would such a note say? And was I really free? Confined by Pedar's rigid rules, and now with Mrs. Saberi's threat looming, I would be the last person to define 'freedom'. 'Thinking' seemed to be forbidden, no matter which side of town one lived on.

At the end of Golestan Avenue, I looked back and made sure no one had followed me, then turned into our alley. What was wrong with me? Did I think SAVAK had nothing better to do than chase me home?

Years ago, another *joob* had run through the middle of this alley, but when the narrow passage forced a few cars into the water, the city cut the trees and covered the stream, turning our shaded alley into just another paved cul-de-sac. The rapid increase in Mashad's population chiseled away at what little charm it had: Horse-driven carriages turned to hideous orange taxis, iron gates replaced aged wooden doors, and the one-of-a-kind stores that used to be full of copper pots, clay jugs and burlap sacks piled with herbs, now sold mostly imported plastic goods. Only the beauty of the surrounding Kooh-Sangi remained – a majestic mountain reflecting shades of blue, purple and orange against the backdrop of a sky that, at sunset, took the color of saffron.

The iron doors leading to our garden were wide open and I saw Mammad, the gardener, carrying an armful of twigs and looking like a tree with long legs.

Not the most graceful home in Mashad, ours originally had only one building. But with three children, we needed more rooms. When my mother refused to sell the house, Pedar joined the town's architectural trend by building a white modern structure adjacent to the old brick one. Not only did the new construction fail to complement the old, its tin roof and stucco exterior clashed with the charm of the verandah, tall columns, and French windows of the original. Unattractive as it may have been, the new building, equipped with a modern kitchenette, running hot water and a small indoor bathroom, offered the conveniences the old one lacked. Only Hassan, the cook, found no use for it as he continued to do his cooking in the old kitchen on wood stoves.

"Roya," my aunt called out before I had climbed the stairs, "go and hang up your uniform, lunch is about to be served."

The mere sight of her, standing at the top of the stairs, leaning on her walking cane, gave me a feeling of security. Had I felt closer to my aunt, I might have confided in her about what had happened at school, but loving as she was, she also kept her distance. I said hello and turned toward the old building.

The hallway felt cool and I noticed Mitra's door was still closed, indicating that she had not arrived yet. I imagined her making a stop at the local ice cream shop, where the boys also hung out. My aunt did not approve of it, but that seemed to make no difference to Mitra. I wished she would hurry home. Should Pedar have any questions, I didn't want to face them alone.

In my small room, I put the books on my dresser and shed the grey denim uniform from over my clothes. This thin, gray dress served much like a lab coat and Auntie insisted I remove it at noon to make sure it stayed clean.

With no previous experience in parenting, my aunt made up her own rules as she went along. Years ago, when my mother died, Pedar had asked Auntie to move in and help to raise her late sister's children. Despite my grandmother's what-will-people-say protests, Aunt had agreed. Crippled from childhood polio and with no plans to marry, she must have grown tired of living with Grandmother. Sometimes I dreamed of romance between her and Pedar, but I never saw any signs to give merit to my childish fantasy.

In the family room, Pedar sat in a wing chair, reading the Kayhan newspaper. My brother, Reza, was on the rug with a pile of torn envelopes, searching for stamps to add to his collection. The math textbook next to him reminded me of my promise to help him with an overdue assignment. The eldest of three children, he was not a good student and had failed frequently enough to now be one grade behind me.

"What took you so long?" he complained.

"Sorry, Reza-*joon,* I was just putting away my uniform."

He made a face.

"You boys are so lucky," I said. "No uniform for you. All you need is a suit."

"Why, Miss Roya," he said mockingly, "you don't seem to have noticed *this.*" He pointed to his shaved head, a boys' school requirement.

I felt sorry for Reza. With a face covered in pimples, a mustache that hadn't decided if it would fully grow or not and the shaved head, he looked more like a convict.

"Baldness suits you," I said. "You look like that movie star Yul Brenner."

Reza put the crumpled envelopes in the trashcan. "Thank you. Now Yul's going to wash his hands before lunch." He picked up his stamps and left.

Pedar smiled at me over his newspaper. "Reza's lucky to have you," he said, his green eyes shining behind silver-rimmed glasses. "I swear, each day I see more of your mother in you.

My physical resemblance to Maman brought about similar comments from everyone, but Pedar thought I also had her demeanor. Aware of the gap her loss had left in his life, I didn't know if this pleased or saddened him. Or both.

Mitra arrived last. I never understood how that girl managed to break every rule and get away with it. Not only did she refuse a ride to school, she ordered tight-fitting uniforms, wore little under them and kept her uniform on throughout the day. Regardless of how many times people complimented me on my eyes, I would gladly have given one of them for Mitra's figure. Taller than me, with all the curves in the right places, she had no trouble turning heads, especially when walking past the boys' school.

"How was your meeting with the Mayor?" I asked Pedar.

He folded his newspaper and put it away. "Same old thing. General Nazemi was there, too," he smiled. "I have a feeling he wants to join our Poker group."

"Everyone seems to want to rub elbows with you," Reza said with a smile.

"Not just with Pedar," Mitra said. "Big shots love to rub elbows with all the other big shots." She frowned and asked Pedar, "Didn't you say General Nazemi was a thief?"

Pedar chuckled. "He is. But we're not talking about a group prayer here, are we?"

Mitra crossed the room and I noticed a small book sticking out of her pocket. Intrigued, I pulled it out and read the title, *The Little Black Fish*.

"How cute," I said.

"Give it back," she shouted, but before she had a chance to take the book, Pedar rose from his chair and snatched it away.

"I'll have none of that trash in my house!" He hurled the book at a wall and it landed open on the rug. All happiness was sucked out of the room.

Mitra took a step toward her book, but my father grabbed her arm.

"It's *my* book," she said.

"Not if I have anything to say about it. Where did you get that?"

Confused by his rage, I asked him, "Isn't it a fairy tale?"

"A fairy tale?" Pedar grunted, then pointed to the book as if the author himself were sitting there. "In his father's grave!"

He let go of Mitra's arm, but neither of them moved.

"That man was nothing but a damn communist. I don't want any of you near a word he had to write." He glared back and forth at Mitra and me and, raising his index finger, he added, "This, young ladies, is not a request. It's an order."

"That's not true," Mitra said in a defiant tone. "He was a harmless teacher, SAVAK had him killed because –"

"Shhh!" Pedar wrapped his arm around her head to cover her mouth. His next words were a harsh whisper. "The affairs of the secret service aren't any of your business!"

Mitra's skin turned red under the pressure of Pedar's hand and her eyes welled with tears. When he finally let go, his fingers left a white impression on her flushed face. Despite the warmth of the kerosene heater, I started to shiver.

"For your information," Pedar went on, "that man died in a swimming accident."

"Swimming in winter?" Mitra gave an angry laugh. "In a frozen river?"

For a brief moment, Pedar seemed as surprised as I to hear that detail.

"Rumors and murky stories are not my concern," he said.

"Not your concern?" Mitra's voice had gained new courage. "Don't you see? Innocent people are put in jail for speaking up, students disappear for no reason." Her lips quivered. "Why, just today there was another arrest, this time right in my school." She sounded as if she thought Pedar could have done something about that.

"An arrest at *your* school?" Pedar's eyes found mine. "You knew this?"

"I didn't believe it," I lied. "Mrs. Saberi said that girl left willingly, and with her father."

"Ha!" Mitra said. "You're so dumb, Roya." She turned to Pedar. "SAVAK came for one of my classmates and nobody knows why."

Pedar sat back in his chair. His expression softened a little, he took a deep breath and said, "Nothing happens 'for no reason'." When he looked up, his face had regained its tender expression. "My job is to make sure my own children won't disappear."

But my sister didn't know when to shut up. "If you don't – "

No sooner had she opened her mouth than Pedar's anger returned. He raised a hand in the air. "That will be quite enough from you!"

I thought he was going to strike her, but instead he lowered his hand and touched the back of his neck.

Pedar, though powerful and temperamental, never raised a hand to his girls. I felt ashamed for having allowed the thought to cross my mind.

"If any of you should ever do a thing to shame me, I will kill you myself!" he said, one hand shaped like a revolver, pointing at us. The look he gave me penetrated deeper than a bullet.

What would Jenab have to say to this? Think? No, not in my family. Once, when Reza had mentioned his thoughts on taking a part-time job, Pedar stopped him in mid-sentence. "Your job, young man, is to study. Leave the thinking to me." Pedar did most of my thinking for me, too. The one time I gathered enough courage to express my passion for the pursuit of a career in literature, it became clear he had other plans. "You'll be a doctor," he had said, his fierce tone ending the discussion.

As Mitra flopped onto the sofa and covered her face, I knew she was crying but didn't dare go to her. It had been such a strange day, I couldn't guess what might happen from one minute to the next. I stared at the garden beyond the sheer curtains. We could have frozen in that position if my aunt had not interrupted.

When Auntie opened the door, she let in a whiff of cinnamon and stewed tomatoes from the dining room. She studied us for a few seconds and then walked over to me and put a hand on my shoulder as if to make sure I was okay.

"I thought I heard the two of you," she said to Mitra and me. Then she asked Pedar, "Are they having another one of their silly quarrels?"

Pedar shook his head.

My aunt must have heard more than she'd admit, but I figured she was trying to diffuse the situation.

"Lunch is served," she said.

Pedar left his chair and we followed him.

Sitting across the table from my father, I played with my food and took a few bites, but I could not bear the heavy silence and, halfway through, I excused myself and went to the garden.

The yellow Dodge was parked in the driveway, where Akbar seemed to be drying it after a wash. The chrome sparkled in the sun. "A bride for the street," he pronounced, pointing to the car. When I didn't share his enthusiasm, he said, "That was a quick lunch, Miss Roya. Is something the matter?"

Akbar had been with us since before my birth and we considered him a member of the family. I nodded to the building. "Mitra and Pedar had one of their squabbles."

He sighed. "Ah, that Miss Mitra!"

"No," I objected. "This time it was me who started it."

"You?" Akbar shook his head and laughed. "You couldn't start a fight if your life depended on it! Miss Mitra needs no help to make your father angry."

I forced a smile and went to sit in the shade of an old mulberry tree. If I had not made such a mess of things, Mitra might have even let me read the forbidden book. I dreaded Pedar's anger and couldn't bear the sorrow that came into his eyes after such outbursts. I knew that for the following days he'd be extra nice, as if trying to mend a broken link.

Unlike my uncle, who thought beating my cousins was the best way to discipline, Pedar had so far saved the whippings for poor Reza.

Still, each time he punished Reza, I could not rule out the possibility that I might be next. That little book with a fish on its cover had been like a raindrop plopped from a gathering cloud. Though I read many books, their full power was unknown to me and it had never crossed my mind to look for answers in forbidden books. My father ruled over his family with one eye on how the king ran our country: One man, one law. Not only was there a large portrait of the Shah in Pedar's office, but also he talked about "His Majesty" with pride, as if he idolized the man.

I had seen the Shah close up. It had been during one of the royal couple's visits to Mashad when I, as the top student in second grade, had the honor of representing my school. The following week, a picture of me in my ruffled dress, offering a bouquet of white gladiolas to ex Queen Soraya, appeared on Pedar's desk. When the Shah divorced her, that picture remained, but as he remarried, Pedar added a picture of him with his new bride, Queen Farah. However, my father's patriotism went beyond displaying pictures or naming his only son Reza, after the late king. Every time the radio played the national anthem, he made us stand to hear its praises to the Shah.

"May our King of Kings live forever. Pahlavis made the land of Iran a hundred times better than the ancient times..."

But were things really better? Oh, thankfully SAVAK couldn't hear my thoughts! Deprived of open discussions, my mind returned to the scene in the hallway, with a girl named Alieh. Like the impending blackness of a moonless night, my horror grew and grew.

If the mention of police brought to mind a sense of security, the addition of the word, "secret," gave it an ominous resonance. When the Shah appeared in public, several men in dark sunglasses followed him closely. Nobody spoke about them, but most people knew exactly who they were. For years I had assumed them to be bodyguards, but one day, while my friend Nelly and I watched a newsflash, she presented the details.

"They sure act like bodyguards, but those are the SAVAK agents, and they're not just looking out for possible assassins. They watch everybody and wear those obnoxious glasses so no one has a clue where they're looking." Then, as if discussing a horror movie, she described SAVAK's treatment of political prisoners. "They burn their bodies with cigarettes. It's the worst burn because tobacco holds a high temperature," she explained. "I've even heard they rape them," she whispered.

At the time, I had dismissed Nelly's exaggerated report, but now wondered if there might be some truth to her stories. After all, her father worked in the city and he came home every day with such accounts. Not my father. Cooped up on his sugar beet plantation, he only encountered such information during his brief stays in town, when he socialized with other big shots. Then again, if he did hear anything newsworthy, we would be the last he might share it with.

I had to push away such dark thoughts. Whatever Alieh did to concern the SAVAK must have been serious. I had done nothing wrong and there was no reason for this fear to run through me. I dusted myself off before heading back inside. Maybe Alieh didn't have the kind of father who watched over her the way mine did. As long as I stayed away from matters that Pedar considered none of my business, no one would come after me.

Not exactly free, but perhaps it was enough to feel safe.

Two

LOOKING BACK, I can't understand what I liked about my school. With no fun included in its rigid curriculum, our school didn't even have a gathering place for the more than five hundred attending students: no gym, no lunchroom, not even a library. As an improvisation, I had created a private sanctuary at an isolated window. We passed by it on our way up to class, but no one seemed to notice it other than me. The old window on the staircase landing overlooked the mud roof of the greenhouse. Its pane was cracked and paint had started to peel off the sill. When the old custodian clumsily applied duct tape to the broken glass, I knew it wouldn't be replaced any time soon. But, as neglected as it was, in spring my window transformed into the frame for a magic garden.

Every year in March, gentle rains drenched the roof of the greenhouse. In a matter of weeks, awakened by the soft drizzle, hundreds of red poppies magically appeared on the mud roof below. I could even smell their toxic scent through the broken glass.

A week after they took Alieh, I realized I was still looking for her. Every morning I stood by my window and checked students as they climbed the stairs. When she never showed up, most of us began to believe the rumors of her transfer.

"Transferred?" Nelly had said. "That's nonsense. Nobody has seen her since that day, not even the girls who live in her neighborhood."

When the last of the students came up the stairs, I decided it was time to stop searching. After all, I didn't even know the girl. Facing my window, I rested my forehead on the cold glass and stared at the now-green roof, where a few poppies had already opened. Soon, hundreds of buds would transform that ordinary roof into a fairyland. Persian New Year was approaching, and the poppies had come to celebrate *Norooz*. Year after year, at the moment of vernal equinox, nature promised a fresh start – but now I could only think about the end: end of a year, the end of feeling safe at my school.

The poppies and I had a connection. Of all the flowers, regardless of the variety and array of colors that made our garden so spectacular, this fragile bloom came the closest to my heart. Each day, the poppies seemed to reflect my own feelings of joy, sorrow, even fear. They spoke of hope, yet the danger hidden in their essence, that mysterious scent of opium, frightened me. With no gardener to care for them, they rose from that mud with pride, yet bent their heads in modesty. And, although I didn't know a happier shade of red, they reminded me of sorrow.

Sensing someone's presence, I glanced over my shoulder and saw Shireen Payan standing a few steps away. I turned back to my window, hoping she would leave.

"I see you like my flowers," she said and took a step closer. "From one poppy lover to another, I'd like to share a poem with you. Want to hear it?"

Taking my silence for a 'yes,' she unfolded a piece of paper and began to recite, waving her free hand in the air as if to conduct the words into their best performance.

You are gone, yet so many flowers come with spring
I am not the only one serenading you; thousands sing.
I scatter on your path one sky of red poppies.
Red poppies, the mirthful gems of the evening brimming.

What a bitter contrast those words carried, a mixture of hope and deep loss. I had no idea what Shireen was trying to say, or to whom the word 'you' referred.

That poem had the sound of a serenade written for a love lost, and from the first verse, my mother's image came to my mind. I listened to each word as if it were meant for her. Maman had left a big hole in our lives and although we lived our days outwardly in a normal fashion, none of us were the same. My family avoided talking about her, but like a cloud, her absence cast a shadow over our home. Shireen's poem had touched a deep chord, too deep for words, too private to share.

"That poem is pure nonsense," I said.

"Nonsense?" She looked at me, wide eyed. "Of all the things to say!"

"Modern poetry," I chuckled. "One *sky*? Exactly how many poppies is that?"

"Gaaaa!" She threw her hands up in the air. "You're no different from the rest of Jenab's class."

"What's that supposed to mean?"

"I bet if he read this out as his own, everyone would want a copy, and you'd be no different."

I stuck to silence. She'd never know what went on inside me.

"Imagine," Shireen spread her arms wide. "One sky! That means beyond measurement, more than one can imagine. One sky, damn it!"

After a long pause, I said, "I'm sorry. I did not mean to be rude."

"There's no need to apologize. I shouldn't have presumed you'd let me inside your thick shell."

"Oh," I said and was not going to say more. But when she stood there without another word, I added, "There's no shell. I just don't have anything to talk about."

"Everyone has something to talk about. I know what it's like to feel lonely."

"I have lots of friends," I said and sounded defensive.

"Friends?" She said with a sneer, but then dropped her sarcasm. "It's all right, Roya. You don't have to say a word if you don't want to." She patted my back and left.

I looked at my flowers one last time before going to class. A breeze fluttered their soft petals, revealing their black hearts.

~

Shireen's strong perception had impressed me. She had seen right through the jolly demeanor I displayed. Although neither of us mentioned our conversation, from that day on we had a connection.

In a society where poems seemed to be woven into the fabric of our lives, a major segment of literature studies focused on classic Persian poetry. We had to memorize the works of masters such as Saadi, Hafez, and Rumi. Teachers encouraged us to share our favorite poems, and those of us who experimented with poetry, read samples of our verses in class. Of these, Shireen's were the best and Jenab made no secret that she was his favorite. As time went by, I also noticed a peculiar relationship between the two, a combination of antagonism and mutual respect.

Jenab praised her poetry, but sometimes his critique came across as harsh.

"You have a talent for stringing your words, Miss Payan," he said after she had read a poem about a child found frozen under a bridge. "But I'd strongly suggest a revision on the part about people's indifference. Isn't it possible that others may share some of your concerns for the poor?"

Looking back, it's now clear that Jenab had known the difference between Shireen and the rest of us. He must have seen her potential, perhaps wagered that she would be the one to leave her mark. However, at the time, I thought he pushed her too much.

A few weeks later, I was again at my window when Shireen joined me.

"Something about our school is changing," she said while watching the students rush to class. "Or could it be me who sees things differently?"

For an instant, I had the urge to tell her about Alieh's arrest. But I didn't know Shireen enough to trust her with such a dreadful secret.

"Maybe it's a little of both," I said.

~

Pedar announced that his work wouldn't allow him to be in town for Persian New Year and suggested we join him at our summer home at the farm during the spring break.

So far, we had only spent our summers at the village, so this would be my first *Norooz* there.

"What kind of a family would celebrate Norooz in a remote village?" Mitra had protested. But Pedar, disregarding our objections, had the last word. "I want my entire family around me to ring in the New Year."

On the three-hour ride to our farm, Reza, Mitra, and I were packed in the back of the Land Rover among suitcases and boxes of food. Auntie sat in front so she could stretch her bad leg. Akbar swerved around the potholes with ease, as if he had memorized every one.

"I hate going to that damn village," Mitra said. "It makes me sick to think of all the fun I'll have to miss."

"Oh, stop whining," Reza said. "We do what we have to."

"That's just it. Why do we have to?"

"So Pedar can continue his work and still have a bit of a celebration." Then, as if finding his own reasoning inadequate, Reza added, "Besides, I'd rather be with Pedar at Norooz, wouldn't you?"

"With all the new films during Norooz?" Mitra said. "You must be joking. With or without Pedar, for once staying in miserable Mashad could have been fun."

I agreed with Mitra. I loved the cinema, and even enjoyed the visitors who called by on New Year, not to mention receiving crisp new money from the elder relatives.

"City folks would give anything to switch places with you," Akbar offered.

"You're a fine one to talk," Mitra said. "You go on rounds with Pedar all the time, but we are prisoners."

Reza chuckled. "Some prisoner. Fussing with your hair, reading magazines..."

Mitra hit his chest with the back of her hand. "Shut up!"

Auntie turned around and glared at her. "That's quite enough, young lady."

That put an abrupt end to their quibbling, and for a time we rode in silence.

When I recall those road trips, I can still see the back of my aunt's head, her graceful neck, and wavy brown hair. The image has remained so vivid that even now on road trips her fine silhouette almost remains a fixed part of the view ahead.

I turned to the side window and gave my attention to the vast desert.

~

The next day, I woke up to the sound of birds in the orchard. After taking some tea and a small breakfast of *lavash* bread and quince jam, I selected an old book from Pedar's bookshelf and went outside. Spring had barely begun in this cold mountainside village and only a few trees showed early signs of a pale green. I found a clean rock by a tree and sat down to read. I don't know how much time had passed before I heard rustling and looked up to find my childhood friend, Zahra, approaching. "God bless you, Miss Roya, what are you doing out here?"

"Hey!" I screamed before getting up to embrace her.

She smelled of dust and burnt wood. Her cotton shirt felt warm against my cheek. She stroked my face with calloused fingertips and flashed her white teeth. "It's a blessing to see you, Miss Roya." Her deep blue eyes blazed from her dark skinned face. "But I can't stay," she said. "I'm expected back to work at the loom."

"Can I come? I promise I won't try to help."

The memory of the previous year's disastrous experience made us both laugh. One day, I had tried to give her some help and ended up ruining her day's work. The effortless moves of her hands had led me to believe anyone could do it. When she left the loom for a few minutes, I gave it a try. But the heavy bobbin slipped and dove to the floor and, as I tried to retrieve it, I broke more lines. By the time Zahra returned, her fine arrangement had tangled into a mess and I was in tears. Hours later, the damage had been repaired before her grandmother discovered it.

"Please take me with you," I insisted.

"You'll be bored, Miss Roya."

I felt uncomfortable with the formal way she addressed me, but Auntie had said I must get used to that. "Bored around my Zahra?" I laughed. "Never."

The villagers worked for my father and they acted as if he owned them. As a child, I had enjoyed the fuss, but now the undeserved attention made me anxious. I imagined how Shireen would frown at me for being treated like a little princess.

Outside the orchard, Zahra walked with confidence and led the way through the field. Barefoot, she found the best path, avoiding pebbles and tumbleweeds. The ruffles of her long cotton skirt swayed with each step. She seemed carefree.

From the distance, a cluster of mud huts came into view. Beyond the pale green willow trees, a dilapidated stone wall separated the houses from the field. As we neared, curious children came and watched. A baby left under a tree fussed as flies stormed her face. I wondered if Shireen had ever seen such a village. Nearby, someone burned cow manure and the smoke made me cough.

"Oh, may death strike me!" Zahra said. "I brought you through this smoke. Come, *khanoom*. Come inside and I'll make you some tea." She shooed a rooster away and pushed open the cracked, wooden door.

Zahra and her grandmother, Bibi, lived in the center of the village. Her mother had died from tuberculosis before she turned one. Her father – a shepherd – spent most of his days in the mountains. Maybe what made Zahra so special, indeed why I had singled her out in a crowd of native children, was our shared miseries. But I never mentioned it to her because I had a feeling that in her mind, the rich had no cause to feel miserable.

We ducked to enter and stepped into the cool semidarkness that smelled of old clothes. When my eyes had adjusted, I looked around the familiar room. A column of light shone through the round opening in the mud dome and dust particles danced in it. With no furniture, the large loom took most of their living space. A bedroll placed against one wall and a thick felt mat in front of it provided a place to sit, sleep, and live. The corner wall was blackened with soot from a wood-burning stove. An indentation in the wall served as shelf and there sat a ceramic dish of newly grown wheat grass, the one and only evidence of a Norooz.

I thought of all the food my aunt had packed, all those cookies, candles, and frills. I imagined Zahra and Bibi, eating what was left of their cumin candies, admiring their bowl of wheat grass, and saying prayers to thank God for their blessings.

The summer before I started high school, Auntie had put a stop to my "inviting village people to *the big house*." Her words laid the first brick for the big wall that now separated Zahra's world from mine.

I put my arms around Bibi's bent back as she held my face between rough hands and kissed my face. Her misty eyes, now covered with a gray film, resembled a dying candle. The year before, Pedar had sent her to town to see the eye doctor; unfortunately her condition could not be helped and she was going blind.

Bibi took the black kettle from the stove. "I'll get some water for tea."

I halfway rose to help, but Zahra pulled at my sleeve.

"Let her be," she whispered. "It makes her feel useful."

By the time tea was ready, a crowd of children had gathered at the door. Zahra wiped the felt mat with the palm of her hand and put a small ceramic bowl of black tea before me. She put a few pieces of yellowing candy next to it and shooed the flies with the wave of her hand. Had Bibi saved that candy for Norooz?

Wispy giggles came through the door as children peeked through its cracks to get a glimpse of the master's daughter. I wanted to offer them some of the cumin candy, but figured that was all Zahra had. Besides, she kept cautioning me not to encourage them.

"It's bake day," Bibi said before she left. She lifted a copper pot filled with flour and balanced it on her head.

"For God's sake, leave the heavy stuff for me," Zahra said and rushed to take it.

Bibi's hand stopped her. "I don't need help." And away she walked.

"Thank you for the tea," I shouted after her.

Bibi turned around and smiled her toothless smile. I watched her, balancing the pot on her head with one hand, swinging the other at her side. As she waddled away, her long denim skirt made lazy waves around her ankles.

Zahra sat at the loom and was soon absorbed in her fine work. The rhythmic tap and click made for a pleasant beat. Her old scissors lay on the floor, the handles padded with faded rags.

I focused on asking the question that had been bothering me since I came in. "Zahra, what's your salary?"

She gave me a bewildered look. "Salary, miss?"

"You know? Wages. How much does Pedar pay you?"

Apparently, I had asked a ridiculous question. "*Agha* owns this entire village," she said, as if stating that he also owned everyone in it.

"How much?" I insisted. And at this she looked up.

"I guess as much as everyone else," she said.

I looked at her, saying nothing.

"We have this house," she added, and gestured to the bare room as if it were a castle. "Two goats, a good ration of grains and some kerosene during cold weather. . ." She thought for a few seconds. "At the feast of *Ghorban*, the pilgrims coming back from Mecca sacrifice lambs, and we get free meat and–"

"That's *it*?"

She glared. "I forgot, we get a year's supply of tea, sugar, and tobacco, miss."

"What about clothes?"

"Bibi sews mine, but every Norooz, the master – may God keep his shade over our heads – sends us money for new ones." And she smiled with pride.

My full and cluttered closet flashed before me.

"Are you telling me that you don't get a fixed salary?"

"Me? No. My father does."

"What if you get sick?"

Zahra chuckled. "The things you ask, miss! Sickness and health is in God's hands, but second to Him, we have the master to turn to."

I wondered how many of her answers were programmed, and if she was the little parrot, repeating what her grandmother had said over and over. *Think!*

As Zahra gave her attention back to the loom, her peaceful expression told me that perhaps she had found better things to think about, things that had nothing to do with the world beyond the dilapidated walls of Golsara. What was it like to believe that the world consisted of a desert and a few villages here and there? Could one wish for things that we did not even know existed?

Later, we shared a lunch of rye bread and yogurt. While I did my best to chew the stale bread, Zahra sprinkled some water over hers and ate with a hearty appetite. By the time I left, darkness had set in. Bibi returned in time to bring some fresh-baked bread and she sent some to my family. She asked Zahra to take their only lantern and walk me home.

The evening had just begun, but the sleeping village gave the impression of late night. Even the animals were quiet, except for a dog barking in the distance. The temperature had dropped and a cold desert wind wrestled among the bare trees. Zahra wrapped her large scarf around her head, covering the lower half of her face. We took hurried steps and did not talk until we had reached the orchard.

"Won't you come in?"

Zahra smiled and shook her head. "*Inshallah* another day."

I reached into my pocket for the only bill I had on me and pushed it into her hand saying, "I didn't get a chance to buy your present. Please buy a scarf on my behalf."

She took a step back. "God have mercy! I couldn't possibly accept."

"It's only a gift, Zahra."

She studied the money in the light of her lantern. "All *this* for one scarf?"

"Please, Zahra. It'll make me so happy."

Petty charity is another form of bigotry, Jenab had said a long time ago. Guilt made me want to give her everything I owned, but now we were in my father's territory, where the invisible barrier once again rose between us.

"May God pay you back in Heaven for your kindness," Zahra said. She kissed the money and touched her forehead before tucking it in her vest pocket. She held the lantern higher and I found my path in its fluttering glow.

At the pond, I turned to her. "I know my way from here," I said and waved.

The desert sky was like black velvet with millions of sequins sprinkled on it. Except for the sound of crickets, the garden was quiet. A few servants prepared to leave, taking home what must have been discarded fruits and leftovers.

Inside, the heat of kerosene burners was more than we needed. I found Auntie in the family room, working on her cross-stitch. Mitra lay on the rug, listening to a play on her transistor radio.

"Where were you all day?" Auntie looked up over her reading glasses.

"At Zahra's."

Mitra glanced at me with a smirk.

"You're no longer a little girl, Roya," my aunt said without looking at me. "Time to act like a lady."

I imagined staying home, doing needlepoint, or helping her to make preserves.

"Do you mind if I skip dinner?" I said. "I've already eaten."

"You didn't eat too much, I hope."

I shook my head, but wasn't sure. Even a morsel from Bibi's limited supply would be too much. There was no way to justify the abundance that my family had.

~

I awakened at the sound of the car horn and it took me a minute to believe we were already back in the city. The gardener opened the gate. He had lived at our home during the two-week holiday and, from the look of the garden, had earned his keep.

The colors offered a bold contrast to the bare village we had left behind. The arch over the driveway had new grown foliage and it would soon burst with blooms of red climbing roses. A variety of pansies lined the flowerbeds and pots of pink geraniums had been moved out of the greenhouse to line the edge of the veranda.

As if life had paused for two weeks, I was soon back in motion preparing myself for school. The next morning, as I saw Shireen enter the schoolyard, I broke away from Nelly and ran to her.

"How was your Norooz?" she asked me.

I shrugged. We were at a farm.

She took a small booklet from among her books. "Look what I've got here." And when she showed it to me, it was a diary-type notebook. "We can talk in this during class," she said with a mischievous smile.

"What?"

"You know? Write down things during class time."

I studied the little diary. It was a promotional calendar for Phillips medical equipment, no bigger than a pocket book, the kind that drug companies gave out.

Shireen imitated a radio commercial. "Trust a Phillips!" And she giggled. "If a class is boring, we can write back and forth in this, pretending we're taking notes."

"How clever."

She grinned. "Yes, I am!"

Shireen's tendency to speak few words had led me to misjudge her as too serious. What a pleasant surprise it was to discover her subtle humor. While she would not resort to anecdotes or make fun of others, her wit made me smile, even in my darkest moments.

The following week, a class project required that we stay overtime. My study group decided to bring lunch to school and work during the two-hours break. In the past, the only times I had stayed in for lunch were during heavy snowfalls, so I looked forward to the change, especially now that Shireen would be there too.

We were still working when she checked her watch. "Time for my prayers." She took her chador from under our desk. "Going to the prayer hall. Will be back soon."

I had been to that room in the basement before. On hot days, it provided the coolest shelter at recess. But the thought of using the prayer hall to actually pray had never occurred to me. I wondered how the old custodian, Baba, a strict Muslim, saw the rest of us giddy girls who never prayed.

"I'll come with you," I said.

"As you wish."

The basement smelled damp and had no furniture. A single bulb hung from its ceiling. We entered just as three girls were leaving. Tahereh Ahmadi, who must have just finished her prayers, gave me a baffled look, then turned to Shireen and said, "May God accept your prayers."

"And yours," Shireen responded and proceeded to remove her shoes before stepping on the kilim-covered floor. I did the same.

Shireen peeled her socks off, rolled up her sleeves, and went to the small sink.

"Can I watch?" I asked, following her into the hallway.

She gave me a bewildered look. "Don't you ever say your *namaz*?"

"Only when I go to the Shrine."

This seemed to puzzle her even more. "If you're not religious, then what business would you have in the holy *Shrine*?"

"Visiting my mother," I said, and while she rinsed, I told her about Maman's tomb, located on the premises of the shrine. "We share the space with another family I don't know. The room faces the drinking fountains. Sometimes I just sit there for hours, leave the door open, and watch the pigeons in the old courtyard." Shireen turned off the tap. Her keen eyes encouraged me to go on. "My aunt says Maman never missed a prayer, not even when she lay sick in bed."

Turning the water back on, Shireen was soon so absorbed in her cleansing ritual that I felt invisible. With each elaborate movement, she whispered verses in Arabic, as if to purify her body and soul in preparation for facing God.

"That water must be freezing," I said when she was done. "Look at your maroon hands!"

She dried herself and pulled her sleeves all the way over her fingers. "It's not too bad now. It gets much worse in winter."

Back in the prayer hall, Shireen draped her *chador* over her head and asked me to pass her a prayer seal. Reaching into the shelf she pointed to, I chose the only unbroken rectangle *mohr* with Arabic verses on it. Made of the soil of Mecca, it felt cold and slick. She thanked me, then kissed the seal before placing it on the floor and stood facing west, where the sign on the wall advised *Kiblah*. Now with her eyes closed, it looked as if she traveled to a different place in her mind and resembled a pale angel, bandaged in the wrong cloth.

I pitied and envied her at the same time. Pity, because she was stuck with a ritual, and envy, for her strong conviction. What did it feel like to believe you had God's full attention?

When finished, I asked her, "You enjoy *namaz*, don't you?"

"It brings me peace." Her smile confirmed that. "Believe me, if you lived at our house, you'd need it, too."

"Peace aside, what exactly do you pray for?"

"Not what. *Whom.*"

Shireen looked as if my question had taken her far away. I wasn't sure I could ask more.

She put the prayer seal back on its shelf and we left.

~

By the end of our junior year, Shireen and I had become the best of friends.

As we more frequently entered the classroom together, Jenab began to address us as a pair. When he asked questions, regardless of which one of us raised her hand, he would point to our bench. "Let's hear it from our two *scholars*." Sometimes I wonder if he had foreseen the rise of a friendship, or worse, if he had deliberately paired us to seal our fate.

While the school authorities pretended nothing had happened, the SAVAK incident seemed to be forgotten. My town went back to its dormant life and school continued as if nothing were wrong. We were but hundreds of girls in gray denim uniforms living in *The Lagoon* – another one of Jenab's favorite poems.

My life is like a lagoon
Still, silent, calm and quiet
Not a wave of anger rushes through
Nor rage roars within...

Despite the calm, I could sense a roar rising somewhere within our quiet lagoon. New rumors were whispered about Alieh. Nelly had heard disgraceful details of a rape, even pregnancy. But no more authorities showed up at school, the police were not involved, and the entire matter stayed out of the press. No one, not even Jenab, mentioned her name.

I replayed that scene over and over in my mind. Each time I descended the stairs, I saw Alieh down below, struggling, begging for help. In Mrs. Saberi's presence, I did my best not to look into her eyes for fear I might still see the warning in them.

Like a picture slowly developing in the darkroom, the injustice around me became clearer with time. Forbidden thoughts grew and multiplied in my head. How many other Aliehs had disappeared before her, and who would be the next?

Three

SOME TEACHERS DON'T DESERVE to be remembered. I think the profound contrast to such teachers might have been what gave Jenab his grandeur. In most classes nothing worth remembering happened, but I'll never forget the day Jenab proposed the review of a forbidden book.

Skipping his usual monologue, Jenab wiped the blackboard and wrote in his best calligraphy, "*The Little Black Fish.*"

When he looked at us, the mischief in his eyes was hard to miss. "How many of you have read this book by Samad Behrangi?" Jenab knew better than any of us that such discussions were taboo at school.

The dreadful scene that had occurred the day Mitra brought that book home played back in my mind. Back then Nelly had filled me in on a few facts. That Samad Behrangi had been a Socialist was a matter of public record.

"His fairytales were cute, but Papá agrees that they also carried a hidden message," Nelly had said. "Soon after the banning of *The Little Black Fish,* his body was found in the icy waters of a river."

Whether or not Nelly made up stories, I had learned enough to know we shouldn't talk about this book, especially not in class.

Jenab waited until the initial shock had passed and then a few uncertain hands were raised. Only Shireen's hand shot up with confidence.

"Miss Payan, would you like to tell us the story?"

Shireen stood. "I wouldn't call it a story, sir."

Jenab smiled. "Indeed." And he nodded. His eyes danced as if he already knew where this was going.

"Written in the format of a children's story," Shireen began, "the little fish is only a metaphor. Most people don't realize this and before its ban, I saw copies of the book in the children's section."

A few students giggled.

"Please stay on the subject, Miss Payan," Jenab interrupted.

Shireen swallowed hard and for the next minute seemed puzzled. "The tiny fish is stuck in a shallow stream," she went on, now with less confidence, "but in fact he seeks the freedom of a vast ocean. He has everything he needs to reach his goal; hope, vision, and courage."

As Shireen captured her audience, I knew exactly where she had learned that and, if only she could mimic the crooked smile, the whole class would know it, too.

"I disagree," Nelly interrupted.

"Oh?" Jenab raised an eyebrow. "You have *read* the book?" He sounded as if he didn't believe the girl could read. "Then do share your wisdom."

I felt sorry for Nelly.

Shireen sat down and we both turned around to look at Nelly, who stood behind us and spoke directly to Jenab, ignoring the rest of us.

"He's just a dumb fish. The book is a childish story and not even well written. But these days, people read something into everything."

A few others voiced their agreement. Nelly smiled at the girl sitting next to her.

"What about symbolism?" Shireen argued. "Behrangi chose

his metaphors with such care that not every reader gets it." She pronounced "reader," as if it meant "idiot."

Others whispered, but before class became disrupted, Jenab spoke.

"Simple, maybe," he said. "But Behrangi's style is far from juvenile." He returned to the blackboard and read the title again, pointing to each word. "Little. Black. Fish," he annunciated. "Not a word wasted. Our protagonist is neither big nor strong; he isn't colorful or showy and, in fact, he is just another being among a crowd, living in an ordinary river. And, most importantly, he has *no voice*."

The pride in Jenab's smile was as if he had created this impeccable metaphor himself. "There is a little black fish in you, and me, and every one of the insignificant people in our world. In a society that suffocates its youth, Behrangi dares to suggest that they matter, that even without a voice, they can make a difference. But above all, he is saying that in order to make such a change, one must have a goal and strongly believe in it."

Jenab sat behind his desk. "If you ask me," he said and shrugged, "the book need not be banned at all. Its message is of nothing but hope."

Shireen rose again. "Then why deliver it in such an obscure manner?"

A murmur followed.

"Quiet!" Jenab commanded, then turned to Shireen. "What obscurity are you referring to, Miss Payan? Tempting as such speculations may be, this is a literature class and I'd like to discuss this exclusively from a literary standpoint and pay attention to its poetic style. Following Antoine de Saint-Exupery's footsteps in *The Little Prince*, Behrangi has written his book using simple prose to describe the philosophical aspect of life."

A few voices rose, but Jenab raised both hands. "I'm not finished!"

He then lowered his voice adding, "Like the power in a whisper, the splendor of Behrangi's story is indeed in its simplicity."

None of that trash in my house, Pedar had said.

I raised my hand.

"Yes, Miss Afshar?"

"Why was it banned then?"

A murmur followed in support of my question.

Jenab dismissed it with a wave of his hand. "Cynicism has caused the ban of numerous works of art. If indeed this book is not simply out of print, if it has been banned – and I'm not saying that's the case – it's a pity, indeed a shame."

A heated discussion followed while Shireen sulked in silence. When the bell rang, she stood and said to Jenab, "I'd like to know if there's an ocean out there at all? And if so, which one of us will dream enough to dare swimming in it?"

Jenab continued to gather his books, so Shireen shouted over the classroom noise, "Sir?"

Jenab didn't even look at her, as if he had not heard the question altogether.

~

That evening before dinner, Mitra and I were doing homework in her room. I didn't have a separate desk, so we shared hers.

"I have one sky of reading to do," I complained, paging through my Physics book.

She looked up. "What was that?"

I laughed. "Sorry. Shireen and I have this silly code, 'one sky,' to mean beyond measurement, like the abyss. It's from a poem that mentioned one sky of red poppies."

Mitra put her book down. "You know that poem?"

Overwhelmed that for once I knew something she didn't, I started to deliver with pride, "You are not there, and how many flowers are—"

"Did that girl teach you this?" She sounded furious.

"Teach?" I chuckled. "We share poetry."

"Not that one, you don't."

"And why not?"

"Because you're not a follower of Behrangi."

"You don't even know what you're talking about," I said and went back to my book, but her hand came down on the page.

"That poem was written in honor of Samad Behrangi and is being circulated among his followers," she said and poked a finger into my chest. "You're not one of them."

"That's silly. I bet Shireen doesn't even know that."

"She knows."

"She never said a word."

"Good!" Mitra picked up her book. "And neither will you."

Much like Nelly, my sister tried hard to sound informed. She considered herself an intellectual, read forbidden books and discussed social problems over a *caffé glassé*. But I saw right through her façade because she showed more concern for a broken fingernail than the lives of people like Zahra. Intellectualism to Mitra was nothing but another fashionable import from France.

I let her read for a while. "Speaking of Behrangi," I said at last, trying to sound casual. "I'd like to read that Fish book, if you still have it."

She stabbed her book with her pen. "What's gotten into you?"

I had to tell her about the discussion in Jenab's class, but I tried to dilute the intensity and surprised even myself at how calm I sounded. "I think if I had read it, I would have understood today's review much better. It sounds like a good read."

"That Mr. Elmi is really asking for it," she said, and added in a softer tone, "Even if Pedar had let me keep it, I wouldn't give it to you. There's a reason they ban such books."

"You're just mean."

"Better mean than stupid," she said and turned back to her studies.

I returned to my textbook. The words on the page made no sense at all. Somehow, Mitra had awakened me to danger lurking over my favorite teacher. She had a point. At a time when people got into trouble for speaking up, why would Jenab take such a chance?

~

The following day it rained and rained. All along the hallway where muddy shoes had left their marks on the mosaic, people left their umbrellas open to dry. At recess, Shireen and I stayed in class and she gave me a copy of Hafez, opened to a marked page.

"Will you test me on this poem?"

"Why?"

"My father makes us memorize at least one a week."

I studied it and found the verses rather hard to read, let alone memorize.

"This is so intense. Do you ever do anything silly, just for fun?"

"Does fun have to be silly?" Then as if regretting that, she said, "Reading can be fun, too, not to mention the interesting debates it can spark."

"What kind of debates?"

"You know, discussions, exchanging ideas, even taking sides."

"On poetry?"

"No, not just poetry. It could be anything: headline news, art. Anything, really."

I laughed. "Sounds like school to me."

"No, it's a lot of fun. We have our laughs, munch on snacks, and play poetry games. My father gives us cash rewards to make it worthwhile." She smiled. "But *Agha-jan* can be tricky. Whenever we start to gain on him, he switches to Rumi, a topic he knows more about than the rest of us put together."

Even though others called their fathers *Agha-jan,* meaning "Dear Sir", to hear Shireen refer to hers that way sounded formal.

"So, that's why you know so much," I said. "My family mostly reads magazines, and the debate is over who gets to do the crosswords first." I laughed.

The profound difference in our experiences should have been enough to imply that Shireen and I lived in divergent worlds. Like parallel lines, we walked side-by-side, together, and yet alone.

From Shireen's descriptions, I imagined her father to be someone worth knowing. But her mom remained a mystery. Whenever Shireen mentioned her, I sensed caution. And one day in the midst of telling me about an argument, she exclaimed, "I'm afraid of Maman."

"Of your own mother?"

Wide-eyed, she nodded. "She can be frightening."

I thought of my mother, bed-ridden and weak, yet smiling angelically. I could still remember putting my head on her bed to receive the gentle movement of her fingers stroking my hair. Weren't all mothers a symbol of tranquility and the source of unconditional love?

"You're just angry," I had said. "Soon you'll both forget about this."

"My mother never forgets."

Shireen seemed increasingly at ease around me and began providing details of her family life. After a while, I thought maybe it was time for me to enter the next level of friendship, the one where I could finally let her inside my "thick shell" as she put it.

~

With final exams approaching, I stayed home and worked hard to memorize the Latin names of fossils. Sitting under a tree, I read my biology book, ignoring the strong scent of jasmine and honeysuckle in order to concentrate.

My father took pride in having one of the best gardens in town.

He had hired Mammad to take care of it and often invited his friends over to show it off. A brick driveway ran down the middle of two large flowerbeds with metal arches overhead to support red climbing roses. Well-manicured flowerbeds burst with pink geraniums, white petunias, and dahlias of all colors. The surrounding high walls were covered with fragrant honeysuckle, isolating this private paradise from the world outside.

The blare of a horn interrupted my reverie. At the sight of my father's car, I was grateful for an excuse to quit studying. The car halted in the middle of the driveway and Mammad rushed over to open its door for my father.

"*Salaam*, Pedar," I shouted and ran to him.

"I see my smart daughter is studying again." Pedar wrapped one arm around me and I saw an older gentleman in the back seat. Turning to his guest, my father said, "Mr. Sa'ad, let me introduce my youngest, Roya."

The man's dark lips opened to a denture smile and he stepped out. He was tiny and, judging by his cotton-white hair, too old to be Pedar's peer. Then again, Pedar seemed to know many of the prominent seniors in our town.

"Your father has been raving about you," he said, catching my hand in a firm handshake. "The valedictorian?" He turned to Pedar. "I must say, Rafi-khan, you have every right to be proud of this young lady."

I thanked him and felt the heat rise to my ears.

My father looked as pleased as when he showed off his garden. He tapped my back. "Dear Mr. Sa'ad, when she becomes a famous doctor, we can all be proud of her."

As they walked away, I gathered my books and went up the back stairs to the family room. The French doors led onto the semi-circular veranda and I opened them wide. My father's room also connected to the veranda, at a right angle, and I could hear the faint trick-track of dice from a backgammon game. I grabbed a cushion and stretched out on the floor of the family room, in a patch of sunlight in the doorway.

"Rajab!" my father called out to his manservant.

I heard the sound of a latch being opened and glimpsed Rajab appearing at my father's doors. Now with both sets of doors open, only the width of the veranda stood between my father's room and me.

"Bring me my iron box," Pedar said to Rajab.

For a while the rolling of dice was all I heard. With the warm sun on my eyelids, I imagined Rajab going down the hall to retrieve, from the closet, my father's heavy safe. That closet was in fact a small pantry that served as storage for nonperishable food and household supplies, as well as a few family heirlooms. It had two keys, of which my aunt kept one, and Rajab the other. What Pedar called his "iron box," was a large steel case with gold paisley designs, containing Pedar's documents, cash, gold coins and such. He alone had its key. Though no one spoke of it openly, we all knew he also kept his stash of opium in there.

Pedar never smoked opium in the presence of his family, though we were all too familiar with its strong smell. Once, when two of Pedar's friends were over, I had asked Auntie, "What's that stench?"

My aunt dismissed my curiosity with a wave of her hand. "Distinguished male guests enjoy being treated to an occasional *puff*."

Whenever Pedar was home for more than a few hours, especially if he sent word that he did not wish to be disturbed, I expected that smell to rise. None of us dared discuss the subject – as if by denying it the whole matter would become less real. But ever since I had started to examine things in the way Shireen might have, denial seemed to become increasingly less possible.

Pedar's voice had a hint of pride as he now proclaimed, "Nothing but the best for my good friend."

I peeked. At first, the bright sunlight blinded me, but then I saw them, sitting on the rug across from a silver brazier. Pedar's back was to me, leaning on his side over a rolled pillow. Now in their loosened shirts and with no jackets, both men seemed more relaxed. Pedar sat up and his keys jingled as he unlocked the safe. The box opened with a single sound of a bell.

He reached into the case and removed a box. "They don't get any better than this," he bragged.

Mr. Sa'ad took the cigar-shaped object. "Nice color," he said and, passing it under his nose, he gave an exaggerated exhale. "Ahh. Really nice."

Rajab came back with a tray, placed a glass of tea before each man, and put the teapot on the brazier. "The charcoal should be ready, sir," he said, and started to untie the cord from around a leather pouch. Out came an assortment of long pipes and jingling little gadgets. I had seen those pipes before, when Rajab cleaned them. They resembled a porcelain egg attached to a long wooden stem.

Mr. Sa'ad picked one up. "The Qajar pipes are hard to find."

"True," Pedar said. "But even if there were many left, who'd dare show them in their store?"

"True," Mr. Sa'ad replied. "Especially now. I wish I knew what's going on."

I listened for more, but they seemed too absorbed in Rajab's preparations.

"I thought we had seen the end of it after they got rid of Mossaddegh," my father finally said. "But now, even *I* worry."

I had heard about the ex-Prime Minister and the conspiracies to get rid of the Shah, but with Mossaddegh long dead, I didn't know what Pedar was referring to.

"Are you worried about the land reforms?" Mr. Sa'ad asked. The Shah had a new plan to divide farms among farm workers.

"Not really," Pedar said. "The land I fear for is that of the whole country."

Conscious of my eavesdropping, I closed my eyes and prayed they could not see me. With my heart ready to explode, I waited a few more minutes before curiosity made me look again.

Rajab heated the porcelain pipe on the charcoal, cut a piece of the opium stick and, using what looked like a doctor's pliers, held the piece over the charcoal before putting it on the pipe. Pedar poked at it with a long needle before passing the pipe to his guest. I shuddered with unease. Something was awfully wrong with this entire poisonous ritual. I wanted to leave, but the magnetism of the scene held me.

Mr. Sa'ad took a long drag. He blew the smoke toward the French doors before giving the pipe back to my father, who took a longer drag and inhaled. That dreadful smell filled the air again – bitter coffee mixed with tar and burning charcoal.

"You know something, Rafi *khan*? I haven't touched this stuff in two months."

Two months? Something in the casual way my father's guest said that horrified me. Pedar seemed to smoke the stuff every time he had a chance. How wrong my aunt had been. Pedar's opium habit was far beyond "an occasional puff."

~

Shireen feasted her eyes on the last poppies of the year and said, "Soon this will go back to being just an ordinary roof."

"That roof will never be ordinary," I replied. "The flowers may be gone, but the roof is their home. It keeps a part of them, season to season. Year to year."

"You're right. They may seem fragile, but their lifeline is strong," she said. "Other flowers can only dream of such freedom."

"Freedom?" I chuckled. "They're as stuck in that mud as we are in this Godforsaken school."

"Think again. No florist harvests them, they aren't bought or sold and they will never be forced to spend their last days in a vase." She bobbed her head, just like the poppies. "Absolutely free."

What did Shireen know of their poison? The vision of my father, hunched over his silver brazier, was as vivid as the day I'd actually seen it. I could still feel the air in his room, heavy with the essence of poppies. My father's addiction, with or without his elegant pipes, humiliated me. I wished I could talk to Shireen about it, but the shame of it prevented me.

One sky of sorrow.

In her poetic way, Shireen had given me a phrase to gauge the immeasurable. At an age when nothing made sense, our days went by with *one sky* of anxiety while a simple word from Jenab could fill our hearts with *a sky* of joy. We exploded with *one sky* of rage and yearned, equally, to escape our oppressive surroundings.

Maybe the poppies' secret, their significance, indeed what made them so unique, lay in their brief existence. Like the misty memory of my mother, something about the poppies both dazzled and troubled me.

Shireen saw their freedom and resilience.

I saw only their vulnerability.

Four

LOOKING BACK, the monotony of my uneventful teenage years is hard to believe. But as boring as the majority of remembrance may be, where Shireen is concerned I have to probe deep and try to understand where things went wrong. Our friendship began as softly as drizzle, and little did we know that if a light rain lasted long enough, it could turn into flood.

I entered my classroom seconds before Miss Bahador arrived. Expecting Jenab, I thought the Geography teacher had made a mistake, but she walked to the desk and put her purse down.

"Mr. Elmi and I have switched classes this morning," she said.

A few students mumbled protestations. I noticed Shireen had taken out her Phillips diary, an indication that she had something to talk about. When Miss Bahador turned to the blackboard, Shireen wrote something down, then slid the diary across the desk to me.

"School is facing a serious problem," it read.

"What?" I whispered.

Miss Bahador glared in our direction.

Before Shireen could respond, there came a crackle from the speakers above the blackboard, followed by Mrs. Saberi's shriek. "Shireen Payan to the office immediately."

The entire front row turned to our bench. To be called to the principal's office was never good, but after what Shireen had just written, I panicked.

Miss Bahador nodded and Shireen flew out of the room.

Students murmured, but the teacher started her lesson and soon everyone seemed to be listening. I watched the door and prayed my friend would return soon. I had no reason to fear SAVAK, but somehow since the day they took Alieh, I imagined any call to the office related to them. I listened carefully to sounds coming through the window, but other than distant traffic noise and the usual come and go in the schoolyard, I heard nothing, and certainly nothing that would validate my qualms.

At recess, I noticed Shireen had left the Phillips diary open where it lay. Knowing she'd not want to leave it unattended, I took it from the desk and carried it with me while looking for her. She was nowhere around.

As I passed by the office I could hear the teachers' chitchat. Acting casual, I peered through the open door, but saw no Shireen there either. I felt sick when she didn't show up for the rest of that morning's classes.

School went on as usual, indicating others hadn't heard about the problem Shireen had mentioned. Maybe I had misunderstood her. But when one of my classmates said that Jenab had not made it to any of his classes, I became more deeply concerned. Before going home for lunch, I looked for Shireen in the prayer hall, but no one was there.

I had never been to her house. Given our social codes, that wasn't unusual. I treated most of my school friends as just that: Friends whom I saw at school. Most girls were allowed to socialize only with friends known to their families. I could visit Nelly any time, but Shireen? If it weren't for her address being on the first page of the diary, I wouldn't even know where she lived.

Akbar was waiting for me in the yellow Dodge. I copied the address out and passed it to him. "Would you mind going by my friend's house? I have to return her book."

I heard him mumble something, which made me think the detour was an inconvenience, but he made a U turn anyway.

Shireen had written that the *school* was in trouble, but what kind of trouble? Being called to the office could possibly be unrelated to whatever she meant to tell me. Maybe the school needed some document for her file or something, and had sent her home to get it.

Contrary to my assumptions, Shireen lived in a prestigious neighborhood, even though her house seemed to be the smallest on the block and lacked the big gate her neighbors had. Akbar parked the car in the shade of a tree just a few feet away.

I had never met Shireen's family. The Payans didn't seem to attend the meetings of Home and School Society. As devout Muslims, I wondered if they would be appalled with my lack of *hejab*. Reminding myself that I did not have to go in, I climbed the three steps to the narrow door and rang the bell.

Shuffling slippers approached and a woman's deep voice called, "Who is it?"

"Roya Afshar, a friend of Shireen's."

There was a pause, and I heard the latch before the door opened. A tall woman with broad shoulders filled the doorway. Giving me a bright smile, her pink cheeks revealed deep dimples. Relieved that the caller was female, she let her chador slip to her shoulders and I noticed the buttons on her tight sweater were about to lose the battle with her large bosom. A floral scarf covered her hair, leaving out only one thick lock on her forehead.

"Hello, Roya-khanoom. Please, do come in."

Surprised by such a warm welcome, I entered the narrow corridor, but stopped short of the foyer. The aroma of steamed rice and melted butter brought lunch to mind.

"I just came by to give Shireen her books," I said, determined to keep hold of the diary if I could not hand them to Shireen directly.

Mrs. Payan dismissed my comment with a wave of her hand. "Oh, but now that you're here, you must visit. Our home is yours. Come in. Come in and stay for lunch!"

She continued, stringing her words rapidly, and calling out, "Shireen-joon, your friend's here." Then she turned to me. "Go on in, dear. Her room is just down the hall." She removed her slippers before stepping onto the rug. I did the same. Auntie would not be pleased to hear of this visit, but by now, curiosity had the best of me. I had to make sure Shireen was okay and personally give her the diary.

"This'll cheer her up," Mrs. Payan said. "The past few days have been tough."

Overwhelmed by such friendliness, I wondered what could have made Shireen be so afraid of her. What hid behind such a jolly smile?

"You go on," she said. "I'll get you two some tea." And she disappeared into what must have been the kitchen.

Just then, a door to my left opened, and a young man came out. Shireen had two brothers and I figured this must be the older one, Ali. A little taller than me, his dark hair was cut close to his scalp. With his head bent down in modesty, I could only see part of his face, but even from that angle I could see his uncanny resemblance to Shireen.

"Hello," he said in a low voice, then turned around quickly as if changing his mind, and went back inside. Before he closed the door, I had a quick glimpse of the interior. A few men sat around the smoke-filled room, seemingly engaged in serious discussion. The way they sat in a circle made it appear to be a meeting and, for just an instant, I could swear I saw Jenab. He was talking to a red-haired man who had his back to me. If Shireen hadn't come to greet me, I think my bewilderment would have held me frozen for some time.

"Hey, what a surprise!" Shireen said in her usual, friendly voice.

Still in a daze, I didn't respond.

"Is everything okay?" She sounded alarmed.

I tried to smile. "Yes. Yes, everything's fine." I offered her the diary. "You left it in class, I just came to give it to you."

"And what happened?" She kept staring at me.

"You're going to think I'm crazy, but..." I shook my head.

"But what?" she insisted.

I nodded to the room. "I thought I saw Jenab in there."

"You're not crazy." She pulled at my sleeve. "Come. Let's go in and I'll tell you about it."

Shireen's room was small. White lace drapes on her single window partly softened the view of a brick wall behind it. Her books were stacked on the floor, except for one laying open on her bed. The room's meager furniture consisted of the bed, an ironing board, and an old dresser with a fan and more books sitting on top. The oval mirror on the wall showed blotches of faded mercury. A copy of the world map and a few random pictures and postcards were displayed on the wall. An enlarged portrait was stuck there with a single pushpin, allowing the edges to curl up. It showed Shireen and a younger girl standing on the stairs, smiling at the camera.

"That's my little sister, Nasrin."

The word 'little' made me smile, because in that picture Nasrin stood much taller, making Shireen the little one.

"Okay, tell me. What's Jen–"

I stopped as Mrs. Payan entered the room.

"I'm so embarrassed," she said while setting a tray of tea, sugar cubes, and dates on the floor. "Those men seem to have finished all my cookies."

I thanked her. "This is more than enough."

As soon as she had left and closed the door, Shireen said, "The way Maman talks, you'd think there's an army in there. It's only my family, my uncle and cousin, plus Jenab. They've been at it all day and I bet nothing is solved." She placed a glass of tea before me. "Lately, Jenab's been coming here every single day."

"He has?"

"For several reasons." Lowering her voice, she added, "Remember I mentioned there's trouble at school?"

I nodded.

"Well, it all has to do with him. Jenab has run into some problems with the Ministry of Education. Someone must have been telling SAVAK things, you know? Trying to make a *dossier* on him."

"What's he done?"

"Nothing, but if they want to make trouble, they can find things. Like that whole book discussion, for one, and oh, remember how he seemed sympathetic about... that girl? God only knows what else they have on him."

Jenab was a remarkable teacher. To hear of him having problems with the Ministry of Education was almost as if someone had told me God was in trouble for the way he ran the world.

"Come on, they won't dare touch him," I said.

"They will if we let them."

Shireen told me that Jenab and her father knew each other through poetry gatherings and philosophy meetings. She hadn't mentioned their acquaintance at school for fear that people might accuse him of favoritism. Now her father was trying to help Jenab.

"Strict as Agha-jan may be, he's going to let me testify."

"Testify, like in a court?"

She nodded. "But not in the court house, it'll be private. That's what I wanted to tell you before they called me out of class."

"Yes, what was that all about?"

"Jenab's lawyer had come to see the principal and see if they could find a few witnesses. He asked me a few questions and then the principal sent me home in a taxi and told me to stay here for the rest of the day. When I saw Jenab's car in front, I thought there would be more questions, but now I know the principal just wanted to make sure I didn't talk to other students about it."

"Why did they choose you?"

Shireen shrugged. "I have a feeling it was Jenab's idea. Maybe it's because I have the biggest mouth in class."

And the most bravery, I thought. Jenab sure knew how to pick his team.

"Won't this make trouble for you?"

She nodded. "It may, but I don't have a choice. After all, Jenab did try to look at *The Little Black Fish* for its prose and not the message. Someone has to tell them that and I may need everyone in class to back me up on it. We must join hands to save him."

She told me that the men had gathered there to compose a petition. She was to bring it to class the next day for everyone to sign.

"You'll be the first, Roya, won't you?"

I thought of Jenab sitting in the next room and for some peculiar reason, I pictured his children, whose livelihood had to be their father's job. My father would never understand if I got involved. But how could I refuse?

I nodded.

"I don't think it's all that bad," Shireen said, as if sensing my uncertainty. "In fact, Ali guarantees that no one will get in trouble." She smiled. "Well, maybe I will, but then again, I have a safety net. My father won't object to something he himself has instilled in his children."

"And what's that?" I asked.

"Courage."

—

Soon, most of Jenab's time seemed to be taken by meetings in the principal's office and trips to Mashad's Department of Education. Our favorite teacher arrived late and he appeared to be preoccupied during class. As always, Nelly reported detailed accounts of what she had heard from her father. "It looks like they'll get rid of Jenab," she predicted, shrugging with indifference.

One afternoon, Jenab arrived much too late and, for the first time, offered no topic for discussion. Holding onto his briefcase, he glared at us and then, pointing a finger at the whole class said, "I hold every one of you accountable for *this* mess."

A heavy silence followed, lasting several breaths.

"School is where you learn," he said at last. "But there's not a book in the world that can teach you how to be responsible." Taking a book off his desk, he tossed it into a corner. "Don't be book-carrying donkeys!"

A few students in the back giggled, but his glare silenced them.

"Even in this so-called 'backward' country of ours, people have rights." He suddenly turned to the Shah's portrait hanging above the blackboard and added, "Though *some* appear to have more than others."

His eyes scanned the room. "We must stand for our rights. Otherwise," he gave a sad smile, "we deserve what comes to us."

Not bothering with a lesson, he stormed out of the classroom and slammed the door so hard I thought it would come off its hinges. The knot in my stomach told me this was serious. I felt a silent danger, a creeping presence, as if a deadly snake was hiding nearby, waiting to strike.

~

With the news of our petition, the school's atmosphere changed. For the rest of that week, class cancellations and teachers' conferences became frequent. Mixed reactions escalated. Even at home, each time a friend called, I heard Mitra's heated discussions over the phone. However, apart from signing the petition, most students remained inactive. I had signed it too, but when Shireen said it would appear in the newspaper, I panicked.

"Pedar will be sure to kill me now," I said, and I was considering it more than just a figure of speech.

I think that must have been when Shireen decided to stop telling me what went on behind the office doors. I saw other students going in and out, but each time I asked Shireen about it, she changed the subject. It seemed as if she had become the one with the tough walls around her, and I felt helpless, left on the outside.

~

We were gathered for a late dinner and Pedar seemed happier than usual. Once in a while, he enjoyed a drink with his dinner and it seemed to put him in a jolly mood. He told anecdotes, talked about his youth, and I hoped that he might strum his *tar* later on.

Pedar poured himself a glass of whiskey, turned to the mantle, and stared at my mother's photograph. In that black and white portrait Maman was much younger than all my friends' mothers. Her arched eyebrows, the neat curls in her hair and that shiny lipstick presented a contrast to the pale face and sunken cheeks of my memory.

When Pedar turned, sorrow had crept into his eyes. He took a swig.

I went to him and gently touched the frame with my fingertips. "Why don't you ever talk to me about Maman?"

He stared at me with darkened eyes, but did not speak.

Auntie stepped in. "This isn't the best time, dear."

Losing my temper, I yelled, "There's never a good time to talk about her." My eyes welled with tears. "How will I know my mother if no one ever talks about her?"

Pedar looked away. Mitra and Reza exchanged a look and Auntie just went back to the table and took her seat.

"How is school going these days?" she asked.

I was too mad to respond.

Mitra sat down next to Auntie. "It sure is more fun with all the chaos."

Pedar put his glass down. "Chaos?"

"Yes, it's that teacher of theirs," Reza said. "Mr. What'shisname. It's all over the place. Everyone talks about it, even at *my* school."

Pedar ignored him and continued to stare at Mitra.

"They're going to fire Mr. Elmi," Mitra offered. "And if you ask me, that man should have been kicked out years ago. But most teachers are protesting. I guess it's a union thing." She turned to me. "Isn't it great with no classes?"

"No class?" Auntie stared at me. "So, what do you do all day?"

"Study for finals," I said with a shrug and wished she would change the subject in her clever, subtle way.

"It has turned into a real movement," Mitra went on. "I think it's great to see the students involved in school politics."

Pedar leaned forward and studied me. "Not the two of you, I hope." His eyes pierced through me.

I shook my head.

"She doesn't have the guts," Mitra said. "I just saw their class petition in the paper and Miss Goody Roya's name wasn't even on it."

If what she said was true, it could only mean that Shireen had removed it.

"Good," Pedar said. "Keep your head in your books. Leave school politics to the school."

Mitra put her glass of water down so hard a few drops spilled out. "But students *are* the school, Pedar. Compliance seems to be what's wrong with this country."

"Do tell!" Pedar said, using his stinging sarcasm again. "What exactly *is* the matter with our country?"

I shrank back in my chair and feared the worst.

Mitra stared at Pedar. "Everybody expects somebody else to solve our problems. Why should people leave politics entirely to politicians?"

Pedar chewed the corner of his mustache. Not a good sign. He wagged a finger at Mitra. "Let there be no doubt in your feeble mind that politicians know a hell of a lot more about the needs of this country than the likes of you do."

Mitra did not dare say more.

"Students," Pedar said and chuckled. "Children, barely out of their dirty diapers, trying to tell their king how to run his country."

"He is not my king and this isn't just *his* country," Mitra snapped back.

"Oh, but it is! Who else but the king would shepherd this dumb flock?"

"Someone who really cares, someone like Doctor Mosaddegh–"

Pedar's fist hit the table so hard that we all jumped. The bulging vein on his forehead told me Mitra had gone too far.

More than a decade after Mosaddegh had died, his followers kept his memory alive and they still seemed to be the strongest anti-Shah group. This wasn't the first time the subject had caused such a rage in my father. I recalled a similar argument between him and my uncle the year before, just about when I had heard that Dr. Mosaddegh's election to Prime Minister had in fact been against the Shah's will. "The fact that he took the oil out of the hands of the British, is a milestone in history," Uncle had said, to which Pedar had responded with anger, "Out of the ditch and into the well we go."

Ever since that day, Pedar prohibited the mention of Dr. Mosaddegh's name, but now too outraged to say another word, he raised an arm and just pointed to the door.

Mitra pushed back her chair and left the table.

My father took a gulp of his drink before his eyes pinned me down. "You're a good girl, Roya."

The "good girl" would not dare talk of the storm within her. Grateful and relieved as I felt that Shireen had removed my signature, I also had the uneasy feeling that perhaps in doing so, she had cut me off altogether.

"Glad to see one of you has a good head on her shoulders," Pedar said at last, and from his tone, I had the feeling he wished for his own head to be on all our shoulders.

Reza spoke with a mouth full of rice. "What about me?"

No one responded. Pedar took the last sip of his drink and stared out of the window as if he could see through the darkness into the distance. My aunt passed more food around. For the rest of dinnertime, I listened to the sound of spoons hitting china plates.

Five

I READ OUR PHILLIPS DIARY now and it is as if the notes belong to someone else. In a strict society where you had no choice but to exchange your best years for a worthless diploma, Shireen and I tried to build memories on the pages of a discarded, outdated diary. The exchange of sentiments on those pages became an outlet that hardly made up for the after-school activities we didn't have. On some pages, our coded language is hard to understand, for I have forgotten whom we had named "the candidate" or "butcher." Reading it again, I still see an abundance of joy, but there's also a deep sorrow that seems more than our share to have carried at such a young age.

Now that the fog of ignorance has lifted, what used to be hope for the future has turned into regrets of the past. The lion's den had been there all along, in clear view, and only a step away. Years later, it is so easy to see the many signs of danger that we missed. I open the diary to a page where I have written, "Hooray, Shireen is coming to my house!" And all of a sudden, I am seventeen again, anticipating the thrill of finally having my friend over.

"Is it okay if I come to study with you tomorrow?" Shireen had asked me.

Up until then our friendship had remained within the school walls, aside from the one time when I'd dropped her books off. I wasn't sure my family would welcome a girl they didn't know, nor could I guess how they'd view her shrouded figure.

"I would love that," I said.

The following afternoon, Shireen and I walked home together. The iron gate was ajar and as soon as we entered the garden, she exclaimed, "Oh my! Look at this heaven."

I laughed. "My father would love to hear that."

"Did he do all this?"

I smiled at the naive question and shook my head. "But it's his ideas."

She walked to the pond with the fountain, before going over to the roses. I followed, but she stopped so abruptly that I thought she had seen a garden snake. Her face turned white. I followed the direction of her gaze and saw the skinny son of our gardener – I didn't know his name. He, too, had a look of incredulity on his face. After a few seconds, he looked at me, said a quick hello, turned around, and rushed back to the greenhouse.

Shireen continued to stare at where the boy had stood. Her mouth opened, but no words came out.

"What's the matter?"

"He looks..." she sounded baffled, "...familiar."

"You know our gardener's son?"

"He looks like one of Ali's friends."

"Him?" I laughed. "Don't be silly, he's just a kid. Fifteen at the most."

Ali was older than Shireen, but even if he had known the boy (perhaps from school), that wouldn't explain why Shireen would recognize him, let alone justify the boy's bewilderment. I wanted to ask her about it, but didn't want to be rude.

We stayed in my room, studying until dusk. Auntie peeked in once to meet Shireen and to advise it was time for a break. Later, she sent us tea and cake. If she noticed Shireen's *chador,* neatly folded and sitting on my bed, she did not show it.

During our tea break, I asked Shireen, "Are they still meeting at your house?"

"They are, but for the last few days the topic has changed."

"Oh?"

She smiled a sly smile. "I'm not supposed to tell, but..." She lowered her voice to a mere whisper. "Last night, the supreme court was there to discuss my future."

"What court?"

"The family," she said. "The ones who make big decisions for my pathetic life."

I had no idea what decision she was referring to, and shrugged.

"Marriage," she said.

Oh, no! I prayed they had not found her a rich old man.

"There's this guy..."

I had never seen Shireen blush that way before. The dreamy look in her eyes, the way she said "this guy," and those downcast eyes could only mean one thing.

"You're in love!"

She laughed and shook her head. "No, nothing like that. You could say he has asked for my hand in marriage, you know? A suitor. I had kind of hoped." She took a deep breath. "Remember when you asked me what I prayed for?"

I nodded.

"I know one should keep faith separate from personal gain, but I've actually been praying that Agha-jan will say yes."

"You *are* in love," I repeated, this time with certainty. "What's his name? How well do you know him?"

"I've known Eemon all my life."

"And you waited 'til now to tell me?"

"He's my second cousin. We grew up together." She paused, clearly looking into the past. "I don't even remember when I started having these feelings."

"So, if he's a relative, what seems to be the problem?"

"My father wants me to marry someone more established." She smiled a sad smile. "I have a feeling by that he means someone more like himself: same income, same moral standards." She chuckled adding, "Same age!"

I laughed too, amazed at how alike our fathers sounded.

"If it weren't for Jenab's intervention, I doubt Agha-jan would even consider Eemon's proposal."

That Jenab. He seemed to be at the core of everything.

"At Eemon's request, Jenab had a talk with my father." She looked up and smiled. "Looks like he's done some magic."

"Wow," I exclaimed. "This means you'll be getting married!" I stopped to think. "What about university?"

"Nothing's decided yet. Besides, I'll continue my education no matter what."

Talking of education reminded us of our current study load, and Shireen suggested we go back to our books.

Shortly before dusk, I walked Shireen out. The air in the garden smelled of cut grass and felt clean and fresh from recent watering. Without mentioning him, Shireen and I both looked for the gardener's boy, but he was not there.

As soon as I had returned to my room, Reza came in with his T-shirt over his head to resemble a chador. "Hellooo! I'm Roya-joon's friend," he said, in a high pitch voice.

"Shut up!"

Reza released his mock hejab and sat on my bed. "I'd be careful around those fanatic Muslims," he advised. "I hear they don't take kindly to the likes of us."

"She's my best friend," I snapped.

Reza hesitated for a moment. "Where did you find her, anyway?"

I didn't dignify that with an answer.

~

Shireen didn't come over to study again. In fact, after that day, she seemed more distant. Our conversations dwindled to mere words here and there. One day when she seemed to be in good spirits, I dared to ask, "Any news of your suitor?"

"Let's not talk about that," she said, and sounded so miserable that I figured Eemon's proposal had been refused. I didn't ask again. She seemed to have enough on her mind, and her body language told me she wanted to be left alone.

I turned to my other friends for companionship. Nelly didn't seem to care about having me back, but a few others welcomed the return. I spent most recesses with them.

~

"Roya Afshar to the teacher's lounge," the speakers echoed.

Oh, dear, was it my turn now? I did a quick mental check of my actions and couldn't think of any reason that would make them call on me. My chest tightened as I neared the teacher's lounge adjacent to the office. The door was closed and I could hear no sound. I knocked, and exhaled in a gasp at the familiar voice.

"Come in."

Jenab stood by the window, back to the door, watching the volleyball game outside. No one else was present. The smell of mortadella, onions and pickles left behind from the teachers' lunches lingered in the air. Through straw shades I saw the girls outside in their blue uniforms, yelling, jumping and passing the ball across the net.

"Sit down, Roya," Jenab said without facing me.

In the three years he'd known me, this was the first time he'd used my given name.

"These are difficult times," he said. "We're all more or less under pressure." He turned around and studied me. "Do not abandon your friend at a time like this. Shireen needs you now more than ever." And he pointed an accusing finger at me.

What did he know? I opened my mouth, but decided to say nothing.

"A friendship like hers is rare," he said. "Few are worthy of such a gift."

I resented the implication that I may not be one of those "few."

"Sir, I don't know what Shireen has told you, but–"

"She hasn't told me anything, Roya, but it doesn't take a genius to figure it out."

"It's she who doesn't want to be my friend." My voice broke.

"But she does," he said, his voice regaining its familiar warmth. "The key to a good friendship is in tolerating what we don't understand."

If I said another word I would cry.

"You don't have to do, or say, anything," he went on. "Just be there. Listen to her."

"She doesn't talk."

Instead of a response, Jenab recited a verse from Rumi, "The language of hearts is hardly ever wrong. Better to share hearts, than seek a common tongue."

The bell rang and Jenab motioned me back to class.

Before leaving, I turned to him. "Sir?"

He looked up from the desk.

"What about you, sir?" I said realizing there were no good words to substitute for being fired. "Are you going to be okay?" I said.

"Only time can tell." His heavy tone combined with the dark look in his eyes told me he, too, was losing hope.

I nodded and left.

At recess, I found Shireen down in the prayer hall, not praying, just sitting there, reading a book.

"Why won't you tell me what's the matter?"

Shocked at my candor, she closed her book, gave a soft sigh and said in a low voice, "Eemon left."

I plopped down next to her. "He's gone? What happened?"

She didn't answer.

"I can't understand your secrecy," I said. "If I ever had a boyfriend, you'd be–"

"He's not my *boyfriend.*"

"No? Then what is he?"

"I don't know."

Was I jealous? And why not? Her life was filled with mystery, and it sure seemed much more exciting than mine. With the prospect of a marriage, soon she'd forget all about me. I tried to stay calm and, remembering Jenab's advice, waited patiently just in case she wanted to talk.

She did not.

~

The week before final exams, the office meetings came to an end and Jenab returned to his class, but we all suspected the matter was unresolved.

"No decision before summer," Nelly the ever informed said. "They just can't afford more student protests."

One day, when Shireen and I were both late to class, Jenab gave us a mock bow. "Let's begin, now that our *scholars* have graced us." His scorn stung. "Teachers can wait," he went on. "They seem to be a dime a dozen these days, don't you agree?"

Ignoring the laughter of a few students, he turned to the blackboard and wrote.

There is so much pain gathered in my heart,
That if from this maze I should survive
I'll limp my way to the portal of existence
And not allow one soul to come alive.

He turned in our direction and I had never seen him more devastated. I looked for Shireen's reaction, but her downcast eyes indicated she was evading him.

Jenab read the poem in his deliberate fashion before analyzing it. "Pain," he repeated. "What Kashi means here by 'pain' is indignation, but what is he referring to?"

He waited, but no one volunteered. "Anyone?" He looked only at Shireen.

Shireen did not stand up the way we all did when responding to a teacher. She looked away and said, "He is talking about the most unbearable pain. The kind Alieh's mother must have felt when they told her the remains of her daughter had been found."

The entire class gasped as one. That single word, "remains," was enough to send a cold prickling under my skin. How easily I had put that whole incident out of my mind.

A murmur rose and the classroom started to sound like a beehive. I realized this was the first time Shireen had mentioned Mitra's classmate by name.

I looked at Jenab.

"Yes," he said. Everyone stopped talking. "That indeed is pain, one so profound that we can only guess its depth, but nothing is 'most unbearable,' Miss Payan. No matter how bad it is, life can always come up with worse."

Shireen bent her head, and drop–by–drop, tears dotted the front of her uniform.

"There are many kinds of pain," Jenab said with less feeling, as if reading from a textbook. "For example, there is a kind that we all need to be conscious of." He pointed a finger at class and moved it from row to row, like the barrel of a machine gun. "The painful realization that we could have done something." He went to the blackboard and drew a line under the word, 'existence.'

"Enclosed in *this* word alone is much injustice. We see unfairness everywhere, all the time, but somehow we choose to stand back." He shrugged. "I'm comfortable, so why take a chance?"

Shireen shot out of our bench so abruptly that her books dropped. She bolted out the back door, slamming it behind her.

Someone gasped. Leaving a classroom without permission was unheard of, especially in that manner.

Jenab shook his head as if to imply he understood. Encouraged, I raised my hand and pointed to the door. He nodded. I picked up the books Shireen had dropped and left.

Going down the stairs, I found her at our window, looking out at the dried up mud where the poppies had been. I stood by her side and we watched a crow strut along the roof.

"Where did you hear about Alieh?"

Shireen did not respond.

"I mean, there was nothing in the news, was there?"

She shook her head and whispered, "There wouldn't be."

I could sense she was leading to something more important, but she seemed hesitant.

"*They* don't want more trouble," she said. "Better to pretend it was a case of rape and murder."

"They? Who?"

With her finger, she wrote on the dusty window, "SAVAK" and quickly wiped it.

I looked down the stairway and into the floor below, remembering the polished shoes and Alieh kicking, struggling.

"I'll never forget Mrs. Saberi's face," I whispered. "She just stood there and watched them take her."

"You *saw* them?" Shireen asked, wide eyed. "Why didn't you tell me?"

"Madam Executioner. She threatened me." Whispering, I gave my friend a brief account of the scene that had haunted me for months. "Sometimes I can't fall asleep, thinking I could have done something." The remembrance made it hard to breathe.

Shireen put her arm around my shoulders. "Done what? Don't let Jenab give you this kind of guilt. There was nothing you could do."

Regardless of what Shireen said, had she been there, she would have acted differently.

"It isn't only the university students," Shireen went on. "People are ready, and those who take a chance are prepared to pay the price."

"Alieh paid dearly," I said.

She looked away. "In a way, I've paid, too."

"How?"

"My father was seriously considering Eemon's proposal. But when both Ali and Eemon joined the demonstrators, he changed his mind." The expression on her face became so helpless, it was as if the young man had died.

"I don't know what to think," I said. "I feel terrible about Alieh, but maybe what I feel is more for Alieh the schoolgirl, not the insurgent."

I regretted my words as soon as I saw the change in Shireen's expression. She took a step back, the cold look in her eyes shutting me out.

"I have to go," she said and turned around. I watched her walk down the steps and out of the building.

On my way back to class, I passed the old custodian. He stared at me with what I took to be a question on his wrinkled face.

Had he overheard our conversation?

~

On the last day of school, students gathered in the yard to view their final grades, which were posted on the first floor windows. Some cheered with relief, while a few girls cried in disappointment. I looked around for Shireen and, not finding her, I went to clear my desk. Our classroom, not used in more than two weeks, smelled of dust and chalk. Shireen sat at our bench, and only when I stood next to her did I realize she was crying.

"Hey, I saw your grades," I said jokingly, "and they're no crying matter, buddy."

She started to gather her things and said in a calmer voice, "Eemon has enlisted in the army. He will be away for two years."

"What about your plans to marry?"

"Oh, that's no longer a plan, at least not for some time. Maman got married when she was only seventeen. She is determined that my sister and I wait."

I was on her mother's side.

"The worst part is that Agha-jan has forbidden me from seeing him." She shrugged before adding, "It may be just as well he's going away."

"He doesn't sound like the army type," I said. "What use is it to him?"

Shireen thought about that. "One never knows when it may come in handy." She stuffed her books in a shopping bag. "I guess two more years won't kill me, will it?"

"I'm really sorry," I said.

"Me, too."

Outside, the summer sun had risen higher, spreading overpowering heat. "We will soon be going to the farm again," I told Shireen. "Promise you'll write."

"I will, but I'll have none of that goodbye business. It's best to say 'see you later,' no matter how late 'later' may be." She reached into the folds of her chador and handed me the Phillips diary. "Would you mind keeping this over the summer?"

I took the booklet and felt as if she had trusted me with her life. Maybe she was worried that her brother might sneak a peek, or that her mother would find it. I stroked the cover and the corners that had started to shred.

"It'll be safe with me."

We saw Jenab coming out of the building with his briefcase

tucked under one arm and a thick file under the other. Baba followed, hauling a huge box over his shoulder. Closer, I noticed the box was full of books, files and stacks of paper.

"Well, scholars," Jenab said as he reached us. "I guess this is goodbye."

"Yes, it is," I said. He seemed exhausted. Was it the heat? Or was he tired of so many end-of-the-year activities?

"Mr. Elmi, where did you park, sir?" the old custodian asked.

"Not too far," Jenab said without moving. "The end to another good year," he said, smiling his distinctive smile. He followed Baba, leaving without another word.

When Baba came back, he tucked the tip Jenab must have given him into his pocket, shook his head and sighed. "I guess that's that."

I laughed at his morbid tone. "Baba, if I didn't know any better, I'd think someone had died."

He shook his head in sorrow. "Mr. Elmi lost."

I found that no less a shock than someone dying and turned to Shireen for her response, but she didn't seem surprised at all.

"You knew this?" I said. "Thanks for preparing me!"

"I wanted to," she said in her calm tone. "But you're the one who asked not to make this *your* problem." She sighed. "Besides, you seemed so happy about your grades, I didn't want to spoil it."

I was too devastated to respond.

Baba shook his head in sorrow. "No one can take that man's place." He pointed to where Jenab had stood minutes ago.

"What do you mean?" I said. "So he lost, and there will be reprimands, but he'll be back." I turned to Shireen, "Won't he?"

Shireen seemed equally surprised as she asked Baba, "Do you know something *we* should know?"

"May God break my hand," the old custodian said, and he held up five calloused fingers. "I myself delivered his letter of resignation."

With that, he left us and went back inside, his head bent down, his back more pronouncedly curved. I didn't even notice when Shireen left.

I just stood there, my feet glued to the asphalt, the hot sun scorching my brain. I looked at the old school building, now appearing so dilapidated. Who cared how old and ugly it looked? Without Jenab, that place might as well crumble and fall to the ground.

Part Two

The Kiln

Six

MY AUNT HAD STARTED packing weeks before, and this time I understood Mitra's resentment of spending another summer in Golsara. It was as if, along with the clothes, bedding and boxes of food, a good part of my youth was also being shipped to that remote village, where it was utterly disconnected from city life.

Respecting Shireen's wish, I didn't say goodbye and before I knew it, we were on that long road again. I still couldn't believe Jenab's resignation and since Mitra dismissed it as, "Not a big deal," there was no one else to discuss it with. Baba could have it all wrong. If Shireen didn't write to me, it might be months before I'd know if there was any truth to his story. I couldn't imagine someone else teaching Jenab's class. Without him, I might as well do as Pedar wished and forget literature.

Halfway there, where the asphalt ended, a tanker kicked up clouds of dirt, the sun reflecting on its chrome body. I could taste the dust through the opening of the side window.

Akbar honked.

"Let him go," my aunt said. "It isn't safe to pass right now."

"It's never safe on these roads, ma'am. Hundreds get killed every year, but the Road Ministry doesn't care." He looked around the vast desert where a few curving lines suggested beaten paths of horses and mules. "None of these are going to be paved, unless His Majesty happens to pass this way."

"A little at a time, Akbar," Auntie said. "No country is developed in a day."

"They're not developing anything, ma'am. They just take the money and pretend the job's getting done."

Was that how things worked? I wondered if my father's foreman cheated in the same way. Maybe Pedar didn't even know the level of poverty among his villagers.

"His Majesty's smarter than you think," Auntie said. "Look how much he has accomplished in just decades."

"Accomplished indeed," Mitra sneered. "Other countries are putting a man on the moon and we are dreaming of paved roads for our donkeys."

Reza and I laughed.

Akbar shook his head. "The Shah has good intentions, I'm sure, but he's just not his father – God bless Reza Shah's soul." He sighed as if he had known the late king personally. "They say he went around in disguise just to make sure things got done."

Mitra said, "Unlike this one with his dozens of bodyguards."

The glass on the side window felt hot against my forehead. All that talk about roads reminded me of a long ago conversation with Zahra. "Is it true that the streets in town are as smooth as the edge of your pool?" she had asked. At this rate, Zahra wouldn't live long enough to see a paved road in her part of the world.

I looked through the back window. With each kilometer, my school would move farther and farther away and I imagined it being somewhere on the other side of the Earth, a blob on one of Miss Bahador's maps.

My aunt reached over and dialed in the news on the radio.

"...new Symphony Hall, His Majesty, king of kings, love of Arians, personally cut the ribbon with golden scissors. However, students demonstrating outside made the—"

Auntie turned it off.

"No! Let's hear about the students," Mitra said and sat up with newfound energy.

Auntie shook her head. "Students! Their bark doesn't mean a thing. Those youngsters are provoked by the enemy."

"Who's the enemy?" Mitra said, sounding ready for another one of her debates. "All we hear about is the Shah and his golden this and bejeweled that. Who cares about him when the majority of this nation remains hungry and illiterate?"

The mention of "golden scissors" had taken me back to Zahra's loom and her old rusty scissors, frayed rags wrapped around their handle. Just how many pairs of new scissors would the Shah's gold ones buy for the likes of Zahra?

"It's His Majesty to you, miss," Auntie said.

"But of course." Mitra made a face. "His Maaajesteee!"

What would Pedar say to that? *"Nothing happens for no reason,"* he had said. Alieh must have spoken as carelessly as Mitra did.

Auntie changed the station and for the rest of the trip, we listened to music and snacked on roasted watermelon seeds.

Soon after our arrival, the caretaker and his wife served a simple lunch by the shallow pool. In the shade of an old willow, wooden platforms created a makeshift deck, now covered by several tribal rugs. The gardener's little girl sprinkled water on the ground, making sure no dust rose. The earthy aroma of dampened hay particles revived me and I sat down to my favorite meal: Hot bread, churned butter, goat cheese, and fresh herbs. Skillets of sizzling fried eggs followed as we ate with a hearty appetite.

The next weeks could not have passed by any slower. Reza went to check the farms with Pedar, and he sometimes told me about his little adventures. Disinterested in the village life, I stayed in with nothing to do. Each time someone came from the city, I rushed to check if there was a letter. There never was.

Finally, I wrote to Shireen. "Thoughts of that last day trouble me and unless I hear otherwise, I'll continue to imagine the worst." I also told her about our monotonous life. It was a brief letter, but she'd know why. I would ask Reza to deliver it when he went to town on an errand for Pedar.

The next day, I took the letter with me and looked around for my brother. I spotted the car down the narrow road and, judging by those weird swerves, it had to be Reza practicing his driving. I waved at him.

He made a turn, drove toward me and stopped just short of hitting a tree.

"Could you please deliver this to Shireen?" I gave him the letter. As he glanced at the envelope with no address, I added, "Akbar knows where she lives."

He studied my face. "Are you okay?"

I nodded, but he killed the engine and got out. "What's wrong, sis?"

I shook my head. "Nothing."

"The truth."

"It's not about me," I said. "It's everything else."

"Like what?"

I threw my hands in the air. "Look at us. We live on a different planet. Thousands of students are trying to voice their discontent and here we are, safely tucked away."

"Oh, that," he said, scratching his chin.

He sat under a tree and clasped his knees in both hands. "So, my little sister is turning into a mushhead. I bet that Mr. Elmi had a lot to do with this."

I shot him an angry look. "This isn't about Jen... I mean, Mr. Elmi."

"No?"

"No! Anyway, he's no longer my teacher. I heard he resigned."

"You're joking!"

I shook my head.

"Good," he said.

"Why good? What did he ever do to you?"

"I've been to a couple of his classes back when he used to teach at my school. I don't like his influence on students. I bet he's behind some of the voices."

"Well, maybe what this country needs is more voices."

He held my arm a little too tight. "Don't you even think of getting mixed up in what's going on," he said, sounding just like my father.

"And how am I going to do that?" I chuckled. "Oh, yes. Why don't Zahra and I take a couple of brooms and march in protest around the village?"

"I'm serious, Roya."

I pulled my arm away and frowned. "Did Pedar put you up to this?"

He shook his head. "I haven't even mentioned the latest riots to him." He shrugged. "You know how worked-up he gets about these matters." His brown eyes were filled with care. "I'm out there, Roya *jan*. I see what's going on. It isn't about voicing your opinion. One wrong move and your name will be on SAVAK's list."

Who was he to patronize me? He may be older, but Reza was still the same boy who needed my help to do his math homework.

"They wouldn't dare touch Pedar's children," I said, "and even if they would–"

"Oh, grow up, Roya. Where the Shah is concerned, his own children wouldn't be safe." He got up, brushed the dust from the seat of his pants and walked back to the car.

I trotted after him. "So what? Is my blood redder than others'?"

Reza stopped and faced me. "The way you're acting, we'll soon find out, won't we?" I wanted to move away, but he didn't let me. "When did you become so damned selfish? This isn't just about you."

He shook his head. "They'll hit you where it hurts. It could be anyone you care about: your father, your best friend, anyone at all." Reza spoke as if his words described dark images from his mind. "Cigarette burns, rape, and whatever torture they can think of. That's what Pedar is trying to spare you."

My job is to make sure my own children don't disappear, he had said.

Reza put my letter in his pocket. "I'll deliver this. But you have to promise you won't get mixed up with the likes of Shireen Payan."

"I'm sick of people treating me like a child."

"Then start acting more grownup." He gave my cheek a peck and got in the car. I stayed by the willow trees and watched him drive back to the orchard. Soon, Akbar came out and they traded seats. As they drove to town, the dust behind the old Land Rover blended into the desert.

Shireen Payan.

My whole body felt ice cold and off balance. It was as if I was standing at the edge of a cliff with the earth being pulled from under me. How did Reza know her name? They were never introduced, I had not mentioned her last name, and it wasn't written on the envelope. Where had my brother heard the name, Payan?

~

The summer could have been a total waste, but when Zahra informed me of her imminent arranged marriage, it gave purpose to my useless days in Golsara. That evening, after I announced the news to my family, it seemed to put Pedar in his best mood.

"Let's have a real celebration," he said to my aunt. "That girl grew up with us and she has been Roya's playmate and companion. I'll subsidize the cost and we could add a few guests from town, too."

Mitra raised her eyebrows, "Unbelievable! A real ball?"

I regretted ever having doubted my father's compassion. This would give Zahra the wedding of her dreams, and me a chance to make sure she had everything she needed. Other village weddings had been fun in the past, but Zahra's meant so much more.

As I mingled among the locals and helped Bibi with her preparations, I noticed a drastic change in the atmosphere of this calm village. The news of upcoming land reforms imposed by the Shah seemed to have made the farmers' behavior toward the landlords less submissive. I didn't know the details of the Shah's "White Revolution," but understood it promised a better future for the workers and a reduction of the existing social gaps. As part of the plan, farm owners could maintain only one plantation and, as dictated by the Shah, any additional land they owned would be divided among the farm workers.

Shortly after the news about land reform, Pedar stopped calling the king "His Majesty" and instead, like everyone else, he referred to him as "shah" – king. It shocked me when one evening, during a TV interview with the royal family, he yelled at Reza, "Turn that thing off!"

Reza did as told and later asked Pedar, "What will happen to our farms after the land reform?"

"No more Golsara," Pedar had said. "You and I may have new problems dealing with farm workers who feel equal to us."

"Why?"

"Because the ignorant perform best under a dictatorship."

~

The morning of Zahra's wedding, a few women from the village took her to the bathhouse for the henna ceremony. When I joined them later at her house, for the first time I saw my friend in crisp, new clothes. Her hair smelled of soap and rosewater and it had a new reddish hue from the henna, as did the palms of her hands. Bibi had sewn a new thinner scarf for her, which she secured on her head with a colorful silk headband. I helped her put on a new jacket – an added luxury despite the heat. She rubbed a hand over its smooth velvet and smiled.

How plain the city bride's white gown would be next to Zahra's red jacket and colorful ruffled skirt. A woman carried a brazier on a tray, filling the air with smoke and spreading the aroma of burning wild rue over the bride's head to ward off the evil eye. Guests put money on her tray. Children sat on the walls or climbed trees to view the festivities.

"Here come the *doholi,*" someone called out and people pointed at the small band approaching, consisting of a kettle drummer and two oboists.

Women formed a circle for their tribal dance. Even the old grandmothers looked graceful as they swayed to the beat of the drum and clapped their hands this way and that. Dust rose under their light feet. Twirling and turning, their long skirts swayed and the assembly resembled flower petals in a whirlwind.

There goes my Zahra, I thought. In my mind, I could see her with a baby tied to her back, working in the fields beside her man, never questioning destiny.

~

We arrived in Mashad late in the afternoon. As soon as the gate opened, I sensed trouble. The grass had grown tall, the flowers looked wilted, and many had dried out. Weeds grew between the driveway bricks. A layer of dust over the trees and rosebushes gave the place the look of an abandoned garden.

At the sight of Hassan, the cook, opening the gate, my father rolled down his window. "Where is Mammad?" he asked.

Hassan hesitated, as if afraid to respond, but he was rescued as Auntie's voice responded from farther down the driveway. "I gave Mammad a few days off," she said, descending the stairs to greet us. "He's having some problems at home."

Pedar nibbled on his mustache, but said nothing.

"Mammad's problem has to do with his son," my aunt explained when we were in the family room.

"Is something wrong with the boy?" Pedar said, sounding disinterested.

"Not exactly... SAVAK took him," she said softly. The news came as such a shock, she might as well have said he was sucked into a black hole.

Pedar stood up. "What in heaven's name would SAVAK want with a gardener boy?" he roared. Then without touching the tea my aunt had offered him, he opened the window and called out, "Akbar! Turn the car around."

After my father left, I asked Auntie what had happened.

"You know how it is," she said and sounded vague. "Naive kids thinking they can hold the world on their shoulders." When I continued to sit there, she added, "I'm sure your father will sort it out. There's nothing you or I could do."

I thought of Mammad's son, pushing a wheelbarrow, helping around the garden. How could that meek boy do anything that would concern the secret police?

It wasn't until much later when I recalled Shireen's reaction to him, the shock on her face, and... oh, no! My heart skipped a beat as I thought of her words. *"Ali's friend,"* she had said.

~

Pedar called to say he wouldn't be home for dinner, so there went my chance to learn more about the fate of the gardener's son. Later that night, restless and worried, I went down to the kitchen for a glass of milk. The floor was still damp from a wash and stacks of copper pots sat beside of the stove. No one seemed to be around. On the way back to my room, I overheard the cook talking to other servants in the basement. They seemed to be having their tea and, with the well windows open, I could hear him clearly.

"Must have been lunchtime," Hassan said. "Three men in a jeep. Mammad's wife says the boy ran behind the house and hid in the tool shed. One man held a gun to his mother's head and ordered her to hand him over."

"Oh, the poor woman!" our old nanny said.

When it became quiet, I moved a little closer.

Someone whispered, "And, did she?"

"She didn't have to. When she started crying, the boy came out all by himself, and they grabbed him."

Someone gasped.

Hassan went on. "She pulled at her hair and begged them to wait for her husband. They hit the boy with a gunstock and dragged him to the Jeep. By the time Mammad came home, it was too late."

Thoughts of Mammad's family and their hopelessness stayed with me for hours into the night. Now I was curious about the boy's connection with Shireen's brother. When I finally went to sleep, I had a dream about being in a large square, somewhere familiar, yet I didn't know the surrounding alleys. People with flashlights ran down the cobblestone alleys, their screams drowned out by the crackling noise of machine guns. I saw flashes of explosion and heard heavy boots chasing me. My knees turned soft and I could not take a single step. My body folded onto the stones of the alley and I tried to crawl on all fours. That was when I saw Auntie, her good leg severed, blood gushing. She waved her walking cane in the air and opened her mouth, but no sound came out.

Covered in sweat, I woke up with a cry, my heart was beating so fast that I thought my chest would explode.

~

Mammad returned the next morning. He looked tired and had the stubble of a beard. He walked with his back bent. His tiny eyes were red and now seemed even smaller.

From my window, I watched him move about the garden like a sleepwalker. His steps lacked vigor, as if his mind were somewhere far away. When he picked up his shears and started to trim the overgrown grass, I went to him. "Want some help?" As a child, I used to remove the clippings for him, but it had been years since he had let me help.

"No, thank you, Miss Roya," he said.

To my surprise, he sounded calm, almost resigned.

I sat in the shade and watched him cut the tall grass by hand. The snip-snip echoed off the high walls and the hot sun made his face turn red.

"It should have never happened, Miss," he said at last. "I work hard and all I expect of him is to finish school, get a desk job, and live a better life than mine." He looked at me apologetically. "You get my meaning, Miss. Job security."

I nodded.

"He keeps bad company, Miss," he said, and began to recite a verse from an old poem, "A shrewd enemy, though he will cause you pain

Is better than any ignorant friend you may gain."

I smiled at his wisdom. An illiterate, he probably used his fingerprint in lieu of a signature, yet he had memorized verses, and what a brilliant line he had selected. Even Jenab couldn't have done better.

Mammad finished the main lawn area, put his tools in his rusty wheelbarrow, and let it squeak all the way to the greenhouse.

Whispers and signals continued throughout the day, but none of us mentioned the gardener boy out loud. I had a feeling Pedar had told my aunt what followed, but unsure if this fell into the none-of-your-business category, I did not dare ask questions.

The next day, on the way back from school, Akbar gave me the good news. "They let the boy go. Your father sent me there to pick him up this morning. He's home with his mother."

"Is he okay?" I asked.

He shook his head. "I'm not sure what they did to that poor boy, but he sure walks funny now."

I never saw the boy again and for the rest of that summer, Mammad hired a new helper.

Seven

On registration day, we showed up in our street clothes and treated it as the social gathering we never had. I asked my aunt's permission and walked to school.

A few maple trees had already changed color, the bright sun enhancing their golden glow. Mashad's gloomy fall weighed heavily on my heart, still, I welcomed the rustle of a few leaves under my shoes as a pleasant reminder of the school days ahead. I had only walked a couple of blocks, when the sudden screech of car brakes ended my calm. A dusty green Jeep came to a stop a few paces ahead of me.

At first, I thought it must be schoolboys borrowing their father's car to show off, but then three men dashed out and lunged into a group that was gathered on the sidewalk. I froze as one of the men grabbed a boy and slammed his face against the wall. Blood spilled out on the white brick and I was sure his whole face was smashed. The boy grabbed his nose with one hand while throwing punches in the air with the other. Dust rose as another of the men joined in, and together they dragged the boy on the unpaved sidewalk while he continued to kick.

I took a few steps back and waited. It was too similar to the scene with Alieh. No one made any attempt to help the boy and most onlookers seemed to be as stunned as I was. Just before they reached the Jeep, a heavyset boy lunged forward as if to intervene, but he was pushed so violently that he lost his balance and fell into the irrigation stream along the sidewalk. Water splashed and I heard the rev of the engine. Only then did I taste blood and realize how deeply I had bitten my lip.

Someone whispered, "SAVAK," but I wasn't sure which direction it came from. Pedestrians stopped and soon a sizable crowd had gathered around.

"Hold my hand, son," an older gentleman said, reaching down for the boy. Water dripped from the boy's soaked suit and his chubby face had lost all color. He bent his head, avoiding the curious gaze of spectators.

"Go about your own business," the man said, dismissing the crowd.

The policeman at the junction of Jaam Street gave up his post and walked over. He blew his whistle and shouted, "Scatter everyone!" But no one paid attention.

He glared at me. "What are you waiting for, girl?" And he waved his baton. "Shoo! Go to your school." From the way he kept on staring, I knew he wanted to make an example out of me. Humiliated, I looked away and quietly left.

In the schoolyard, I spotted Shireen among a group of students. As I got closer, I was surprised to find Nelly among them. I heard a girl saying, "He resigned."

Someone's voice rose in fury, "Jenab would never do such a thing!"

"But he did," the girl insisted.

"Not true," Nelly jumped in and I thought she was in an exceptionally good mood. "He was fired," she went on, sounding happy about that. "Mind you, if it weren't for my father, he'd be sure to stay fired."

Shireen turned to her with an expression of bitter resentment.

"I'm not sure what's going to happen," Nelly continued. "They've been trying to resolve this problem all summer and Papá is still working on it."

"You mean, Jenab may not teach this year?" I asked, unable to hide my anguish.

"I don't think he's in town," Shireen said, doing her best to sound disinterested.

"Oh, he's in town all right," Nelly said with disdain. "Though I seriously doubt he'll show his face around here just yet."

Shireen and I exchanged our frustration in a sharp glance.

"Papà is using all his power to get that man his job back."

"He is?" I said with newfound hope. A lawyer, Nelly had convinced me her father had enough influence to do anything he set his mind to. Shireen wouldn't look at me.

According to Nelly, there had been parents' meetings throughout summer to solve Jenab's problem, and her father had been at the center of it all.

"Why fire our best teacher?" I asked Nelly.

Nelly waved a hand in the air. "Jenab doesn't exactly follow the regulations, does he? Maybe that's why. I mean, maybe it's because he's such an eccentric."

"Or maybe because he won't allow regulations to interfere with his principles," Shireen snapped back.

Nelly rolled her eyes. "*Papà* says Mr. Elmi is a phony."

"He does?" Shireen asked. "So why's he trying to keep such a phony around?"

"Because of the upcoming university. Mr. Elmi's help will get me through if I decide to take the entrance exams."

"Couldn't your *Papà* hire him as a private tutor?"

Nelly seemed to have missed Shireen's bitter sarcasm. "He couldn't," she said and, to my amazement, she blushed. "I mean, Jenab refused."

This was the first time Nelly had ever called him *Jenab*. Shireen smiled broadly and I had a feeling that if she liked Jenab before, she worshipped him now.

Someone called Nelly from across the yard and as she left, I thought she was saved from being torn to pieces.

"Oh, those rich people and their power struggle," Shireen said. "They make me sick!"

I felt sick too. Sick to realize that, as much as I resented Nelly's arrogance, somewhere deep inside I had identified with a girl who relied on her father's power. No matter how I looked at it, everyone in my family was among the people Shireen despised.

After registration, I told Shireen about the incident on Golestan Avenue. To my surprise, she seemed unmoved by it. I had barely finished when she interrupted me in her matter-of-fact tone. "Get used to it."

Taken aback, her forewarning made every hair on my arm stand.

~

My prediction of a school without Jenab couldn't have been more accurate. With a variety of substitute teachers, the emotional spirit was sucked out of literature class, and as I lost hope for his return, school days became more and more tiresome. Shireen and I read bits of poetry during recess, but unable to analyze some of the more complex verses, our little sessions lacked the needed passion.

Nelly came up with more of her stories every day and I had conditioned myself to believe only what made sense. One day, she came to me in class and whispered, "Did you hear? SAVAK has officially summoned Mr. Elmi."

"What for?" I asked.

"Maybe to squeeze out information about students."

The word 'squeeze' brought to mind all the gory images I had imagined following Alieh's abduction. The thought of any harm done to Jenab was inconceivable. I saw no point in sharing that piece of news with Shireen, as I could just see how she might react to anything coming from Nelly.

At the start of fourth week, I was in class when a lot of noise rose below the windows: cheers, claps and even a loud whistle. I rushed to the window and looked into the schoolyard. Students were gathering, pushing and making their way to approach someone. When I finally got a glimpse, I could not believe my eyes. Jenab, who had just broken free from the crowd, was about to enter the building. That one glimpse was enough to know how much I had missed him. I rushed out to join the crowd, but was pushed back as classmates stormed into the room.

I waited for Shireen, but she wasn't there. I asked someone what was happening, but nobody, not even the students who had seen Jenab downstairs, seemed to know if Jenab was back to stay or not. After what felt too long a wait, Jenab strode in and the entire class erupted in loud applause. He had on a suit and tie, and his face, though clean-shaven, seemed too pale and unwell. He put his briefcase on the desk and started to wipe the blackboard, as if the past few weeks hadn't happened at all. Before beginning his lesson, he hesitated and said, "For those of you who put curiosity before education, let me explain that I'm here to waste another year in this Godforsaken institute." He nodded in appreciation to our cheer and then wrote down the topic of his lesson. "The Significance of Solitude in Poetry."

How I had missed my Jenab's intriguing presence and the way he conducted his class. I watched him with intent, trying to memorize every single move just in case he disappeared again. He seemed to have grown much older over the summer, but there was more. I noticed he no longer studied his audience and throughout the lesson, he made references to our textbook as if to make sure his talks were confined to their subject matter. Unsure if the long absence hadn't made me glorify his image, I tried to focus on the lesson and even took some notes on the differences between solitude and loneliness.

Where was Shireen?

"So you see," Jenab concluded, "Solitude is never lonely. It is rather a sanctuary where one learns to draw wisdom from the company of *self*." He turned to the blackboard and underlined the word. "That is precisely where Rumi stands when he writes, *'Dear heart, get used to your solitude…'*"

As soon as the bell rang, Jenab closed his book and students began to shuffle out of their benches.

"Miss Afshar?" He motioned me forward.

I approached his desk, feeling anxious and excited that he had singled me out.

"Your friend is not well," he said when everyone had left. "Nothing serious, I hope, but I suspect she won't be back for a few days."

His voice lacking the care I had come to know, he now sounded more like a news reporter.

"Yesterday, I went to meet with her father," he went on. "And I happened to run into Miss Payan. She requested that you keep her updated on homework."

Baffled by his formality, I nodded. "I'll call her."

He opened his briefcase to put the textbook away and I noticed the stretched leather had now collapsed into the almost empty compartment.

"Maybe a phone call isn't the best way," he said.

I didn't know what he meant, but thought I'd look for her sister, now a freshman at our school, and give her the assignments. Trailing behind him as we walked to the door, I noticed he dragged his right foot a little. Nelly had spoken of SAVAK's tortures on many occasions. So far I had attempted to ignore her horrific accounts, pretend they couldn't be true, but my confidence was wavering and I felt closer to the brink of fear. Then again, maybe I was just looking for signs, reading too much into things.

"Sir?"

Jenab turned and gave me a sideways glance. For an instant, his eyes met mine and I thought I saw panic in them, as if he dreaded my next question.

"It's good to have you back," I said.

He tilted his head, gave me a crooked smile, and left.

Eight

By the time Shireen came back, the initial energy had died down, our uniforms no longer looked crisp and school had settled into its routine. I had called her house many times without any success. Whenever I gave a homework assignment to Shireen's sister, I asked about her and, "She's okay," was all the answer I got out of Nasrin. It didn't take much to figure that something had happened, something dreadful enough to take away her phone privileges.

Shireen arrived a few seconds after our Geography lesson had started. As soon as she sat down, I took out a sketch I had drawn on a card for her and put it on the desk. It showed a woman in a floral *chador,* holding a bunch of flowers. Under it I had written, "She's Baaaack!"

She smiled, her calm expression unyielding. I nodded to the Phillips diary, hoping she'd write something in it for me, but she just tucked it away and stared at the teacher. It wasn't until later, during recess, when we went to the prayer hall that she told me what had happened to her.

"My parents locked me up," she said. "Three whole damn weeks!"

Despite the warm sun outside, the room felt chilly. Pedar had once locked Reza's door for a day, but three weeks?

"I don't know enough words to describe what I've been through," she said in a hurried tone, as if she could no longer hold it inside. "A couple of weeks ago, I went home to find Maman busy in the kitchen. She said she needed help with dinner because Ali was home, visiting. Then, as if reading my mind, she added, 'Eemon, as well."

"Great!" I said, but Shireen's grim expression stopped me.

"Maman wagged her paring knife at me and said, 'Don't you dare do anything to shame your father or me, you hear?'" Shireen sighed and leaned against the wall. "So, I gave her my word."

I found that hard to believe. The Shireen I had come to know seldom made promises, and for her to give up the chance to see Eemon was out of character.

"I helped Maman prepare the food while thinking of a plan. Finally, when she turned all the burners down to simmer and went to take a shower, I dialed Eemon's number. To hear his voice after all those long months, I thought I'd explode with happiness, but all I said was, 'tomorrow at eight, Goharshad Mosque,' and I hung up."

Shireen had become animated at the remembrance and her face was flushed with excitement.

"He has changed, Roya, aged even. He's not the type to complain, but I could tell the army's been too hard on him. We sat in the crowded courtyard of the mosque and talked until noon." Her lips parted into a faint smile. "That talk alone was worth every minute of being caged."

"How did they find out?"

"Ali told on us."

"Your own brother?" Not to mention Eemon's best friend.

She nodded. "After dinner, we had gathered for tea when Ali just came out and told Agha-jan that I had spent most of the day with Eemon. With no time to prepare a response, I just told them the truth. I guess I must have felt like a trapped animal because I remember shouting back, 'What do you want from me? It's my damn life.' And that was when his hand came down and slapped me." She looked as if the remembrance hurt more than the actual blow to her face. "He hit me, Roya. My father actually hit me!"

Instinctively, I reached up and gave her cheek a gentle stroke.

"Maman just stood there, her piercing eyes a reminder that I had been forewarned. Though later she dismissed it as 'just one little slap,' that single slap was enough to break the barrier of respect and annul all the rules my father had set over a lifetime."

With each word she said, I found a million new questions, but her breathless, hurried recount prevented me from interrupting.

"Ali came to my room in the evening to explain that he had done so for my own protection, that he did it only because he loves me. What in the hell kind of love is that?" She sighed. "For weeks, all I did was cry. Nasrin brought in my meals and left without saying one single word. I had no phone, no books, not even a watch. And all that homework you sent wasn't delivered until just two days ago."

"I'm so sorry."

"Why should you be? I don't regret it one bit," she said firmly and I noticed she had remained dry-eyed, as if isolation had made a stronger Shireen out of her. *One learns to draw wisdom from the company of 'self'.* Weren't those exact words Jenab's interpretation of solitude?

"I'm no longer fighting my father alone," Shireen continued in a calmer voice. "Ever since that day, Ali's attitude has changed, as if he's lost respect or at least sees fault. The other day, Agha-jan was shouting, 'In my time soldiers wouldn't dream of a protest against their Commander in Chief.' I don't know how my brother got away with it, but I heard him say, 'maybe times have changed.'"

"Good for Ali," I blurted out.

Shireen smiled. "Better yet, he went on to finish with this verse, *'If I shall rise, and if you would rise, everyone will.'*"

I knew that poem, though I couldn't remember the poet's name.

"What did your father say to that?"

"The same thing he always says when he doesn't have a better answer. He just told Ali to shut up!"

I wanted to ask what had prompted them to let her go, but her next words gave me my answer. Her parents had threatened her with what my father used as a bribe: Freedom, and love, the lack of which provided them with enough ammunition to make Shireen break down and do the unthinkable. She apologized.

"When Maman brought me to him and said go and kiss his hand, Agha-jan wouldn't even look at me. He kept staring at the television screen while I bent down and kissed those cold, stiff fingers. I said, 'I'm sorry,' my voice betraying me. He just pulled his hand away and said, 'Let's hope you've learned your lesson.'"

I thought of Pedar's melancholic eyes after each outburst and thought if I ever did that, it might make him cry.

"I sure did learn a lesson," Shireen said in a bitter tone. "In pursuit of freedom, I will have to lie, even to my own father."

After a long silence, I asked her, "What about Eemon now?"

"Nothing!" she said. "He is back at the base with no plans for another visit."

~

Before I left for lunch, Shireen gave me something wrapped in a newspaper. It had the feel of a notebook.

"What's this?" I asked.

"You'll see."

I figured it must be another diary, maybe some notes about her horrendous experience. Still, curiosity made me peek. Halfway across the street I had a glimpse of what it was and the shock stopped me right there. Someone cursed as a car swerved by. I tucked the thin book inside my notebook and ran to the other side. For the rest of the way, as if carrying an explosive, I held my books away from my body. Shireen had given me a copy of *The Little Black Fish*.

In my room, I hid the tiny book under my mattress and went to join the family for lunch. Too preoccupied to enjoy the meal, I hurried through it and asked to be excused to go and study. Having locked my door, finally I sat down to read.

The story began with a few baby fish, listening to a bedtime story about the vast ocean. When they all went to sleep, a little black fish continued to think of the ocean and decided to find it. His adventures were sometimes a challenge and many times scary, even funny, but at no time did the story strike me as extraordinary.

I enjoyed reading it and had to agree with Jenab on the power of its simple prose, but like Nelly, I was unimpressed. Nowhere in the entire twenty pages did I find a suspicious message. What had I missed? The little fish was motivated by sheer curiosity. A careless little character, he broke some rules, yet he wasn't even brave enough to cross simple barriers. He never found followers, did not start anything that resembled a movement, and at times his character annoyed me.

I read the book twice more in search of something that might justify its ban, not to mention the possible assassination of the author. There was none.

That afternoon, as soon as Shireen had arrived, I returned her book.

"Finished already?" she asked.

"Yes, and I don't see a reason for all the fuss."

Shireen seemed neither offended nor surprised. She only continued to give me an inquisitive look.

"So what if a fish goes to the ocean?" I said. "Am I too dumb to get the message?"

"Maybe you're looking for the wrong message," she said in her calm voice.

"You're right." I laughed. "I expected to find Karl Marx going fishing and taking all of Tehran University with him."

She didn't laugh at my joke. "What do you know about Marx?"

I shook my head. "Not much, but I was hoping the fish would teach me."

She looked around to make sure we were alone before taking the book out of the newspaper wrapping. She paged through it and took her pen to scribble something before giving it back.

She had underlined the part where the little fish faced danger. *"Death can come at any moment, but... what matters is that my life, or death, should have a profound effect on the lives of others."* She had also marked the ending, when, back at the stream, someone told the same story to a different school of fish. *"All the baby fish went to sleep, except for one little goldfish who stayed up. All night long, he thought of the vast sea."*

"Okay," I said. "So those are pivotal points in the story, but dangerous? Taboo?" I laughed. "Now we're really reading things into this."

She tried to remain calm, but I could sense her frustration.

"Don't you get it? Had he been any clearer, the book would never go to print."

All afternoon, I thought of that book and imagined daring to learn more about illicit topics. What would happen if I broke the rules and did everything that Pedar had prohibited? *"They'll get you where it hurts. It could be anyone you care about,"* Reza had cautioned. But how would they know?

Then I thought of SAVAK, watching a nation from behind those dark sunglasses. Their mysterious presence now a constant in our daily lives, they seemed to be everywhere: in a taxi, inside the telephone line, within the walls of our classrooms and even under the bed.

Nine

HAD I KNOWN THE VALUE in those last days of school, I might have stayed in the moment, but as it was, all I saw were long days, monstrous exams, and my endless worries. I could not wait to put them behind me.

By the time the diplomas were handed out, most students had already dispersed. I realized I might never see some of my classmates again. Few would continue their education, while the rest planned to stay home, wait for suitors, and get married. On the last day, with no uniforms to blend us, our social differences became more noticeable.

As I cleared my desk, I imagined that must be how people felt when they moved. Soon strangers' voices would echo in the hallway, others' hands would run over the worn wood of my desk, and someone else would look out the window on the landing. I was no longer a part of this place, yet even back then I knew it would forever be a part of me.

On the far side of the schoolyard, the old custodian carried a pail and dragged his broom behind him. How ghost-like his presence had been! For six years, Baba had cleaned my classroom, brought charcoal for the fireplace, and watched over us. Yet I knew nothing about him, not even his real name.

After high school, few would bother to go back for a visit and a 'reunion' was unheard of. I watched the sun's reflection on the greenhouse and took one last look at the weeds on its roof, now shriveled. For all the springs to come, I would have to look elsewhere for my poppies.

"There you are!" Shireen's voice interrupted my summation. She had come out of the building, Jenab by her side.

"You wouldn't leave before I had a chance to thank you," Jenab said as they approached, and I knew he was referring to a painting I had left in the office for him. Not my best, but it showed a man, holding a little girl's hand, walking her through a dark forest. The attached note read, "Dear Mr. Elmi: Thank you for illuminating the way."

True that Jenab had kept his distance throughout that year, but his class remained interesting. Some said his problems were political, that SAVAK continued to watch him. Others claimed Jenab had sold out, but none of us knew enough. What mattered was that we had him back and I would not say or do anything that might jeopardize that. My favorite teacher had stamped his name on all the good poems I was to read in the years to come and his voice would echo in many expressive words I might come across. In return, I hoped my painting would remind him of me.

He shook my hand. "Good luck scholars. And, good-bye."

The terminal implication in that phrase reminded me of Shireen's witty bypass. I returned his handshake, forced a smile and said, "See you later, Sir."

~

That summer, we did not go to the village. Mitra's decision to continue her education in England and study European History came as a huge surprise. Tradition dictated that a girl leave her home only when married. How Mitra managed to get Pedar's consent to ignore the old custom was a mystery to me.

Mitra's departure came faster than I was ready for. One day she was there and the next, my sister had gone away. Despite my newfound freedom, not to mention the bigger room I acquired, it surprised me to feel lonesome without her. My father's long absences became more noticeable, Reza was always out with his friends and Auntie spent her days on useless projects such as sewing bed sheets.

Reza seemed to look forward to being a senior at longlast. When he brought home his first impressive school report, Pedar wanted to know if he had cheated. "I didn't need to," Reza said and something in his tone told me my brother had finally matured.

~

The whole world seemed to be preparing for the university exams, known as "concourse." Unlike school exams, which were dispersed over the year, this test covered all the subjects in one day. "Concourse fever," as everyone called it, spread everywhere. On some streets, boys studied under the streetlamps, reading aloud, buzzing like bees.

"How can anyone concentrate with all the noise?" I said to Akbar as we drove by.

"It isn't by choice, miss. They're out here either because they've got no electricity, or they live in a cramped space."

"What about girls then?" I asked. "They can't study on the streets."

"Most of these families won't allow their girls to continue. And, those who do will just have to study under a kerosene lamp."

I imagined school children, small bodies on the floor around a single lamp, its flame casting long shadows on the wall, the air in the room filled with oily fumes.

That night, I found it even harder to study. All of a sudden, Mitra's desk seemed much too big for one person and the room appeared to be ridiculously large. The next day, I called Tahereh Ahmadi.

The only known fact about Tahereh was her poverty, something that even her old uniform could not mask. Her socks were sewn in several places, and she wore shoes that clicked and tapped from the nails used to repair and re-repair them. She hid her mound of frizzy hair under a wrinkled scarf and when she smiled, she covered her mouth with her worker's hands that had chapped and cracked all over.

"Would you mind coming over to study with me?" I asked. We barely knew each other, but she seemed to be overwhelmed as she accepted my invitation.

Night after night, her father gave her a ride to and from my house on his squeaky bicycle. I cleared part of my desk for her, but she preferred to sit on the floor. Not bothering with chitchat and hunched over her books, she studied the entire time. As her focus and determination rubbed off, I studied harder and the distinction of who was helping whom quickly disappeared.

Tahereh's father worked longer hours on Fridays, so when Friday rolled around, I offered to pick her up.

Akbar studied the address I had given him, then took a look at my outfit and said, "You better get yourself a chador, miss."

Trusting his judgment, I ran back inside and found my only chador, and as we neared the south side, I draped it over my head and wrapped it around me.

Fridays being a time for special prayers, the main street, Bala Khyaban, was at its busiest. Pilgrims crowded the sidewalks and vendors' displays spread along the messy pavement. Women gathered by the wide stream that ran along the street, using its smelly water to do their wash, rinse dishes, and even bathe their children. A man led his donkey across the street, impervious to traffic, transporting a heavy load of watermelon.

With the windows down, I heard the melancholic recital of Quran at a nearby mosque. Something about this area of town always made me sad, and it had nothing to do with my mother being buried nearby. Pilgrims came from faraway places to fulfill their dream of touching the shrine's golden doors. A nonbeliever, I felt like a stranger, utterly out of place.

Akbar turned into a cobblestone alley where vendors had opened their carts on both sides. He honked and one woman grabbed the hand of her child and moved to make way, but when a few vendors refused to budge, he stopped.

"I think you should walk the rest of the way, miss."

I agreed. The alley could barely accommodate one car. What if someone drove in from the opposite direction?

"I'll back up and wait for you on the main street," Akbar said. "Unless you want me to park the car and come along."

"I'll be fine."

Even with my chador on, people seemed to know I didn't belong. They stared and I sensed little respect. Maybe my chador was too short, showing bare ankles. Or could it be the clank-clank of my high heels on the stone that set me apart from other women in their thick socks and quiet galoshes?

The alley had a sour smell and I could see urine stains on the whitewashed walls. The only time I came close to anything pleasant was when I asked a shopkeeper if he knew which was the Ahmadi's residence.

The man's face lit up with a smile, showing his few remaining teeth. "Of course, ma'am," he said. "Everybody knows the Ahmadi family." And from his endearing tone, I gathered they were well liked. He pointed to an old door that still had traces of a fading blue paint. There were two brick platforms on either side of it. I didn't see a doorbell and as I hit the heavy brass knocker, its sound echoed in the dome above the door. I heard hurried steps and soon Tahereh's head peeked through.

She opened the door wider and motioned me in. "My mother is eager to meet you. She's made some tea." Tahereh, now more at ease, seemed much happier, even animated.

Afraid that refusing the invitation might offend her, I stepped into a courtyard surrounded by rooms. A few curious heads peeked through half-opened doors, a woman sitting by the tiled pond pointed to me and whispered something to the child on her lap. In the shade of the east wall, a man was asleep on the ground, using his turban for a pillow.

Tahereh, perhaps noticing my stare, whispered, "Those are our neighbors. We all share the courtyard."

"Nice," I said and didn't know what else I could add.

A door facing the entrance opened and a small woman came out to greet me. She had on a black chador and, like Tahereh, she covered her mouth with one hand as she smiled. "Come on in, it's your own home," she said.

I was ashamed at feeling far from being at home. She ushered me into a single room, separated from whatever was beyond it by a blanket nailed to the wall.

No sooner had I sat down on the rug than they both disappeared behind the makeshift curtain. The room was bare, with the exception of a pair of cushions in bright colors, a machine-made rug, and a folded blanket alongside the wall. On the single built-in shelf sat a portrait of Imam Ali next to a brass vase containing two faded plastic flowers. I checked the ceiling, hoping to find a light fixture. There were none.

Tahereh returned with a tray of tea, an unopened box of cookies, and some cube sugar. Her mother followed with a half a watermelon on a plate and two forks stuck in it.

"You shouldn't have gone to all the trouble," I said.

"No trouble at all," Mrs. Ahmadi said in a deep Mashadi accent. "I have been looking forward to meeting Tahereh's good friend." She smiled a genuine smile. I pitied my friend for not inheriting her mother's glowing charm.

While I drank my tea, Mrs. Ahmadi told me about her dream for Tahereh to become a nurse. "Not only will she be in an all girls' school," she reasoned, "but she'll also live in comfort and make a little money right from the start." She smiled at the prospect. "In the end, she'll have a job that'll pay enough to put my other two through school." She shook her head. "Her father can't work all his life, you know."

I wondered if anyone ever asked Tahereh what she liked to do, or if that girl had a chance to harbor any dreams of her own.

~

Two days before the exams, Shireen called and asked me to go shopping with her. I thought it was meant as a joke, but she sounded serious.

"Are you out of your mind?"

"I can't do it alone," she whispered into the receiver.

"This better be awfully important."

We met on Pahlavi Avenue. Apart from the bazaar, Mashad had only one other shopping area. Pahlavi Avenue, lined with poplar trees, formed a T-junction with a narrower street whose real name no one bothered to use. With the T not being at a right angle, it had gained the nickname Crooked Street. A variety of shops lined both sides of the two streets, turning the area into the upper town's main shopping center.

I waited by the fabric section, a row of small cubicles with just a countertop separating the vendor from the sidewalk.

At first, I wasn't sure it was Shireen who got out of a taxi. She had pulled her chador all the way down on her forehead, holding part of it over her mouth.

"Thank you for coming," she said when she had reached me. Out of breath with excitement, she pointed across the street. "See that book store? It's his friend's. He's in there." She held my hand and aimed to cross. "Let's pretend you need to buy a book."

So I would finally meet Eemon, but still didn't understand what she needed me for.

We zigzagged across the street through rows of honking cars and swerving bikes. I followed her into the shop. There were three men inside, including the vendor. One of the two shoppers was thin and tall and had a pleasant face and the other was a redhead, a little on the heavy side. If I had to guess, I would have picked the more handsome one to be Eemon.

Contrary to my expectation, Shireen walked straight to the redhead. Was that who I had seen at her house talking to Jenab? He seemed a few years older than Shireen. Tall and slightly overweight, his red curls had already started thinning.

I busied myself with the book display to avoid looking in their direction. How opposite they seemed, this robust man standing next to tiny Shireen. At the sound of soft laughter, I looked up. Unaware of their surroundings, Shireen's chador had slipped to her shoulders and he seemed utterly absorbed in what she was telling him. Despite their physical disparity, at that moment they seemed in perfect harmony.

I picked up a gaudy postcard and wished she would hurry. The vendor seemed to know I wasn't there to shop, as he didn't bother to ask if I needed help. Minutes later, Shireen came away and we left.

Shireen turned into a side street and stopped to catch her breath.

"Thank you for being my safety net in there," she said. "I had to see him, but since you're with me, if any report gets out, I can always say it was a coincidence."

"Don't even mention it," I said, happy to see her enthusiasm back, and happier to find a face for the infamous Eemon.

"I want you to be the first to know," she said, sweetly, sincerely. "My parents have finally set the date for a wedding."

"Hey!" My loud reaction made a few pedestrians look. "How did that happen?" I said, my voice still a bit too high.

"Jenab had a big part in this," she said. "By now, my father is such a fan, he would consult Jenab on just about anything."

"I wonder what he said to turn things around."

A dark look crossed her face. "It wasn't only him. Maman helped, too." She smiled sadly. "Though not in a nice way. She thinks that after the last fiasco I am such a 'marked girl' that no other suitors will come forward." She gave an angry laugh. "She must have convinced Agha-jan that marrying Eemon would save the family honor and get rid of me all at the same time."

"Oh, you're being silly. A marked girl?" I said, as if the insult had been intended for me. "All you did was walk with him. That hardly deserves such a slur."

She waved her hand to dismiss the matter. "In my mother's mind, walking with a boy is bad enough, and spending a half a day with him is even worse."

"So, tell me, when is it going to be?"

"Not for a while," she said. "After several meetings, my father decided we could get married when, and if, my first year of training is successfully done."

"Then why the secrecy in seeing him?"

"Oh, there's another condition," she said and shook her head. "This time, his exact words were, 'Don't you go thinking this is your permit to play around!' Which, as translated by Maman, means I'm not to see Eemon unless one of them is present."

In a society that forbade gender mix, an engagement was nothing but such a permit. I would never be able to grasp the Payan family dynamics.

When Shireen took a taxi and left, I found myself standing there, smiling. I had finally done something positive for my best friend.

~

The night before the exams, Tahereh Ahmadi agreed to sleep over. I went to bed at midnight, thinking no matter how hard I studied, my brain had reached its full capacity.

I woke at dawn to the sound of my alarm clock. Tahereh's bedspread was untouched.

"You didn't sleep at all?"

She looked up from her notes and shook her head. "Plenty of time to sleep tomorrow."

Auntie offered us a big breakfast, and for good measure, passed us under the old family Quran. Akbar made a stop at Jorjani School of Nursing to drop off Tahereh.

Four blocks away from Medical School, we could see a crowd in front of it. At first, I presumed they were also there for the exam, but as we neared, I saw them marching along University Avenue, carrying a banner in bold letters that read, JUSTICE, SOLIDARITY, and VICTORY.

Most of the demonstrators were dressed in dark clothes, two girls wore scarves and a few boys had black armbands. One man carried a photograph of a young boy, whom I did not recognize. Each time the banner rose higher, they all chanted, "Freedom and solidarity."

"They're at it again," Akbar said and shook his head.

"You think they may disrupt the exam?"

"Nah," he said and nodded to an armed guard near the gate. "With so many of those and all the police around, there won't be a problem."

The demonstrators moved past the guard, who watched them, disinterested.

"Miss Roya," Akbar said before I left the car. He turned to face me and I noticed his hair had already turned gray. He smiled and said, "If anyone passes this exam, I bet it's going to be you."

"Thank you, dear Akbar. Wish I had some of your confidence."

The guards checked my admission papers before letting me in. The demonstrators had moved farther, their chants now fading down the street.

By the time I left the examination hall, there was no one in the courtyard. The police were also gone, except for one patrol car with no one in it. Akbar had not yet arrived. I moved to the shade of a tree, and as I leaned my tired back against its trunk, my hand touched something wet on its bark. I turned to look. A shiny smear in dark red ran down the trunk and I prayed for it to be paint. I brought my hand closer to my face. With the smell of blood, horrible images rushed into my head. What had happened here while we were in the exam hall? I saw no sign of the demonstrators on the street. I craned my neck and looked for Akbar. Where was he?

Stepping back, I instinctively leaned against the wall as if to make sure no one could attack me from behind. A few other students came out and passed by, discussing the questions. Finally, I saw my father's car and ran to it, breathless.

"What happened to you, Miss Roya?"

I looked at my white shirt, where I must have wiped my bloody hand. "There," I said, gasping for air and pointing to the tree. "I think somebody was killed!"

He turned off the engine. "You stay right here," he said, and jumped out. Curled up in the corner of the car, I watched him, rubbing the tree trunk, and then bringing his finger to his nose. He looked in the direction of the car and took a handkerchief out of his pocket to wipe his hand. He went around the other side of the tree and examined the ground. When he finally came back, I thought he looked panicked. Without a word, he started the car and drove away.

"Well?" I said.

He studied me in the rear-view mirror and gave me an unconvincing smile. "I don't think there's anything to worry about," he said, but sounded hesitant.

"What do you mean 'nothing to worry about?'? There's blood. I saw you smell it, too."

He didn't look at me. "Come on, Miss Roya," he said and shrugged. "They probably sacrificed a lamb. People have a ghorbani all the time."

"Here? In front of the medical school?"

"Yes, in front of school." He shook his head. "In front of any damn place they please. You've seen them do it."

I leaned back and exhaled. I pictured men, holding down a lamb as a fountain of blood rose into the air. "Yes, I've seen it."

Maybe Akbar was right. All worked up over this exam, I must be imagining things. "I thought it was the demonstrators," I said. "It scared me."

Akbar now managed a hearty laugh. "The daughter of Rafi khan is scared?" He chuckled. "Wait till your Pedar hears about this." He studied me in the mirror again. "Look at your face, *khanoum*! You look like you've seen a jinni!"

~

Weeks later, the concourse nightmare was behind us as Shireen and I were both admitted to our schools of choice and Tahereh Ahmadi scored second best in the School of Nursing.

Pedar could not stop bragging about my triumph. The minute my name showed up in the newspaper among other first year students, he picked up the phone and called his friends. "Have you seen the papers?" The way he spoke of my success sounded as if I had already graduated medical school.

That evening, Pedar cancelled his poker game and took the family out for chelow-kebab. After dinner, he presented me with a gold coin in a red velvet box. "When you graduate, the biggest gold coin in the country will join this one," he said and gave me such a tight hug I thought he'd break a rib. His smile had widened and there was a new bounce to his step.

Mashad University, though one of the best in the country, lacked a real campus. It had started with an old house and by now had expanded through the entire neighborhood. Each school started in whatever large building became available. The Medical School sat a few blocks away from the School of Science. Despite the proximity, I did not see Shireen. Sometimes I passed her at the main library, but we seldom had a chance to talk.

A few months into the academic year, Shireen called and told me about her wedding plans.

"We'll only have a private ceremony to sign the documents, a small gathering of just the family," she said.

Not knowing her family, I understood, but it did feel strange to imagine not being at my best friend's wedding.

"Have you decided on a gown?"

"Just a simple white dress," she said. "I don't want a bridal gown, it's such a waste of money."

"Oh, but you must," I objected. "What's a wedding without a pretty dress, a veil, a lovely bouquet? Oh, and a good photographer to take lots of pictures."

She huffed with disgust. "All that frill is nothing but an imitation of Western fashion. Can you imagine what that kind of money can do elsewhere?"

"Well, if I ever get married, a dress is at the top of my list. I don't care who the groom may be, but you can bet the dress is going to be stunning," I said and laughed.

Shireen was so quiet that I feared she might have taken me seriously.

As the year progressed, I noticed more changes in my friend. On the sporadic occasions when we did talk, she spoke less of her own life and more about society in general. Much to my embarrassment, she became ever more passionate in her criticism of the wealthy, though none of her remarks seemed to include me. It was as if by knowing me, she made an exception and put my family on neutral ground.

"In a society with so much poverty, what right do those useless people have to indulge in luxuries they neither need, nor deserve?" she said.

"Do you ever stop to think that I'm one of those useless people?"

"That's not true," she said apologetically. "Let's say you don't belong there."

Her own lifestyle, though comfortable, was not grand. The Payans lived in an average three-bedroom house and got along without a car. Her father owned a shop in the bazaar selling hand-made rugs, while Mrs. Payan did all the housework. If they needed more, they didn't show it. In fact, I knew of one student in Reza's class whose educational expenses were subsidized by Mr. Payan.

I tried hard to push away my inner thoughts. Why did Pedar own two cars if he had only one driver? Servants cost little and many were happy to work for room and board, but did we need so many?

Wishing to diminish the guilt, I reminded myself of the stories Pedar had told us about his youth, how he started by working for his uncle. "I only had the shirt on my back and a few coins in my pocket," he said time and again. On the other hand, he came from a well-known family and God only knew how many doors had opened for him just because people knew the name, Afshar. Pedar took pride in what we had. "Don't you ever forget that you're really somebody," he said to Mitra.

"And what's a *somebody* if you take the money away?" Mitra asked. "What's the difference between us and *them*?" She pointed to the basement, where the servants lived.

"It isn't as if I stole the money. I've worked hard to get here." He chuckled. "As for *them*," he imitated Mitra, pointing to the basement. "They're not slaves. They're free to go. If God wanted them to earn more, he'd give them bigger brains."

They're not slaves. *Just how different were they? Most farmers worked for room and board. Where was the justice in that? Sometimes I wondered if behind the praise, behind the polite smiles, there was also resentment.*

In an adult world, time flew by. Gone were the days when I saw a long distance between breakfast and dinner. As I spent my entire day at school, came home at dusk, and dealt with a larger volume of work, my measure of time changed from hours to weeks, months to semesters.

Ten

I STAYED AT THE ANATOMY LAB during my lunch break to study for a mid-term exam. The strong smell of formaldehyde reminded me of the disinfectants used at hospitals. Alone with a corpse, it surprised me that I no longer feared the brown mass on the table. In fact, it now looked more like a dummy made of leather.

As I finished my work and prepared to leave, the door opened and sunlight framed a tall figure. Judging by his lab coat, he was also a student.

"What are *you* doing here?" he asked, as if I had trespassed.

"Studying. What's it to you?"

"Ah! A child prodigy, are we?"

I glared at him. "I'm nineteen."

He chuckled. "Sure you are." Walking to the table next to me, he gathered some papers and waved them in the air. "Came for these," he explained, and stood there as if expecting me to talk.

I walked away and left without a word, making sure I slammed the door. Hard.

A few days later, the guy showed up again, this time at the ping-pong tables. "Is there room for one more player?" he asked the group.

I jumped at the chance. "Are you sure you want to play with *children*?"

"Ah, there you are," he said sounding pleased. "I've been looking all over, trying to find you."

I ignored him.

"I believe I owe you an apology." He walked over to me. "But you can't blame me. You do look too young to be in med. school."

I was tired of comments about my childlike looks. If that was his way of apologizing, he'd better forget it. I turned away and watched the end of the game.

As my friends started the next round, he extended a hand to me. "Kyan Ameri," he said, but when I pretended to give all my attention to the current game, he wiggled his fingers adding, "Or not!"

I did my best not to smile. He stepped closer and whispered, "What if I get down on my knees in front of all these people and beg? Will you then forgive me?"

I stole a look at him. In the bright light he looked better than I remembered. A protruding chin and his Roman nose gave him a serious look, but under the bushy eyebrows his eyes showed a playful twinkle.

"What's there to forgive?" I said and shrugged. "People make similar stupid remarks all the time."

"Shame on people." He smiled.

"How old or young I seem shouldn't matter, but I suppose some people's brains are in their eyes."

He nodded. "In that case, let me tell you. I think you have beautiful brains."

I smiled, but tried to focus on the game.

"So how's the anatomy lab going?" he said, standing closer.

"Don't even ask!"

"That bad?"

"It was bad enough to study the blue veins, red arteries and yellow nerves in the textbook, who knew they'd all turn brown on a pickled cadaver?"

"Oh, but there's a trick," he said. When I did not respond, he added, "I'll be glad to teach it to you and make up for my 'stupid remark,' as you put it."

I smiled at the idea of having my very own tutor.

~

Kyan proved to be the anatomy guru. During the following weeks, we met in the lab a couple of times and the way he explained things made it much easier to study. Each time, he made sure we ended our meetings with a tea at the cafeteria, and I enjoyed having my classmates watch me walk in with an attractive student two years my senior.

One day, as I was about to leave the library, Shireen came out the door.

"Is that you, Roya?" She sounded surprised.

I gave her a big hug and thought she looked tired. "Good to see you," I said. "I've been meaning to call. How's the married lady?"

She touched her belly. "You mean the 'Mama'."

"Oh, my God!" I shouted and then, remembering the library, lowered my voice. "You mean I'm going to be an aunt?"

She nodded and her smile had radiance.

"When?"

"Oh, I'm only into my third month."

She started to go down the hallway. "I'm late for my doctor's appointment," she said. "See you around."

I wanted to tell her about Kyan, but she had already left. I stood there and watched the glass door as it swung in diminishing arcs, until it came to a stop.

~

Summer had just begun, but the mercury on the thermometer outside my window had already climbed close to a hundred. Here and there on the street I had seen the ice vendors selling huge blocks of ice and knew that soon the heat would keep me indoors for most days.

Many students had already gone back to their hometowns. Kyan said he'd be somewhere up north near the Caspian. I enrolled in an English literature class at the British Council Library and also planned to spend some time on my artwork, but deep down knew it would be a long, boring three months.

"I'm going to Golsara one last time before I let it go," Pedar announced at breakfast.

"Let it go?" I asked. "What do you mean?"

He did not respond.

Reza looked up and motioned for me to shut my mouth. So preoccupied with school for months, I had not even thought about my father's share of land reform issues. The Shah's so-called "white revolution" was now in full motion. Every day the television showed farmers bending their turbaned heads to kiss the royal hand, and receiving the deed to their own piece of farm.

"Golsara is such a lovely little place," Auntie said. "I hope they'll keep it up."

Pedar grunted. "Unlikely. That village was on its way to ruins as it were. Between us, if not for the orchard and the big house, I would gladly have let it go years before."

I opened my mouth to say something, but Reza glared at me.

Unfair as some considered this new takeover, the Shah's decisions and any amendments he added to the constitution, were indisputable. Pedar seemed so outraged about the whole matter that none of us had dared discuss the details with him. We knew he would keep Ahmad Abad, better known as 'the upper village.' The money generated from its crop of sugar beet had always been Pedar's main income. All the same, his choice for Golsara to be the first to go came as a surprise.

"We'll need to clear the big house," he said.

"One of us needs to be with you to pack our things," Auntie said, "but I couldn't possibly make it on such short notice."

Reza nodded to me.

Picking up on my cue, I said, "What if I go?"

That seemed to please Pedar and so it was decided.

As much as I had resented our long stays at Golsara during the past couple of years, the prospect of never seeing it again was more than I was prepared for.

"That was good of you to offer," Reza said later, as if it had been my idea. "I think we all need to be more supportive." Worry crept into his eyes. "Sometimes I fear Pedar may have a nervous breakdown over this."

"Why don't you come with us?"

He shook his head. "No, not me. Pedar needs someone who can calm him down, someone he really likes, you know? Lately, my presence seems only to agitate him."

Though I disagreed, deep down I knew he was right. For some peculiar reason, Pedar showed no patience for his only son. Did he have any idea how deeply Reza cared?

If anyone could understand my grief over letting go, it would be Shireen. But when I called her, she sounded so excited about her preparations for the baby that I decided not to spoil her mood. "Does one little baby need all this?" she asked. "I think we've made enough clothes for me to have quadruplets."

"I wish I could come over and help," I said. "But Pedar and I are going to the country for a few days."

A man's voice called Shireen.

"I have to go," she said in a hurried voice. "Have a great time," she added before hanging up.

I put down the receiver. "Yes, a great time," I said into the thin air. "I'll have the greatest time saying goodbye to Zahra and to my childhood memories. It'll be a blast knowing I'll never see that place again!"

When I looked up, my frustrated reflection stared back in the hallway mirror. What was wrong with me? Was I turning into an old maid, jealous of my happily married friend? Or, could I be angry with myself? I had taken that orchard, the old village and all those wonderful people for granted. As long as I remembered, they had been a constant presence. I felt something break inside me.

~

We arrived at Golsara in the early afternoon. More than a year had passed since the last time I'd seen the place. Judging by the neglected garden, I thought my father must have given up on Golsara months before. The trees seemed thirsty and Pedar feared the village's single stream would soon dry up.

"Why not dig a new well here?" I asked.

He shook his head. "It won't be cost effective. Golsara has very little farmland and its soil lacks quality."

"Then, what will the natives do?"

"Very few plan to stay. I've provided housing for most of them in the upper village." He pointed to a dying willow. "Those hard working people deserve better than *this*."

Zahra and her family had already moved to Ahmad Abad, but I took a walk to her neighborhood anyway. The place had already assumed the appearance of an abandoned village. The wide-open doors to several huts resembled big holes in the wall, no smoke rose to show any sign of life and there was no livestock around. Hard to believe that these dilapidated mud houses had recently been a happy community. In the orchard, many trees and half of the vineyard had dried up. Even the pool looked mossy.

The drastic change in the attitude of the few remaining servants was hard to miss. While they seemed to be going about their jobs, I saw no sign of the old courtesy. The gardener's little girl showed no interest in our comings and goings. Abolishing her old attire of a long denim skirt and colorful headbands, she now dressed "city style" in a shirt and pants. When I passed by, she just stared without showing the slightest sign of recognition.

During the first two days, I followed Auntie's instructions and went down the list of our personal effects to be packed. Pedar spent most of his time in the room by the entrance, using it as a makeshift office to talk to workers. The day he went to say his good-byes to the remaining natives, he was in such a bad mood that we barely spoke. Late at night, I could smell his opium down the hallway.

My packing was done around the same time as the crows began to circle the orchard. With pictures removed from walls and my father's books packed in boxes, the place looked as though no one had lived there.

Akbar drove the Land Rover with Pedar in the passenger seat and me riding in the back. My father's voice carried a resigned tone. Except for a word here and there, none of us said much along the way, but I sensed a shared grief among us.

Like a camera, the small rectangle of the rear window zoomed out on the playfield of my childhood. With each mile, the village shrank smaller and smaller until the cluster of trees disappeared into a cloud of dust behind us.

I never saw Golsara again.

Eleven

On my first day back, all I could think about was seeing Kyan and I hoped my excitement wasn't too obvious. I had noticed the way other girls eyed him, though he did not seem to return their glances. Sometimes, I allowed myself to think I was more than just a friend to him, but for all I knew, he considered me his pal, a younger student who needed help and leaned on his friendship. I would do nothing to jeopardize what we had.

Only when we drove through University Avenue and I saw a few demonstrators, did I remember the growing wave of oppositionist activities. This time, people gathered at the junction of University Avenue and Jaam Street and there appeared to be equal numbers of men and women. What surprised me was that all but two women wore a headscarf. They held a sign with a young boy's picture on it. As we sped past them I could only read "*Free our...*"

"Slow down," I said to Akbar, and tried to read the rest through the back window.

Akbar mumbled something without changing his speed.

"They didn't look like students," I said.

Akbar glanced at me in his mirror and said, "Who knows who they are these days? It could be teachers, students, even parents." He shook his head. "They're like weeds, growing everywhere."

I turned to look again, but the demonstrators had disappeared around the corner.

Minutes later, Akbar dropped me off in front of the gate where a new guard asked for my identification.

Students were gathered around the courtyard in small groups, talking. If they knew of the demonstration outside, they didn't show it.

In the cafeteria, Kyan waved at me from a table near the wall. When I reached him, he pretended to check the watch he never wore, "Right on time, little lady," he said, smiling.

"Look at you, all roasted!" I knew he had spent most of his summer by the Caspian Sea, where his uncle lived. "Looks like you had a great time."

Squinting, he studied me as if searching for a clue. "I missed you," he said at last.

That flutter was back in my rib cage. Thoughts of Kyan had been a major part of my summer, but only now did I realize how much I had longed to see him.

"Aren't you going to say you missed me, too?" His eyes had a playful sparkle.

"Are you joking?" I said and chuckled. "I had a great summer away from those anatomy lessons of yours."

He laughed.

I told Kyan about the demonstrators I had seen on the way. "From what our driver told me, it sounds as though their numbers have increased over the summer."

"I don't think so," he said. "Though, having been away most of the time, I wouldn't know for sure." He leaned closer and whispered, "It's been hush-hush. But this week, with the start of school..." Two boys neared, and Kyan didn't finish.

I had hoped we could sit there and talk for a while, but someone from the courtyard called Kyan, and he had to leave.

"Tomorrow, same time, same place?" he asked.

I nodded.

Walking to my locker, I made a mental note to call Shireen again. The day I returned from Golsara, I had called her house. She was out, but the woman answering the phone told me that Shireen had given birth to a healthy boy five days earlier than expected. I couldn't wait to see the baby.

That evening, I called Shireen again and this time she picked up. "I've been meaning to call you myself." She sounded rather formal, distant even.

"I'm dying to see the little guy. When can Auntie Roya come over?"

She hesitated for a few seconds. "How about Friday?"

"Perfect."

Friday afternoon, the taxi dropped me off at the opening of a dead-end alley, not too far from the Payans' home. Rows of new construction on both sides of the street resembled identical stamps on a large envelope. The doors were painted olive green with a large white tile mounted above to show house numbers.

Shireen's was second to last. How strange it felt to know this was the first time I would set foot in my best friend's own home. I had a small gift for the baby and now regretted not having brought some flowers from our garden.

Cautious that the doorbell might awaken the baby, I knocked lightly and soon Shireen opened the door. She was in a short-sleeved cotton dress and wore her hair pinned up in a bun. She carried her son, wrapped in a blanket, in the curve of her elbow. With the baby in her arms, we gave each other an awkward hug.

"Look at you," I said, my voice high with excitement. "I can't believe you're a mom."

"Neither can I," she said softly, and closed the door behind me.

The dimly lit hallway smelled of plaster and fresh paint. Shireen turned on the light. "In this dark place, day and night are the same." She held the baby so I could see his face. "Meet Behrang."

Behrang? The only person I had heard of with a name close to that was the author of *The Little Black Fish* – Samad Behrangi. But I had never heard it as a first name. Did it sound masculine enough? I wasn't sure.

Wrapped in a hand-knitted blanket, the baby turned his pink face away, squinting at the light. His miniature fingers wrapped around one of Shireen's. Who knew a baby could be so small?

"He's precious," I whispered and touched his cheek with the back of my finger. His skin felt soft as a flower petal. "And so tiny!"

"Tiny?" Shireen chuckled. "Ask my arms how tiny a five-kilogram baby is."

She opened the door to what seemed to be the dining room. Except for a rug, an oval table and six chairs, the room had no other furnishing. Bare walls with a few holes left from nails gave the place a transitory look. I wasn't sure if they had just moved in, or were about to move out.

I took the chair Shireen offered me.

"How did you come up with such an extraordinary name?" I asked.

"He's an extraordinary boy," Shireen said and I had the feeling my remark was misunderstood.

An awkward silence fell and for the first time, it seemed as though we had nothing to say to each other.

"Can I hold him?" I said, not knowing how else to break the ice.

She hesitated at first, but then lowered her arms and put the baby in mine. He weighed less than a cat and smelled of milk. His out-of-focus eyes did not meet mine. He half opened his mouth, revealing the tiny button in the middle of his upper lip. It was as if the finest work of art was entrusted to my hands. The baby started to frown and squirm. Afraid that I wasn't holding him right, I gave him back.

"The poor thing is so tired," Shireen said. "But I wanted you to see his beautiful eyes while they're open." She nuzzled the baby's head and kissed it gently.

"How does it feel to be a mom?"

"It's the strangest sensation," she said. "He's a gift far beyond what I deserve. I look at him and see a part of myself that I can shamelessly worship." She stopped smiling. "Sometimes I get this hollow feeling that someone's going to steal him."

The baby's face turned red and he started to fuss. Shireen got up. "He really needs his sleep. Be back in a minute."

She left and moments later, I could hear her humming a soft lullaby. I tried to imagine what it would be like to have a home, a husband, and my own baby, but all that came to mind was Kyan, waiting for my answer to a question from the *Gray's Anatomy*.

Shortly after the adjacent room had gone silent, Shireen came back, carrying a tray of tea and homemade cookies.

"I'm still practicing," she said, nodding to the cookies. "You'll be the first to try these."

She seemed content, and the hostess role suited her, but something was missing. As if pre-rehearsed, her words lacked sincerity and sounded hurried.

"Just look at the dust around here," she said and rubbed a finger on the dining table, leaving a shiny line behind. "One tiny baby can take up all of your time."

Her attempt at small talk intensified my anxiety. Had I not called in advance, I might conclude I'd come at a bad time. Shireen went to the window and looked into the backyard. "This would have been much easier by phone," she said at last.

I had no idea what she meant by 'this,' but the chill in her voice stirred a bad feeling in me.

"I guess there's really no good way," she added.

Looking back, I wish a thousand times that something had interrupted Shireen before she uttered the next sentence.

"I don't want you to call me," she hesitated, "or visit."

She had to be joking. While she continued to look outside, I tried to make sense of the situation. A minute must have gone by in silence, and with each passing moment her words lost more of their meaning until they became just sounds hanging in the air, casting a shadow between us. A car horn sounded in the distance.

"What do you mean?" I finally said.

"We can no longer be friends."

I felt the way one feels after dropping something valuable into deep water, wishing to dive in and retrieve it, while there is no doubt it is lost for good.

"I'm a married woman–" My nervous laughter interrupted her.

"I know, I know! You may open my eyes and ears," I said, trying to imitate our vice principal in high school, but now it didn't sound funny at all. "Don't worry, I know all about sex. I'm almost a doctor." My voice was too high-pitched.

Shireen didn't laugh. She stayed at the window with her back to me.

"Eemon doesn't approve of our friendship," she said at last.

I don't know how long it took me to believe she was serious, but overcome with humiliation I said, "He doesn't even know me."

"He knows enough *about* you, your family, and the people you associate with." She hesitated a moment. "Eemon rarely makes mistakes in his judgment."

Why won't she look at me?

"And how exactly does he *judge* me?"

"I don't think he knows you well enough to be able to set you aside, or make an exception." She added softly, "The way I do."

She remained by the window while I stared at her back, waiting for the next lash. After a long pause, she hit me with her cruelest remark. "He thinks you're shallow."

"Shallow?" I hit the table so hard it hurt my hand. Her worried eyes turned to the next room.

Hoping I had not awakened the baby, I repeated in a lowered voice, "Shallow?"

Shireen walked over to me and put a hand on my bent arm.

"That's *his* opinion," she said and for a second I thought her voice had a touch of affection. Resuming her matter-of-fact tone, she added, "I can't be around you without somehow getting mixed up in your society."

I would not put up with any more of her condescending remarks.

"What's wrong with *my* society, Shireen? What did we ever do to you?"

"Roya-jan, please don't make this any harder than it is."

She sounded well rehearsed, as if she had planned exactly the path this conversation would take. Why couldn't we talk the way we used to? What happened to finding our own words, making up our own expressions? Busy at building a divide between us, she seemed to add another layer with each word. "Please, try to look at it from my side. He's my husband and, as a wife, I comply with his rules."

'Comply' had never existed in Shireen's vocabulary before. Had marriage changed her that much?

"Then why did you tell me to come here today?" I asked her.

"I have something to give you."

When our eyes finally met, I thought I saw a trace of my own feeling of loss in hers, deep sorrow, even regret. Then again, I was desperate for anything that might salvage what she was so set to destroy. She rose and left the room in search of whatever she had meant to give me. Alone, I reviewed her words, trying to make sense of what was happening. The blow was so hard that if Shireen had asked me to leave that minute, my feet could not have carried me.

She returned with an armful of papers, notebooks, and letters. Piling them on the table, she said, "I have no use for any of these."

I saw the gray cover of the Phillips diary, but there was more: things we had written together, my letters, and a photograph of the two of us. I should have left before my tears betrayed me, but they now flooded my cheeks, blinding my eyes. I detested those damn tears for making me look so weak.

"I'm sorry," Shireen said, but she didn't sound sorry enough.

I gathered the stack of papers and was in the hallway before she could say another word. I thought I heard her say goodbye as I slammed the door, but I wanted to walk away as fast as my high heels would let me.

The smell of fine herbs filled the alley, coming through a neighbor's window. Children playing behind one of the walls talked and giggled. The main street was quiet and I saw no taxis. Feeling the unbearable weight of the memories Shireen had dumped in my arms, I didn't stop until I was far away from her neighborhood.

At my house, I went straight to the big kitchen. Hassan was busy fanning the lit charcoal in preparation for making *kebab.* He yelled as I threw the stack of the paper into the fire. "What are you doing, miss?" he said. "This isn't a wood stove! Aw, look at the mess you've made of my good charcoal!"

Hungry flames rose and swallowed the remnants of my younger days. The poems, stories, and silly notes shriveled and turned into thin, gray flakes that Hassan considered just a "mess." And oh, what a mess! I wanted nothing to do with the times when I was soft clay. How intense my world had been back then, when everything was either black as the night, or white as innocence! An entire slice of my existence, a time of hope, trust, and pure emotions was burning into oblivion. *I have no use for any of these!* So that was what happened as life moved forward. I wondered if I was the only one who still clung to tender memories.

Tearing the picture of two friends in half, I threw it into the fire and watched our faces distort, as they each burned alone.

Hassan watched me in surprise, but when I threw in the Phillips diary, he reached into the flames, grabbed its corner and threw it on the ground.

"Not this one, Miss," he objected. "It's too heavy. It'll be sure to kill the fire."

I picked it up from the ground. The fire had only made the cover hot, but not yet reached its pages. I wiped the ashes from it. This wasn't Shireen's alone to discard; it was my life too, my stories, and my memories.

The old cook had a point. *Not this one.*

~

There were only a few students around the cafeteria. Despite the large fan on the counter going full speed, the place felt hot. The minute I reached Kyan, he frowned asking, "What's wrong?"

I shrugged. "I'm different."

"Oh?"

"I grew up."

He chuckled and gave me the once-over. "Nope. Still the same cute five–foot-nothing." When I didn't respond to his humor, he asked in a more serious tone, "Did someone dare hurt my favorite girl?"

"What makes you say that?"

"Because for each growth, there's a growing pain, and for each pain, something – or someone – who caused it."

I nodded.

He paused. "No one – and I mean no one – is worthy of your tears, because those who are worth it, will never make you cry."

He reached over and gave my hair a gentle stroke, brushing away a layer of pain.

Weeks later, I ran into a classmate and learned that Shireen and her husband had moved to Tehran. Good. That meant I wouldn't bump into her. Nor would I be likely to hear their names in conversation. At some point, I took the Phillips out of my dresser and put it in a box where I stored old books and magazines. I, too, could discard Shireen from my life and for a while it looked as if I had succeeded.

~

When months later Auntie spoke Shireen's name, I had to actually think before I realized to whom she referred.

One day at breakfast, I realized all eyes were on me. My aunt put down her newspaper and poured me a glass of tea. Then she took the paper, folded the front page and held it in my face. I read the headline.

Bank Roberry Attempt Leaves One Dead
And Three In Critical Condition

I shrugged and reached past her for the bread, but she held the paper steady.

"You'll want to read this," she said, her voice alarming.

"Auntie, dear. You know my bank robbery days are over," I said and chuckled at my own joke.

"It concerns your friend," she said.

"I don't know who you're talking about."

Reza said softly, "You know."

My aunt looked at the article and read the name, "Shireen Payan."

I dropped my bread and snatched the paper from her hand. "Let me see that," I said, still sarcastic. That couldn't possibly be the same Shireen, and I'd soon find out where the misunderstanding came from.

"Last night, the guards at Tehran's Eisenhower Bank shot and killed one man, and critically wounded two others during a robbery attempt. According to the police, the bandits were armed and guards shot them in self-defense. These men are linked to the terrorist group responsible for the bloody incident at Siahkal."

With no names mentioned, so far I had not seen a link. Suddenly, the door opened and hit the wall behind it as Pedar walked into the room.

"I see you've read the paper," he said to me, and sat down.

"I just started, but I don't see what–"

"Keep reading," he growled.

I went back to the article and the next paragraph hit me.

"Three other members of Fadaiyan were later arrested at their residence. Ali Payan, a key member, was shot and killed at the scene. Eemon Arfa, believed to be the mastermind behind this terrorist act, took a bullet to his lung and is listed in critical condition. His wife, Shireen Payan, was later captured at their operation base. Despite the indirect nature of Payan's crime, no bail is set for her release. Her infant son is believed to be unharmed."

Ali shot dead? For a second I saw my own brother, Reza, in a pool of blood. As tears welled in my eyes, the words on the page slid around like dark ink blotches. There had to be a mistake. By now I could believe the political motivation, even in them being members of whatever "Fadaiyan" were, but bank robbery and acts of terrorism? No matter how mean she had been to me, I knew that the last thing Shireen Payan cared about was money. She would never do anything that might jeopardize lives, certainly not for money. And, from what she had told me, neither would Eemon.

Like dust particles in a storm, my thoughts whirled in different directions. The pain of our last visit resurged, as if a scab had been removed from a wound. I blinked the tears away and tried to read more, make sense of it, but it was hard to concentrate with everyone watching me. Pedar stared as if I'd had something to do with the incident.

"I'm waiting for an explanation," he said in an uncompromising tone.

Auntie took my hand in hers. "Roya, dear, the time to tell us is now." She put her arm around my shoulders. "Did you know about any of this?"

I shook my head, unable to utter a word.

"Roya is too sensible to get involved in anything like that," Reza said. But no one seemed to pay attention.

"Stop your crying," Pedar commanded. "What happens to these felons isn't any of your damn concern. Just be grateful you weren't among them."

My father's unfair judgment made me feel protective of Shireen and for just a moment, it helped me to get past my anger. I was still mad at Shireen, but I knew she was no felon. She may have been disloyal to me, but she was not a terrorist. The only possible conclusion was that the whole story had been fabricated to mask something else, something bigger. But what?

Pedar dropped his napkin on the table and pushed his chair back without having touched his food. He came so close to me that I had to lean away. Poking a finger into my shoulder, he whispered, "Listen, and listen well. If I so much as hear of you making a suspicious move, I'll deal with you in a way that'll make the secret police seem like angels."

He left the room and no one said a word until the sound of his heavy footsteps had faded down the front stairs. For a few seconds, I only heard the chime of the big clock in the hallway.

My aunt offered me a tissue and gently stroked the back of my hand. Her next words told me just how little she knew of what went on in my world.

"This is where I'd like to see this friendship end," she said.

Having no response to that, I excused myself and left for school.

I walked along Golestan Avenue. The images that were brought to mind by the article were all foreign. Funny how the only vision that was clear had nothing to do with the report, yet I found that one the hardest one to push away: Behrang's tiny hand wrapped around Shireen's finger, holding on for dear life.

My own mother's face on our last day together had started to fade behind the thickness of time, her pale face lost in a huge pink bed, the pear-shaped charm on her neck chain rising and falling. She had left me long before other memories could be built. I wondered if she ever felt well enough to enjoy her baby Roya, and if she had been the one teaching me my first words. On that last day, I had stood on my tiptoes, hanging on to her bedpost, watching her neck chain and that pear-shaped pendant go up and down, up and down with every breath she took. She gave me a wan smile. "Go away and play," she had said. What were Shireen's last words to her little boy?

A man sat at the crossroads. "Extra, extra! Bank robbery in Tehran," he shouted. I stopped and bought two different newspapers.

On University Avenue, there were four police cars. The sidewalk was covered with pieces of torn paper and pamphlets with large print.

Where had the demonstrators gone?

Skipping class, I headed straight for the coffee shop and spread my newspapers on a table. Now paying more attention to details, what I read was shocking. The report gave an evil, dangerous portrayal of Eemon and Shireen, and what a monster they had made out of Ali! Now, with no one hovering over me, I could at least concentrate on what I read. Shireen was charged for being an accessory to a crime. Posing as the lady of the house, she had taken care of what the newspaper called "the terrorists." Their apartment was referred to as a "team house." Ali had been shot during the raid and was pronounced dead. Others, including Eemon, and Shireen's younger brother, Ahmad, were critically wounded.

"According to a SAVAK's spokesman, the government is working on a plan of action that will tighten the national security. "

"May I borrow your newspaper?" someone asked.

I looked up at three first-year students. For years, I had identified SAVAK by their dark suits and large sunglasses. Now I no longer knew what to look for. Unsure, I handed the paper to one of the students. When the three gathered to read the article with occasional exclamations of surprise, I decided they were as confused as I was.

The reaction around campus proved to be far from what the newspapers had hoped for. Not only did most students refuse to call them criminals, they seemed to view the Fadaiyan with deep respect. A few claimed they knew those boys. One proclaimed he lived next to Eemon's parents. There had been a time when she was my best friend. But I no longer knew who she really was. I pushed the tears away. I would not let my heart break again. She was no friend of mine.

"They can call it robbery, or anything else they want," a boy sitting at the next table said under his breath. "Where else would they get the money to buy ammunition?"

"Imagine that," his friend responded. "They came *that* close..." And he sounded as if his favorite team had just lost.

I got up and went to my class.

Throughout the day, the incident was talked about on campus. At noon, someone said they heard on the radio that Eemon had been taken to the military hospital for surgery. I could no longer guess how Shireen would react. *"Sacrifices are what this society needs,"* she had said. How silly of me to think she had meant charity.

Shallow.

That evening, my family did their best to avoid mentioning the news.

"You didn't talk to anyone about your friendship, right?" My aunt said casually.

I only shot her a look.

Pedar, disenchanted as he may have been with the land reforms, continued to be a loyal subject and saw the country and the king as one. His patriotism seemed to blind him to the point that he would not allow himself to even consider anything that might jeopardize the security of the throne.

After dinner, I went to the basement in search of my Phillips diary. Hiding it inside an old magazine, I took it to my room. I lay down on my bed and read some of what Shireen had written, especially the parts that had previously seemed obscure. Maybe the news had influenced me, but now I found a whole different connotation in her words and could not fathom how I had missed it before.

On one page, Shireen had written a quotation from Nietzsche's *Thus Spake Zarathustra.*

"Learning to look away from oneself is necessary in order to see many things: this is needed by every mountain climber. He, however, who is obtrusive with his eyes as a discerner, how can he ever see more of anything than its foreground?"

Wow! I needed a dictionary to grasp the full meaning, and yet, she had been barely eighteen when she copied that. While I was fascinated with the obvious, "its foreground," she had seen deeper – much deeper. How long had Shireen been a mountain climber, a revolutionary?

On another page, she had paraphrased Antoine de Saint-Exupéry.

"To love is not looking at one another, but together looking in the same direction."

The word 'love' now took on a whole new meaning. I saw Shireen and Eemon, standing side-by-side, fighting for what they believed. As if peeling an onion, with each page I read another layer lifted, helping me to reach the core. Eemon was not just a husband. Their love began with "looking in the same direction," their marriage uniting them to the point of being one and the same.

I fell asleep with the Phillips still in my hand and I dreamt of a dark road. A group of people, all in black, marched toward me. They carried two coffins. Closer, I recognized the faces of Shireen's parents among the pallbearers, followed by Nasrin and Jenab. Shireen walked alone between the two caskets. She had on an elaborate wedding gown that glittered with rhinestones, and her long hair was adorned with jasmines. All I could see of Jenab was the top of his head. Passing by, he raised his gaze to look at me, but his face was gone, leaving a huge black hole in his skull.

I awoke with a start. The night was quiet except for the occasional screeching of cats on the neighbor's roof. I had no idea what time it was. Outside, no moon illuminated the pitch-dark garden. I turned on the bedside lamp.

The Phillips diary in my hand brought me back to reality. Shireen's neat handwriting, tiny letters so close together, reminded me of the notes I had destroyed. How I wished I had them now to help me understand better. Still, one phrase was seared in my mind and I did not need the diary to remember the words. "*I've learned my lesson: In pursuit of freedom I will have to lie, even to my own father.*"

I had thought of those words many times, though now they made more sense than ever before. Maybe I had failed to grasp their message because I never read them with such care. I had seen the world through my father's eyes, but why? He belonged to another time. His time. As much as I loved Pedar, he didn't have the right to control my mind and worse, not allow the true *me* to emerge. As the meaning of Shireen's words sank in, I felt the warm excitement of sin. "*I will have to lie, even to my own father.*"

Over the next few days, the atmosphere around campus changed. Many students skipped class and gathered in the cafeteria to exchange news.

"They've captured three more," Kyan whispered as we stood outside the Chemistry lab.

I maintained calm. "Three more what?"

He laughed good-naturedly. "No need to be cautious around *me,* little lady."

"Did you know anything about the Fadaiyan?" I asked, immediately regretting it. Wouldn't it be better if I knew nothing at all?

He gave me a surprised look. Then, as if unsure where to start, he asked, "Do you remember the incident at Siahkal?"

I shook my head.

He opened his mouth, but seemed to change his mind. "Some other time. This isn't the right place and is certainly the wrong time." After a long pause he added, "Let's just say that the Fadaiyan may be our best hope for the future."

"Are you one of them?"

He shook his head. "I'm not selfless enough."

I noticed many students were leaving. "Where are they going?" I asked.

"It's a silent protest. No classes."

I smiled at the realization that by skipping lab, I had unknowingly joined my first protest. *"Do not abandon your friend at a time like this,"* Jenab had said a long time ago. The loss Shireen had endured put her at so much of a disadvantage that I could forgive her. In pursuit of what felt right, I too, would lie to my own father if I had to.

—

Mrs. Payan couldn't mask her surprise at my visit. She craned her neck out the door and looked into the alley before letting me in. When the door was shut, she wrapped her strong arms around me and held me tight. "You smell of my Shireen."

She led me to the living room and took the faded bed-sheets off the couch.

"Please accept my deepest sympathy for..."

"Don't!" she said and held up one hand as if to push my words away. "I'll have none of that. This family does not condone such acts of terrorism," she said loudly. "There will be no grieving around here."

I opened my mouth, but she put a finger to her lips and shook her head in sorrow. "Not another word," she said. Her eyes pleaded with me and that look of resignation on her face was in contrast to her strong voice. She motioned to the couch and I lowered myself to it.

"The government has granted us permission to give Ali a proper burial." She looked at me intensely to make sure I understood. "Most families of insurgents aren't even allowed a line in the obituaries." I took that in. "They've made an exception for the Payans because our family set an example by publicly condemning the actions of our disloyal members."

Looking at her crestfallen eyes, I wished she would go ahead and cry.

"The loss of a terrorist is no loss at all," she said loud enough to be overheard, her eyes disagreeing with every word. "It..." Her voice broke. "...Will be done tomorrow," she finished in a whisper. She slumped on the floor, held her head in both hands and began rocking side to side.

Respecting her anguish, I submerged into the deep silence of my own grief. On a side table sat a black-and-white family portrait in a silver frame – Mr. and Mrs. Payan were seated in separate armchairs while the four children stood behind them: Ali and the younger brother, Ahmad, on either side of Shireen and Nasrin. It must have been taken before I knew Shireen. They were all young and none of them smiled. I saw no other pictures around. Next to the silver frame, a vase held three withered roses.

"That is where Ali Payan's family stands," Mrs. Payan said. "The burial will be small and private, with only the immediate family attending. We shall have a memorial service next week." She offered me a box of tissues. "You may attend, if you wish."

"Will you go to visit Shireen?"

"My sister and I will visit her regularly."

Another silence briefly fell. "I'll be in Tehran in a couple of months. Can I go too?"

She glared at me and said, "Why would you do such a thing?"

I didn't blink. Instead, I stared right back. "Because that's what friends do."

She nodded, but I wasn't sure what that meant. Did she just agree with my statement, or would she take me with her to Evin prison?

Changing the subject, she talked about Eemon's approaching surgery. "They'll want him to be on his feet when he attends the trial. Or maybe the firing squad."

Her words made me shiver, but she maintained a calm tone – finally imprinting on me that their home was surely wired.

"What happened to Behrang?"

At the mention of her grandson's name, Mrs. Payan smiled and for the first time, I saw a resemblance to Shireen.

"At the time, he was with a neighbor," she said. But she did not elaborate. "He'll live with his other grandmother. They'll keep him away from his parent's harm."

Mrs. Payan's sad eyes conveyed much more than the words coming from her mouth. "With the child having their last name, we couldn't claim custody." She paused in thought. "They may want to change his first name, you know? He doesn't need such connection to his parent's idol."

Another missed clue. Now that Shireen was caught among the little black fish in search of the free ocean, I deeply regretted having questioned Behrang's name.

Mrs. Payan stood. "It was good of you to stop by. And I'm proud of you for having the common sense not to ever get involved in their mess."

She spoke those words exclusively for the "bugs." She embraced me again just before I was out the door and whispered, "Be careful, my dear."

Across the street, a man sat in the shade of a tree with his back leaning against the trunk and his cap pulled down. Chewing on a twig, he looked up at me. A window at the neighbor's squeaked as it was slowly shut. I walked faster. Around the corner, a blind panhandler raised his cup and asked for money. As my feet picked up speed, a young boy on a bicycle swerved by.

Which one was there to watch me?

Twelve

THE ENORMITY OF THE POLITICAL EVENTS overwhelmed me. It was as if I had stepped from absolute darkness into blazing sunlight and needed time to adjust to the shock. My father and aunt continued to avoid discussing the news and Reza, despite his deep respect for the Fadaiyan, refused to share what he knew. I had to find Jenab because if anyone could answer some of my nagging questions, it would be him.

More than two years had passed since the last time I had seen my good teacher. Having left his job at my school the year we graduated, he now taught French at a private academy across town from the university.

The taxi dropped me off in front of a two-story brick building. A brown and beige sign above the entrance read Arya Language Academy. There were doorbells on the wall next to a column of names displayed under clear plastic. I found Jenab's, *Mahmood Elmi, Ph.D.*, hand written in that familiar calligraphy of his, and pressed the button for 26B. A few seconds later, there was a faint buzz and I pushed the door open.

The small lobby was bare, with no reception desk and it had a moldy odor. I climbed the stairs, found 26B down the hallway, and knocked.

"Enter."

At the sound of that warm voice, I became sixteen again and my heart filled with joyful anticipation. Would Jenab be half as excited to see his old student?

I stepped into a room that was neither an office, nor a classroom, yet it resembled both. There were six chairs arranged in a semi-circle, facing a small blackboard and to the side sat a desk facing them. Jenab sprang out of his chair and at first, I took that as pure chivalry, a show of respect for a female visitor, but looking at his face, I saw panic.

"What a surprise, Miss Afshar!" he said in a high-pitched voice and offered a clammy hand to shake. "How are you?"

Back to being called Miss Afshar, I didn't know how to respond.

"So nice to see you again, sir."

Except for a little extra weight and more gray hair, he looked exactly as I remembered him. He found a pencil on his cluttered desk and began tapping the cover of the book closest to him. Above the small blackboard hung an oversized portrait of the Shah and Queen Farah and next to it a smaller picture of the young crown prince, whom I guessed was about six years old.

Jenab opened the window and looked at the traffic below. When he spoke again, his voice was smothered in street noise.

"How is the University treating you?" he asked.

"It's okay. Hard work, but okay."

He paused for a few seconds. "Devastating what happened to your friend, isn't it?" he said, still not looking at me.

He knows why I'm here.

"Yes, devastating," I said. "And quite a shock."

"You weren't aware of her activities, were you?" he asked, and now looked at me, his inquisitive eyes searching mine.

I shook my head. "You know how Shireen was. She kept things to herself. I had a feeling you knew her more than anyone else did."

He sat back in his chair. "No, actually I can't say I knew her all that well."

Sure that I had misunderstood him, I said, "I don't think she trusted anyone. At least, not in the way she trusted you."

"Oh? But I was only a teacher." He raised his shoulders and assumed a naive look. "However, it was clear that the two of you were *very* close."

What was his game?

"That's not entirely true," I said, unable to mask my surprise. "Maybe she understood my limitations, but whatever her reasons may have been, she kept me in the dark."

He leaned back. "Well, so much for that." And, putting the matter to rest, he asked, "Now, what can I do for you?"

"I was hoping you'd explain some of what is going on. You know, help me to understand some of these horrific incidents, and what is left to hope for."

His eyebrows rose. "Explain? How could I? There's nothing to explain." He shook his head. "Not a thing."

I had learned to read people's faces, but Jenab did a good job of turning away and avoiding eye contact. I watched him, in search of a clue.

"I tried to guide that girl," he said and shrugged. "But she stopped listening to me a long time ago."

Each time he spoke, I noticed he turned his head to the right, slightly, inconspicuously. I looked around, but saw nothing unusual.

Jenab's dry voice interrupted my thoughts. "I didn't know much about her life beyond school."

"Weren't you and Mr. Payan friends?"

He shot me a look, but his reply was calm, not reflecting his anger. "Indeed we were. But that poor man didn't know what his daughter was up to either. In fact, he was as shocked as anyone by the news."

Now I knew he was lying. Each false word he uttered chiseled away at the idol my young mind had created.

"If you ask me, that brother of hers poisoned her mind."

"Mr. Elmi, Ali is dead," I said, hoping to shame him.

Jenab leaned forward and put a fist under his chin, his half opened eyes regaining some affection. "Yes," he said with a sigh. "And isn't it a shame to see these young people waste their lives?"

Years ago that gaze would have won me over, made me feel he understood the depth of my sorrow. Now I stared back and, like an illiterate looking at written words, I saw nothing meaningful.

"We come across all kinds of students," he said, resuming his fatherly tone. "Each student draws what he or she wants from a teacher's words."

"But you were different. We relied on your guidance," I said hopelessly.

He shook his head. "My hands were tied, Miss Afshar. I could only do so much to save my students."

"But it was you who encouraged us to think, to make a difference."

Panic rose in his eyes.

"She trusted you!"

He chuckled. "So did many others, so did you, dear Miss Afshar. And look how fine *you*'ve turned out."

Oh, how he had changed! I thought of the hardened clay and wondered about his true color. That programmed speech and his matter-of-fact manner were not what I had hoped to find. For the first time, he sounded like all the other teachers: unfeeling, having an agenda.

He pulled up his sleeve a little and glanced at his watch.

I stood. "I believed in you, Mr. Elmi, we all did." It was my turn to sneer. "Call it a child's intuition, but something about you alarmed me even back then." Ignoring his stunned expression, I grabbed my purse. "I hope in the future, when you teach your wonderful metaphors to young students, you'll remember to add that idols are also made of clay. Let them know that the bigger the idol, the more hollow it will be."

Before leaving, I looked back and there he stood, with his pathetic, crooked smile and eyes that were still trying to win me over. "That girl is finished," he said coldly, as if to throw in the last punch.

"Not for me, she isn't." I opened the door. "But you are."

Jenab didn't respond, but for a fleeting moment, I thought I saw deep sorrow in his eyes.

~

The next day, as I prepared to go to school, Auntie knocked on my door. She came in and sat on my crumpled bedspread.

"Your father and I think it best for you to stay home for a couple of days."

I dropped my hairbrush on the dresser. "Why?"

"Let's say he worries for your safety." She seemed uncomfortable acting as Pedar's messenger. "I think it has to do with what's going on."

"What about my classes?"

She shrugged. "A couple of days shouldn't matter."

"It matters to me!" I would have to take this up with my father. "Is Pedar up yet?"

"He went back to the farm early this morning."

"And I'll bet you promised him you'd keep me home, didn't you?" I said and shot her a look. "Reza better be in his room too!" I said and stormed out, but Auntie's voice stopped me.

"He's not here. Your father needed him at the farm."

"Great! The one person I could have talked to while being locked up!" Frustrated, I found nothing more to add.

For two days, I did not attend class. Nor did I join my aunt for meals. I locked my door and only opened it for Naneh's trays of food or to sneak to the bathroom. Auntie knocked on my door twice, asking me to open so we could talk. I ignored her. Thoughts multiplied in my head until it began to hurt. I wanted to know the exact point at which Shireen had become involved with the opposition movement. Had it, in fact, been Jenab's idea? Or was it her brother, Ali, who had planted the first seed as Jenab implied? Pedar had kept me home for my protection, but what he hadn't anticipated was that in my seclusion, more questions would arise and I would become determined to seek the answers. What was my place in a society that knew no justice, and just how long did my father hope to keep me within the walls of his false sanctuary? By the third day, I had decided.

When the house fell into its post-lunch silence, I changed my clothes and snuck out. Our alley was quiet in afternoon slumber and even on Golestan Avenue I saw no pedestrians. An unbearably hot sun baked the sidewalks. A man rode his bicycle, carrying a heap of crabapples on a round tray balanced on his head. I saw no demonstrators, and except for a few empty taxis, there were no cars. Closer to medical school, I noticed the police patrols in their usual spots, though no one seemed to be in the cars except for one, who had pulled his hat down and seemed to be napping.

Kyan greeted me with enthusiasm. Happy to have his buddy back, he skipped class so we could sit somewhere for a catch up.

"I wouldn't recommend the cafeteria," he said. "The new guy working there gives me a funny feeling. Let's walk."

"Another new guy?" I laughed. "Why don't they all just wear a SAVAK badge?"

"Shhhh!" He looked over his shoulder.

We walked along University Avenue. To see the school from outside brought the entrance exams to mind. I told Kyan about the blood I had seen on the tree the year before.

"Doesn't surprise me," he said. "Whenever there's police intervention, they clobber the poor demonstrators. Just wait 'til your hospital rotations. None of it is ever reported, but we see enough in the ER."

We walked for a while in silence. "During the past few days there were many more protests," he said. "All they seem to need to start another demonstration is for the news to call the activists names such as 'insurgents' and 'criminals'."

"Any news on the Payans?"

He shook his head.

We turned into a side street. "I've been saving a few articles for you. Here and there your friend's name was mentioned, but no big news."

I noticed a few shreds of pamphlets and typed notices pinned to trees and lampposts.

"What are those?"

"Announcements," Kyan said. "Students come out late at night and post them just to see the police remove them in the morning." He stopped and studied me. "Now your turn," he said. "Where were you?"

"In my glass bubble."

His face relaxed and he resumed walking.

"Will you tell me what happened back then in Siahkal?" I said. "I feel as if I've just awakened from a coma, but no one is willing to bring me up to date."

"A glass bubble, ha? I wondered about that." He looked at me sideways.

I tried to keep up with the poised stride of his long legs. "Tempted as I may be to put all the blame on my upbringing, I've really never cared much for politics, and maybe still wouldn't if it weren't for Shireen."

"Hmm," is all he said.

Even on busy streets I could feel the limp weight of a sleepy afternoon behind the drawn window shades. The asphalt felt soft under my shoes and the air was still.

Walking under the shade of the high walls, Kyan told me about Siahkal. He started patiently at the beginning as if he were telling a story to a child.

"It began in a small village near the Caspian Sea, with guerrilla warfare in the mountains. Some believe it was modeled after the communists in Cuba."

I didn't mention that I knew nothing about Cuba, either.

"If you ask me," he continued, "that's how the oppositionists got their reputation for being communists. But they really aren't. There are some fundamental differences."

"Like what?"

"Religion, for one. These guys are devout Muslims."

He held my elbow and made sure we cleared traffic while crossing.

"There are several anti-government organizations," he spoke in a whisper and stooped down to make sure I could hear. "Fadaiyan, Mojahedin, Toodeh, National Front, you name it. They each have their own set of ideas, but since Mossaddegh, none of them had done a thing beyond meetings, talks, and distribution of pamphlets. The Siahkal attack on government officials was the first dent in the security SAVAK had enjoyed for years."

"Then why was it considered a failure?"

"Because it was... in a way. All of the involved members were captured and later executed. What makes Siahlak a historic incident is the fact that the oppositionists did rescue two of their previously captured members."

From time to time, someone walked by and Kyan stopped talking, only to resume when we were a safe distance away.

"It was so hushed that no one really knows the details, but rumor had it that a few key members of oppositionists were killed on the spot." He seemed disturbed. "The closed trials were just a puppet show. With so many executions, it was a serious blow to the Fadaiyan."

"So really, it was all pointless?"

"In a twisted way, no. The casualties brought more support than the Fadaiyan had dreamed of. There were hints, vague messages and public demonstrations." He pointed to the pamphlets on the wall. "SAVAK doesn't have the means to deal with all this."

Something about the name, Siahkal, had always brought a dark vision to mind. Now the word *siah* – black – matched the image. I was developing a strong curiosity, an obsession, and wanted to learn more. Unable to ask direct questions for fear I could not handle the answer, I said, "So, what is to become of the... detainees?"

Kyan stopped and looked at me. The dismal look in his eyes told me the answer. "Political prisoners are always convicted. And almost always executed."

I felt the razor's edge in every word. The vision that flashed before me made me gasp: Shireen, blindfolded, standing against the wall, waiting for the gunfire.

"I know you want me to tell you otherwise, but it's best to be prepared."

I shook my head in denial. "Then why would they operate on Eemon?"

"Don't be naive, Roya. They just want him to live long enough to talk."

"There's always hope."

He put a heavy hand on my shoulder. "Don't do this to yourself."

I wondered what I had ever done to deserve his friendship. What had I done to deserve any of my good fortune?

He walked me back to school and before we parted, he said, "Don't build up much hope, my friend. The way things are, no amount of support can rescue your friend."

I wanted to tell Kyan of my decision to visit Shireen in prison, but thought it best to save him the worry. I spent the rest of my day listening to other students, trying to catch up on what I had missed. Around five in the afternoon, I heard a crowd in the distance, "Freeeedom and solidaaaaarity!"

My heart leapt with excitement as I ran outside. Damned if I was going to remain silent! No more, not now that I knew so much, not after what Kyan had told me. Those demonstrators were my peers and, whether my father approved or not, I was part of them. History was being made and I had every right to be out there, voicing my thoughts, protesting, demanding justice.

Outside, traffic had stopped for the demonstrators to pass. Their march must have started at the School of Science because a few trailed behind from around the corner. Police stood all along the street, just watching. I noticed a few had their hands on their holsters.

Someone handed me a yellow pamphlet just as I started to cross the street. Printed in large letters was: Free Political Prisoners. I held it with both hands above my head and ran toward the demonstrators. I had only gotten halfway when someone grabbed my arm, "This way, miss!"

Startled, I turned to find Akbar bearing down on me with a fierce expression on his face. No longer the friendly driver, he held my arm with such force that I thought he was willing to break it if he had to.

"Let go of me!"

He would not look at me and, ignoring a couple of spectators, he raised his voice, "Into the car, Miss Roya!"

A few students stopped and stared, but no one came forward. I wanted to scream and fight, but it was obvious that Akbar would win.

On the ride home neither of us spoke a word. I sulked in the back corner of the car and once in a while, Akbar checked me in his mirror. No doubt my father was waiting for me and it would be best to prepare for whatever punishment he had planned.

The gate was open and we drove straight in. I left the car and found the house a little too quiet. Even the servants didn't seem to be around. Akbar motioned to the family room. "You're expected there."

By now, I had cooled down enough to grasp the gravity of my actions. No one ever dared to disobey my father and, with the exception of Mitra's political comments and occasional whining, none of the Afshars had ever taken part in anti-government activities. In fact, with Mitra being abroad, no one even bothered to initiate a political discussion at our house.

Finding only my aunt in the family room, I wondered where Pedar was. Auntie stood by the mantle, with my mother's picture in her hand. She kept on staring at it without responding to my hello.

I took the chair nearest the door and sat down.

My aunt continued to look at Maman's picture for another minute or so before she put it down and looked at me. "I'm not sure if not bringing your father into this is the right thing to do."

The mere fact that Pedar did not know helped me to exhale, but even my aunt sounded calmer than I expected.

"Maybe I'm wrong," she went on in the same calm tone. "At this point, it might be in your best interest to let him deal with you."

Unable to defend myself, I just sat there and looked at my hands.

"As it stands," Auntie said, "no one but Akbar knows about your foolish act. And, I'm willing to keep it that way, only if I can trust it will never happen again."

When I didn't say a word, she hissed, "What possessed you?"

Finding some of my courage again I said, "You can't treat me like this. I am not a child to be sent to my room. This is my society and those are my peers out there. How can Pedar expect me to sit around and watch them do this to my friend?"

My voice came out stronger than I felt, as if being out of immediate danger had generated new energy in me.

"Oh, I see," she said. "So you're willing to put your life on the line for a *chadori* girl; a girl who came over *one time* to study with you."

I resented the way she spoke about Shireen. "No, Auntie, not for one girl, not for anyone in particular, but for equality and freedom." I gave an angry chuckle. "The kind of freedom that allows me to march peacefully alongside others without having a servant drag me back home."

"Well, well!" she said and the look in her eyes told me I had gone too far. "So much for equal rights. Where do you get off calling the man, who has been like a member of this family, 'a servant?' Let me tell you, young lady. That 'servant' obviously cares more about this family than you do. He'd never do anything that might put the rest of us in jeopardy. As for today, he was only acting on my orders."

"I'm doing what feels right."

She shook her head. "Looks like I may be too late to save your neck after all."

My aunt picked up my mother's picture and, wiping the dust off the top of it, she whispered to the picture, "I won't break the promise I made you." Then she lowered herself into a wing chair, covered her face, and wept.

The mere sight of my aunt in tears, something I had never seen before, was enough to transform me back to the little girl who worshipped her. I rushed across the room and knelt by her side. "Please don't, Auntie. I didn't do this to hurt you. Can't you try to see it from my point of view?"

Auntie sat up and reached for the box of tissues on the table. "Never mind."

"Please finish what you were saying, Auntie. What promise did you make to Maman? What is it that you're not telling me?"

"Nothing." She wiped her tears. "But even if there was a secret, I'd be the last one to talk." She sat taller, as if to regain her poise. "If you ever do anything so foolish again, I'll have to leave you to your father."

"What secret, Auntie? Who will tell me?" I insisted.

She looked at my mother's photograph and said, "Don't pressure me, Roya, I have nothing to tell you." She stood up, and gently put the frame back on the mantle before leaving the room.

Thirteen

KYAN MUST HAVE KNOWN from my face after a sleepless night that my problem was too personal to talk about. When I didn't make an attempt to find him at noon, he kept his distance for the rest of the day.

After an entire night of mulling over the day's events, I concluded there was nothing I could do. Auntie's tears had shaken me. *The ones who are worth it will never make you cry.* For the first time, I questioned whether I had been worthy of my aunt's unconditional love. Indeed, if my actions only upset the ones I loved, maybe it would be best to disassociate myself from what went on. This I would do, not so much to please my authoritarian father, but to put an end to my aunt's grief.

For many days, I was torn between two worlds. I vowed to stay in the shadows and keep my head low, but those were thoughts contained by the walls of my own room.

Once I left the sanctuary of my father's house, I saw and heard too much to remain calm. At school, all I had to do to learn about the different opposition groups – was keep my ears open. Sometimes Kyan offered me a ride home in his beat-up Volkswagen and he talked about the latest news. In a society where most people ignored the demonstrators and kept their distance, I admired the way Kyan cared about their small accomplishments.

As I began paying close attention, the subtle changes around the city seemed more conspicuous. A new version of guards in army uniforms, carrying rifles, circled the campus. Two police cars parked in the alley behind the medical school were now a permanent feature, and once or twice, I saw strange men walk out of the Dean's office.

According to Kyan, many intellectuals were detained in Evin and Qasr prisons in Tehran. Though I never asked questions, any time someone mentioned the Fadaiyan, my ears perked. Their name alone, the 'Devotees,' told me enough. I knew at least one member who had been truly devoted to her cause. Despite the government attempts to label them Marxists, most members had a strong religious background. That in time created a new title, 'Islamic Marxist,' a name Kyan considered meaningless.

"You can't be a religious fanatic and a Marxist at the same time," he said. "This is the government's attempt to appall the general public because nobody likes a communist. The Fadaiyan's goal is to establish true democracy. And, if necessary, they won't hesitate to take from the rich and give to the poor until a reasonable balance is reached."

"Then why won't the poor support them?" I said.

"Support them to do what? With SAVAK being everywhere, the authorities would be informed long before they take any action." His lips parted in a sad smile. "Besides, what kind of support would they get from the poor?"

"Maybe the army will back them up. You know, like they did with Reza Shah."

"A military coup? My dear, back then the Qajars had no secret police, as we know it. So it was easy for the army to sneak up on them and overthrow their dynasty. People welcomed the new Shah, one who had risen from among them. But times have changed. This shah has learned his lesson and his SAVAK will make sure such history is not repeated."

The next day, Akbar and I heard a report on the car radio about the most recent demonstrations at Tehran University.

"I don't know where these young people get their guts," Akbar said.

"Marching on the streets doesn't need a whole lot of guts."

He studied me in the mirror, wordlessly .

I went on, "*I* would have done it if you hadn't butted in, remember?"

"You're lucky I did," he said, now sounding annoyed. "You would have liked it even less if they treated you the way they treated Mammad's son."

"Didn't you say they let him go?"

"They did," he said and shook his head. "But, as I also said, whatever they did to him, he sure walked funny for a while."

I felt a chill. What would they do to Shireen? I still didn't have a clear idea about the depth of her involvement. If Mammad's son was involved in Ali's party way back then, did the fact that they knew each other mean Shireen was, too?

"I haven't seen him around lately, have you?"

Akbar shrugged. "He wouldn't dare show his face. Not now that he's become an informer."

"He what?"

"That's what happens, miss. First they torture them, then make them switch."

So, the groups were to decay from within. What Pedar had once dismissed as 'child's play,' now seemed anything but childish.

~

With Fadaiyan gaining public support, more political messages came through songs, books and pamphlets. Contemporary literature, poetry and prose alike, took a new tone, which ultimately led to more banned books and the arrest of several writers.

Within months, the surge of public awareness had turned a failed robbery attempt into an impressive campaign. Rumor had it that the captured members were offered amnesty in exchange for a public apology, that is, to ask for the Shah's pardon. But neither bribes, nor SAVAK's gruesome tortures could bring them to their knees. The country had not seen such bravery since the fall of Doctor Mossaddegh in 1953. The late Prime Minister's supporters had been hushed through brutal punishment. Now, nearly two decades later, once again people were rising against the monarchy and Mashad was proud to be home to many heroes.

One evening, Auntie and Pedar were at my uncle's house and I went to the family room to watch the nine o'clock news with Reza. I turned the knobs this way and that and adjusted the antenna until a snowy black and white image of a newsman became visible.

"...have been scheduled for next Saturday," the man announced. "We shall report more on these trials as information becomes available." He then moved on to reports from around the world and Reza turned off the TV.

"We just missed it," he said.

I shrugged. "They wouldn't go into details anyway."

By now, Reza had started to talk to me more about politics. He truly believed the political activists in general, and Fadaiyan in particular, were the country's hope for the future.

"How come you were never tempted to join?" I asked him.

"Me?" He laughed. "First of all, those guys are too smart for me. They'd laugh at my ignorance. Secondly, I saw what that deal with Mammad's son did to Pedar. I'd hate to think how he would react to his own children being involved."

"You're afraid of Pedar, too?"

He gave me a surprised look. "Afraid?" He shook his head. "He's all about bluffs, he'd never harm me, no matter what. The problem is in the harm such actions may cause him. Pedar is not as tough as you think. But he really loves his country and thinks a monarchy is the only way to rule."

"Don't be so sure. Pedar has changed, too," I said.

"A little, maybe. But you can't change a man at his age. Pedar was not raised to accept equality. If you ask me, what hurt him most after the land reforms had nothing to do with wealth. He couldn't bear not being the master." He thought for a moment. "What about you? I remember a time when you seemed tempted."

A time? I could not begin to count the number of times I had wished to join the students' movement. When I did not respond, Reza persisted, "I mean, being a friend of Shireen Payan, you must have participated in some way, no?"

"Once," I said, and recalled that awful day. "But I'm embarrassed to even mention it."

"What happened?"

"Auntie sent Akbar after me. She made me promise I would not do that to the family," I said, then to emphasize how strong her reaction had been, I added. "She cried."

"Auntie cried?" he sounded as shocked as I had been when I saw it.

I nodded.

Reza gave me a kind smile. "Whatever works," he said and put one arm around my neck. "I can't imagine what I would do if any harm came to my little sister."

Hard to believe this was the same Reza, who once only cared about his acne and failed grades. Now a first year engineering student, he sounded as intellectual as anyone on campus.

When he got up to leave, I said, "Thanks for the talk. When one of every five people is a SAVAK agent, I don't know whom to trust."

He turned around with a grin. "What makes you so sure I'm not one?" And he ran out before the shoe I hurled could reach him.

~

The next day, I told Auntie I was going to the shrine, and asked if she wanted me to light candles on her behalf.

"Praying to pass an exam again?" Auntie said. "You shouldn't turn to God only when you want something." But she sounded as if she approved of such faith.

I had never trusted the power of prayers, but this time God would listen because I was asking a favor not for me, but for someone who had a better relationship with Him.

As I washed up in preparation for my pilgrimage, visions of sixteen-year old Shireen in the prayer hall came back. "It is the cold winter that helps us to appreciate our warm homes," she had said when the water made her little hands turn maroon. Holding the palms of those hands together, eyes closed, she had surrendered her soul to God. At this moment, He was probably her last hope. Her only hope.

I followed the line of pilgrims, kissed the silver doors to the courtyard of the Shrine, checked my shoes and entered, taking small steps on the slick marble floor.

Arabic chants echoed under the domed ceiling, and although I didn't know their meaning, the melancholic reverberation clutched at my heart. The air was heavy with the scent of burning candles, incense and rose water. From one prayer hall to the next, I kissed the tall, gilded doors and gave a bow to the golden cubical of the Imam's burial. As pilgrims pushed forward, I gasped for air and let the mob carry me. Hands extended over my head toward the golden bars of the tomb. Stumbling against an older woman who had tied herself to the bars in demand for Imam's miracle, I lifted my head upward, but the light reflecting off the mirrored dome was dazzling. I realized that despite the magnificence of the architecture, the place failed to offer the solace I had come for. If anything, it had filled me with awe, even fear.

Minutes later, I pushed my way back to the courtyard and sat on the stony ground, facing the shrine. Minarets reached high, blending with the long rays of a bright sun. A hexagonal room in the middle of the courtyard housed water dispensers. As a child I used to love drinking from those brass cups chained to faucets. Our nanny, among many others, believed the blessed water could cure just about any ailment.

"Please dear God, help Shireen and grant all of them – especially Ali who is now with you – peace and comfort." I chose my sentences with care, hoping I came close to how Shireen might have prayed.

Above the courtyard, hundreds of silver pigeons flew about and rested on the gold dome. They were a fixture around the shrine of this Imam and even considered sacred. With so many people buried on the premises, some believed the pigeons to be the spirits of the deceased. My mother's tomb being across that courtyard, for years I had imagined her spirit in such a bird. I'd extend a hand, waiting for one to land on it. None ever did.

The hum of the crowd indicated that too many people needed the Divine attention. God seemed busy after all, and I had little faith he would hear me.

~

Welcoming the news that the outcome of the trials would be broadcast during school, many students skipped class and gathered in the cafeteria around the radio.

"Don't talk in there," Kyan cautioned me as we crossed the yard. "It's best not to react at all. God knows how many *SAVAKies* are in there."

The cafeteria was packed and most of us sat on the cement floor. Loud conversations killed the music on the radio and the place sounded like a gigantic beehive. I noticed two new workers behind the counter.

"Shhhh," someone said. Others followed here and there. "Shhh!"

As soon as the news came on, and particularly the strong voice of the evening reporter, a dead silence fell. Disregarding the fact that the entire country must be waiting to hear the fate of the political prisoners, the first item in the news was about a train accident in northern Iran. Then came the verdicts in the Payans' case.

"Following days of deliberation, the high court of the Imperial army has reached their verdict concerning each and every one of the recent political detainees." The reporter sounded drier than usual. Each time he repeated "Guilty" with every name and on all accounts, a huge gasp rose collectively from the crowd.

For some reason, I'd had the impression that the incident involved only Shireen and her family, but now more than ten people had been named. The word 'guilty' was hammered over and over.

Six men, identified as the "key elements of this sabotage," would face the firing squad. As feared, Eemon was among them. I didn't know the others, but the crowd reacted with equal shock to every one. Later, Kyan told me three were from Mashad. After all the terrible verdicts, it was small comfort to hear that Shireen's younger brother, Ahmad, would be spared.

The women's verdicts came last. "Shireen Payan, Irandokht Karimi and Atefeh Mehran," he announced. "All three are guilty of conspiracy, and each is sentenced to eight years of imprisonment with hard labor."

The students' objections became a distant hum as the room began to spin around me. The air was heavy with grief and all I could feel was someone holding my shoulders, keeping me upright. *Eight years*! That was twice the number of years that I had even known Shireen. Kyan handed me a glass of water. "Good girl," he whispered. "Not a word now."

Soon after the news, the crowd dispersed and everyone went back to class. Kyan stayed with me and we listened to a more detailed report of the "crimes."

"These women were the collaborators, giving the team-houses their façade of a normal home. Neighbors became suspicious and the recent clean up was the result of a tip from one such neighbor," a female reporter said.

In my mind, I imagined them living in a cul-de-sac similar to our alley. I saw a neighbor's wife peek through the curtains. Shireen carried heavy bags of grocery in one arm, holding Behrang in the other. I saw her hold the edge of her chador in her teeth while struggling with the keys. Did she know she was being watched?

Clean up? I hated the reporter for her choice of words. Oh, the horror Shireen and her friends must have felt when they heard the bang on the front door.

Back to the original reporter, his final words caught my attention. "The Payan family has publicly condemned these activities. Although they plan to hold a memorial service for their son, Ali, Mr. Payan told our reporter, 'Anyone who betrays this country deserves to die.' Their younger son, Ahmad, is sentenced to twenty years without the chance for parole."

~

All I needed for sneaking into Ali's memorial service were some dark clothes and a black chador. I found a T-shirt and skirt to wear, but didn't know whom to ask for the chador, without raising suspicion. I called Tahereh Ahmadi, now a second year nursing student. We had been out of touch for some time and she sounded happy when I told her I was going to stop by and see her.

Jorjani School of Nursing was located adjacent to the Shah Reza Hospital. Everyone there seemed to know Miss Ahmadi and a young girl went to call her. The 'new' Tahereh greeted me with newfound confidence. Her complexion had cleared, her unmanageable hair was neatly tucked under her white nurse's cap, and the white uniform gave her a whole new look. As she smiled, I concluded she was even pretty.

"I hate to come here for a favor, but I'm desperate for a black chador," I said after we had exchanged initial greetings.

She studied me with intent. A smart girl, it didn't take her long to figure out where I might want to go, that my own family would not provide a chador.

"Will you be safe?" she asked. "I don't want you to get in trouble."

"I won't. Promise."

"Let me get mine."

The next day, I told Auntie I'd be late for dinner. She gave me one of her wary looks and it made my heart sink to think that once again she could be on to me.

She went back to her knitting. "Don't be too late."

After the last lecture, I changed clothes in the ladies' room, took a taxi to the Payans' and wrapped Tahereh's chador around me. Made of a thick fabric, it was the heaviest chador I had ever worn and smelled of mothballs. As the taxi pulled to the curb, I saw an older man standing there. From his black armband I guessed him to be a close relative of the deceased. He wore a gray pinstriped suit and his shirt collar was unbuttoned – another sign of mourning. I paid the driver and while I waited for my change, a younger man, also wearing a black armband, came out of the house, approached the taxi and leaned into the side window. "The Goharshad Mosque?" he said, naming his destination.

The driver agreed to take him.

"Wait one minute," he said and turned to the older gentleman, "Mr. Payan, please, this way."

I got out of the taxi and studied the old man with interest. Without a response, he took another drag from his cigarette before tossing it to the pavement. As if grief had shrunken him, his coat hung loosely from his bony shoulders. I found little resemblance between this frail man and the strong figure I had seen in the Payan family photo. He wore round, tinted glasses and leaned on the young man's arm.

As they passed me, I said hello. He looked in my general direction, but it was clear he hadn't seen or heard me.

I approached the house. Unlike other funeral services, no black flags hung outside the home and I did not hear the sound of the Quran's recital, a *rowzeh,* or cry of mourners.

The door was wide open and a small group of women had gathered in the hallway. I thought I recognized a female teacher from high school. I knew this to be the women's service, a chance to pay their respects to Mrs. Payan. Kyan had told me that the men would gather at the big mosque. Although he did not know the family, he planned to be there. "It's the right thing to do," he said. Somehow I had a feeling Reza would also attend.

I spotted Mrs. Payan standing next to the living room. In her white silk blouse and gray skirt, she presented a contrast to the rest of us in black and I saw no sign of grief in her proud face. She shook my hand. "Thank you for coming, Miss Afshar." Then she leaned closer and whispered, "Stop looking so sad, Roya. And remember, there will be no crying!" She motioned to the living room, and ushered me in.

Inside, all the furniture had been removed to make room for a larger crowd. Women sat on the carpeted floor in a circle, leaning against the walls. Someone moved over and made room for me.

A young girl carrying a large tray offered me coffee. The Turkish coffee had no sugar – its bitter taste indicating the young age of the deceased. A few women spoke softly to each other, but in general, the room was much too quiet, even for a funeral.

On the opposite wall hung a large photograph of Ali with a black ribbon tied to its frame. He stared at me, haunting me with eyes that bore strong resemblance to Shireen's. His peaceful expression defied every nasty comment I had heard in the news. Somehow, I could not connect the words "criminal" and "evil" with the innocence in that picture. Those were my friend's eyes, questioning my loyalty, and seeking solace. Shireen and I were never as close as I had presumed. All along, she must have known I leaned on her for strength and at some point she had given up on me.

I recalled the one time I had seen Ali. "Hello," he had said. To me, that would remain the only word he had ever uttered before his voice was hushed.

The sounds of my mother's funeral from my childhood memory contrasted this silence of the Payans' home. I remembered a room filled with women in black, the strong smell of coffee making it hard to breathe. Oh how my grandmother had screamed, slapped her cheek and pulled at her hair! Small enough to hide between the pleats of a velvet curtain, I looked on until someone spotted me and led me away. Later, my nanny took me to my room where I sat on her lap, ate ice cream, and watched her shed silent tears.

Only now did I know why my grandmother had needed to scream. The hush around me, giving way to deafening sounds of memory, was more than I could bear. Maybe the cry trapped in Mrs. Payan's throat had no escape, but unchaining my tears, all I could do was stare at the rug and watch its pattern run in all directions.

Someone tapped on my shoulder and I looked up to find Nasrin. "Come with me," she said, and taking my hand, she led me to the room I knew. Shireen's books were still piled by the bed, her cardigan draped on the chair, her slippers paired at the door, as if she had just stepped out.

Mrs. Payan sat at the edge of Shireen's bed.

"I can't allow this, Roya," she said, pointing to my soaking face. She walked over to me. "No one was to shed a tear today. No one!" She wrapped her arms around me for a warm embrace and I could feel her trembling.

"There are all sorts of people here," she whispered. "We are not allowed to mourn Ali's loss. I have been instructed to publicly condemn his actions." She looked as if she would break down. "If you can't play their cruel game, then I must ask you to leave."

She said the last sentence rather loud and I knew the women standing in the hallway must have heard her. With a gentle stroke, she wiped the tears off my cheek. "Please go."

Before leaving, I recalled something Jenab had once said, "A hero is like an axe in search of water in a mountain. When he has cracked the rock enough to free the first drop, his job is done. Water will remember the axe in its strong flow."

Standing on the exact spot where Ali had once stood, I wondered if down the line, he would be remembered as the axe that broke the rock.

Eight years sounded like a lifetime, especially for a little boy who needed his mother every minute of every day. This I knew. No matter who raised Behrang, no one could take Shireen's place for him. He would grow up to wonder how it would have been to grow up with one's mother present in all the scenes of childhood.

Unable to sleep, I couldn't picture Shireen incarcerated and how they wanted her soul to rot in a jail. Would my father be willing to help? Couldn't he do for my friend the same thing he had done for the son of our gardener? I should talk to him, even beg if necessary, ask if he might use his influence to reduce Shireen's sentence. The more I weighed the idea, the better it sounded. Reza was wrong; when it came to saving someone's life, even my father could change his mind. Besides, with the government's harsh treatment of students, my father had to have altered some of his views... surely.

The following morning, I went to Pedar's room before breakfast. From the inhaler pump at his bedside, I figured he must have had another one of his asthma attacks.

He gave me a weak smile. "How's the doctor?"

"I'm fine," I said and pointed to the pump. "Are you okay?"

"I'm okay now, but I had a rough night."

"I know what you mean. I've been up all night, too." I responded, pleased to find a way to circle around the subject.

"Oh?"

He reached for his box of cigarettes, but only held on to it.

"Horrible news these days. How long do you think it's going to be before we see a drastic change in this country?"

"A drastic change?" he said dryly.

I watched him light a cigarette, and it wasn't until after the first puff that he poured out his anger.

"Let me tell you about a drastic change." He glared at me through the thin layer of smoke. "We had one with Reza Shah's coup d'état before you were even born. We had another when he went into exile. We also went through a drastic change with Mossaddegh." His voice rose with each sentence, his face distorting. "The last thing a country of idiots needs is a *drastic change*. At least this Shah has established a semblance of order." He smoked his cigarette for a while. "I smell trouble, Roya. Mark my words. If there is a change – and I doubt there will be – but if there is, countless lives will be destroyed."

Taking his last comment as an indication of sympathy for the most recent loss of lives, I jumped at the chance. "Then why don't you do something?"

"*Do*?" He squished his cigarette in the ashtray as if he was beating it. "Do what?"

"A few members of the oppositionists could use the help of someone as powerful as you."

He gave an angry laugh. "Are you serious? You expect *me* to help those wolves in the mountains rebel against the best army in the Mid East?" He shook his head. "Trust me, when you've lived as long as I have, you tend to sit back and watch. And that, my dear, is precisely what I plan to do." He wagged a finger at me. "And I'd expect you to do the same."

My father's absolute lack of sympathy sounded unreal. Something boiled inside me and I could no longer hold back the anger. "I can't, Pedar. I won't!"

He shot me a look that a few months earlier would have made me eat my words, but now I stared back.

"Enough!" His hand went up and I closed my eyes instinctively. When he did not slap me, I looked. "What did you think I might do, Roya?" His voice quivered. "Did you really think I would stoop to hitting you?"

Too ashamed to say anything, I looked down.

"I had to ship your sister's butt far away when *she* was getting ideas," he growled. "As God is my witness, I won't hesitate to do the same to you."

Mitra's sudden departure had come not that long after the news of Alieh's death. I could still hear her heated discussions on the phone. I wondered if Mitra had any idea.

"Don't you go sneaking around town, thinking I don't know your comings and goings," Pedar said. He lit another cigarette. "It's one thing to offer sympathy to a grieving friend, but quite another to put your nose in matters that aren't your business."

My stomach formed a knot.

"One wrong move, young lady," he said and wagged his finger. "And I swear you won't know which way the wind will blow you."

The excitement made him cough. At first mild and throaty, then the cough grew deeper and his face turned maroon. Rajab rushed in with a glass of water. Moments later, his cough subsided and with the help of his inhaler, his breathing became normal.

"Remember," he said as I prepared to leave. "I'll be watching you!"

I had barely reached the end of the hallway when I heard him shout, "Rajab! Bring me that damned brazier."

~

Following the news that the executions would be carried out on the following Saturday, street demonstrations escalated. Not only were there more police cars everywhere, but also the army was called in. On Thursday afternoon, as we prepared for the week's end, there came an announcement of class cancellations and we were told there would be no attendance on Saturday. The radio had already reported the closure of both universities in Tehran. On Saturday, Pedar gave strict orders that all of us stay home for the entire day.

I doubted the radio would broadcast the actual executions as they happened. More than likely, it would be an item in the evening news, hours after the fact. I had seen firing squads in the movies and imagined it took place at dawn. Would they make Shireen watch? I pictured her standing in the yard as the prisoners were brought in, blindfolded, lined up against the wall.

No, that was inconceivable. I sat in my room and thought about my friend, wishing she didn't have to be so lonely.

I could almost see her in her cell, standing at her window, waiting for the first glimpse of daylight. Having stayed up all night, at dawn she would pray hard and talk to God in her purest of hearts. In the absence of a prayer seal, she would put her forehead on the cold cement floor and pray that her man feel no pain and show no remorse.

In my imagination, I could see her standing there, her head up in an attempt to maintain a fragment of pride. But as the gunfire shook the walls, she would run to the barred window, a cry escaping her throat before her knees would fold, making her body collapse and fall to the ground in the exact way that Eemon had fallen.

Fourteen

Nelly had moved to Europe, but her family still included me in their Friday luncheons along with other old friends. Mrs. Emadi's parties were different from any other I had been to. Not only was her house decorated in the finest Italian designs, the tables she set looked like a page out of gourmet magazines: Cut geraniums in a crystal bowl, tall candles in silver candleholders, large serving platters adorned with appetizing garnishes. Her touch gave ordinary Persian food a French look.

After lunch, guests gathered around the pool. A few sat in the shade to play cards or enjoy a round of Backgammon while others went for a swim. Such carefree gatherings seemed to go on despite the political turmoil, and guests talked about everything except politics.

I had just settled down in the shade of a willow, sipping my cherry drink and watching others when I heard my name called.

"Miss Roya," the Emadi's maid announced from the terrace. "You have a phone call."

Too excited to look for my shoes, I darted barefoot over the hot tiles on the patio and went inside. Nelly's mother passed me the phone in the foyer, but she didn't leave.

"Mrs. Payan?" I responded to the familiar warm voice on the other end. Nelly's mother leaned in with curiosity.

"Sorry to disturb you," Shireen's mother said. "I called your home and was given this number to reach you." She hesitated for a moment. "We're going to Tehran in a couple of days. I'll be there for about a month. If you happen to be in Tehran, I could take you with me."

"Are you serious?"

"Yes dear, you could go as—"

The line went dead and I noticed Nelly's mother had her hand on the cradle. Looking furious, she took the receiver out of my hand and replaced it. "Did that woman ever stop to think that the line could be tapped?"

Oblivious to all caution, my heart soared with newfound hope. "Oh, but did you hear? This was Shireen's mother. She can take me to see her."

Mrs. Emadi's expression didn't change. "I expect more common sense from you, Roya-joon," she said and turned away.

"I'm not doing anything wrong. She'll get an official permit for me."

"But why, my dear?" she said. "You come from such different backgrounds."

I did not need a reminder to know I was raised to be different from the Shireens of my society, but no longer could my upbringing prevent me from being myself. And, nothing anyone said could change my mind.

~

Mrs. Payan had just washed her hair. With her head wrapped in a large scarf and her cheeks red from a hot bath, she looked healthier, younger.

"You're no stranger," she said with a smile. "Let's go to the kitchen." And she led the way.

The smell of steamed cabbage wafted into the hallway. A small bowl of water on the tile floor suggested the presence of a housecat. Thoughts of Shireen lingered as I sat in a chair she must have sat in at some point, and watched her mother pour tea. Mrs. Payan and I seemed to meet under the most unusual circumstances, yet she always managed to behave casually.

She pointed to a closed door. "Behrang is here today. He's asleep."

Behrang. I smiled at the chance to see him again.

Through the clean lace curtains, I could see the small garden beyond the window. Signs of a good life around this home presented a huge contrast to my last visit and that awful memorial service. Staring at a large enamel sink, I tried to picture Shireen here, helping her mother prepare a meal for Ali and his friends. I couldn't. Shireen's presence was now more that of a ghost, than a real woman's. All that came to mind was my friend in a dark cell, with no heat and a mattress that smelled of death.

For a month now, each time I closed my eyes the same vision had returned: Shireen's body curled up in a dark corner, her face hidden in the fold of her arm, her food decaying on the floor. I would hear the opening of the cell's door, the sound of heavy boots. The jail keepers and torturers were faceless, as if I had trained my mind to stop there.

I took the hot tea that Mrs. Payan offered.

"You were serious about taking me to her, weren't you?" I said at last.

She looked at me. "I am if you are."

"Would they let me?"

"I'll have to pass you off as a cousin."

"What made you change your mind?"

"Nasrin just came back from Tehran. She brought messages from Shireen."

"Is she okay?" I asked and realized how ridiculous that sounded.

Mrs. Payan looked at me. "How can she be okay, Roya-joon?"

She put the sugar bowl before me.

"I mean, how does she handle... it?" I asked, thinking of all the awful possibilities.

She bent over the table, leaned on her fists, and peered into my eyes. “That place changes people. Like a warped mirror, only this one distorts their entire persona. She’ll never be the same.” She shook her head. “Ever.”

Shireen’s mother seemed to plunge into her own thoughts and images and I knew better than to expect more. I also knew that, unless she spoke further, I would be stuck with the horrific details of my imagination: The chain cuts on Shireen’s wrists, the cigarette burns on her body, and the bleeding lines on her bare back. And worse, sometimes I could see, feel and smell the disgusting weight of a guard, forcing himself on her. I wrapped my fingers around the teacup.

“The last time I went to see her, she couldn’t believe you had attended Ali’s memorial,” she said. “I think it comforted her to know that you finally understood the reason for what she did to you. Getting rid of the simplest evidence was all she could do to protect you.”

At first, I missed her point, and by the time I realized what she was telling me, a cold sensation covered my whole body. They were both wrong. I had not understood at all, not until that moment. The pounding in my ears muffled Mrs. Payan’s voice while she went on, “God only knows what would have happened to you if they had found all those notes, pictures, and diaries,” she said. “Or worse, if you had gone to visit her in Tehran while the team-house was under surveillance.”

How grand I had felt at being the forgiving one, the merciful. Oh, how I had hated Shireen for breaking my heart. My best friend, she must have counted on me to take the bait because she knew that a fool is a fool!

The baby cried in the other room and Mrs. Payan went to get him. Moments later she returned with the toddler in her arms. Behrang, now much bigger than the last time I had seen him, yet still smaller than anyone I knew, rubbed his eyes and didn’t seem thrilled to find a stranger present.

He had Shireen’s soulful eyes, and I noticed he had the red curls and severe facial expression of his father. I reached for his hand, hoping he would hold my finger the way he had held on to Shireen's, but he jerked his hand away and buried his face in his grandmother's bosom.

"Don't mind him," Mrs. Payan said. "He's cranky when he wakes up, and even worse with strangers." She sat down and put him on her lap. Behrang pulled one sock off his foot and brought a plump pink toe to his mouth.

"I always thought grandchildren were God's best gift," Mrs. Payan said. She looked beyond the lace curtains and I had a feeling she could still see her own babies playing out there in the yard. "As a grandparent, you're not supposed to feel so responsible or worry so much." She sounded as if she would cry. "All my friends told me the best part of being a grandmother is that you can enjoy your grandchildren and, when they get crabby, you can send them right back to..."

Her unfinished sentence hung awkwardly in the air.

Behrang touched her face, but soon the sugar cubes on the table distracted him, and he leaned over to grab one.

"I used to think her marriage was all wrong," Mrs. Payan said with a sigh. "But Eemon was a good man and she loved him so." She took a crumpled tissue out of her sleeve and dabbed at her eyes. "God only knows how hard I try not to blame him for any of this."

The baby pulled at her neck-chain. She didn't stop him.

"Now I don't know what to think any more," she went on. "Living in the world of the blind, it's easy to ridicule the one who speaks with vision."

I squirmed and looked around the room.

"Don't worry. After the phone company paid us a surprise visit to remove a few wires, we knew they had lost interest in our pitiful mourning."

She seemed so broken, I wanted to reach over and hold her.

"I'll be damned if I let this be a total waste of precious lives," she said. "My children may be dead, but their dream is very much alive." Her words were heavily charged and I knew then that she had joined Shireen.

Before I left, we exchanged phone numbers in Tehran. When I was at the door, she pushed a folded piece of paper into my hand and said, "Shireen sent you this message."

On the ride home, I opened my sweaty palm and studied the wrinkled note. I knew those tiny letters, the neat handwriting.

"If I shall rise,
And if you would rise,
Everyone will."

The quiet Mashad afternoon told me of the peaceful nap of a blind nation. The taxi traversed streets that appeared calm, yet the walls sheltered other Shireens and Alis, masking a revolution.

A few streets away, we passed another group of demonstrators. These weren't students, but a mix of young and old, men and women, marching peacefully on the sidewalk, holding a sign that said, "Justice, Now!"

For a moment, I imagined asking the driver to stop the car. I saw myself running to join them, holding a huge sign: "Free Shireen." I saw Shireen smiling that same smile I had seen on the day I signed the petition. *I am one sky proud of you,* she had said.

When I glanced out again, we had passed the protestors.

As my father had said, it was one thing to be there for my friend, but quite another to become involved. It took self-sacrifice and a strong conviction to rise the way Shireen had. Through repetition, my father's pessimistic forecast had taken away all my hopes. If the poem Shireen had sent me was a summons, I would have to decline.

I smoothed the wrinkles on the note, folded it, and tucked it into my wallet. A simple visit had to be harmless enough. SAVAK had to know I was no revolutionary.

Kyan called the week before his finals.

"Hey, little lady. Remember me?"

"You sound familiar. Is this Dr. Ameri, also known as the bookworm?"

He laughed. "Close enough, ma'am. But I won't be a doctor for another week."

He said he had a little time the following day. "It would be nice to take a short break before I plunge into finals. Let's meet for one last tea before I go away."

Go away? So he must have had some news.

For the past few weeks, every morning I woke up hoping to see Kyan, but he and his study group stayed home and crammed for finals. This being his last year, his future depended on the outcome of these exams. Like many other students, Kyan aspired to be admitted to a residency program abroad. He had applied to several universities. I had pushed the idea of his imminent departure as far from my mind as possible.

Lately, thoughts of him followed me everywhere. He showed up in my books, in my house and even in my glass of tea. Day after day, I went to the library without being able to accomplish much. I kept on watching the door, hoping for his tall form to walk through. I even debated if I should call him or not. I deciphered and analyzed his every word, trying to read more into them. What about those times when he held my hand a little too long? And that time when I caught him staring at me? But in the end, I came away with nothing more than friendship.

~

At the coffee shop, Kyan pulled up a chair for me. "I'll get us some tea," he said. "Care for anything else?"

I shook my head.

As he walked over to the counter, I surveyed his stack of books on the table, as if that would tell me about his destination, but all I saw were textbooks and notes.

Be strong, Roya. You can do this.

Kyan returned with a bottle of yogurt drink and two glasses. "They're out of tea. *Doogh* was the best I could do," he said as he filled my glass.

"Too hot for tea, anyway," I said.

Kyan usually found a lot to talk about, but that morning he seemed too quiet.

"So, how are the studies going?"

"Fine," he said and gave an exaggerated nod.

"So, I gathered from your call that you must have heard some good news."

He nodded again.

"Congratulations!" I forced a smile. "Where will you be going?"

"America."

I could not look at him for fear he would read my thoughts in my eyes. America? That sounded so far away, he might have just as well found himself a program on Mars!

"How soon do you think you'll leave?"

"In a week," he said. "I mean, I'll be done with the exams in a few days, go to Tehran in a week, and then fly abroad when all my documents are ready."

I had no idea what I could say.

He took a sip from his drink, then put his glass down quickly and held my hand. His fingers were cold from the glass, making me conscious of my own sweaty palms.

"I don't know how to say this," he began.

I tried to think of all I had ever learned in cardiology and couldn't remember if the walls of the human heart could cave in.

"Marry me, Roya," he said in a hurried voice.

I pulled my hand away, as if electrified.

He studied my face and repeated, this time slower and with more affection. "Please say you'll marry me."

The whole world must have heard me gasp, but no words came out of my mouth.

"I should have thought of a more appropriate place, perhaps at a better time," he said. "But last night it dawned on me that the reason I couldn't concentrate on anything was the uncertainty. I can't go on like this, at least, not until I know where we stand."

"Of all the things to say," I said at last, my voice shaking.

"What do you mean?"

"A clue. You never gave me a clue."

He kept staring at me.

"I had no idea," I said.

"Oh?" He leaned back a bit. "I had hoped the feeling was mutual." And he sounded hurt.

"It was," I said. "Is." My face felt hot as I repeated more to myself, "It most certainly is."

With my secret now out, it was impossible not to look at him. The pumping in my chest was too loud. All I wanted was to stay in that moment, right there, and with Kyan.

I held my tears back long enough to say, "I can't think of a better man to share my life with." And at that moment, I didn't care who saw us, or heard what we said.

~

Auntie sat by her sewing machine in the dining room. Like all the other times when she had a big project, our dining table had been transformed into a tailor's workshop with scraps of fabric scattered everywhere. I sat next to her, and watched the seam she sewed, feeding the fabric to the machine with one hand, pulling it with the other.

"Hello, Auntie," I said and kissed her cheek. "What are you making?"

"Pajamas for Reza."

"Lucky Reza."

She looked at me from above her glasses. "Shouldn't you be studying?"

"I'm just taking a break."

She went back to her project. Her fingers, now curved from rheumatism, still maneuvered the fabric with reasonable skill.

"When do you think Mitra will get married?"

"Oh, I don't know," she said. "I suppose sometime after her studies are done." She sighed. "That girl's like a wild gazelle, hard to tame."

"What happens to *me* if she never does?"

Auntie stopped working and gave me an inquisitive look. "Why, Miss Roya!" She laughed before mocking me more. "Are *we* in a rush?"

Choosing my words with care, I proceeded to tell her about Kyan. I had to make sure my story met with her approval because, even with a marriage proposal, a respectable girl wouldn't go out and pick her own man. In my aunt's world, by bringing the question first to me, Kyan had disregarded tradition. Besides, my relationship with Auntie was too formal to talk openly about love.

After describing Kyan as my supportive friend and the true gentleman that he had been, I concluded he made a good candidate and that I thought she would approve of him. Conscious of the glass wall between us, I skipped the part about my own feelings.

"He wanted to know if his parents could call you for an appointment."

Auntie folded the fabric, put it aside and started to wind the long thread around a bobbin. "No," she said, sounding distant.

I held my breath, and only exhaled when she added, "Not yet."

Still too shocked to react, I waited for more.

"I know your father better than you do." She placed the wooden hood over her sewing machine and arranged the spools of thread neatly in her sewing basket.

Too much was at stake and I could no longer contain myself. "I won't let Pedar ruin this for me," I blurted out.

Auntie gave my tearful eyes a surprised look and continued to tidy up. She gathered pieces of thread from the table and rolled them into a ball. "If you play your cards right, no one will ruin anything for you." For a minute or so, she continued to clean the table without a word. "Here's what I suggest," she said. "America is on the other side of the world. Let the young man go ahead with his study plans. If by the time you graduate you haven't changed your mind, I'll make sure we gain your father's approval."

I was not thrilled with her suggestion, but said nothing.

Her voice regained the affectionate tone of guidance as she said, "Two years is a long time. It's like throwing an apple into the air; who knows how many twists and turns it may take before it lands?"

~

A week later, Kyan and I said our good-byes in the school cafeteria. Not many students were around and the young man in charge of the café had started to pile the chairs on top of the tables in preparation for closing.

Kyan took a box of cigarettes out of his pocket.

"You smoke?" I said in utter surprise.

"Not really." He took out a cigarette. "They say it's good for the nerves." He lit his cigarette clumsily.

"You'll write to me, won't you?"

He gave me a sideway glance. "As if you had to ask."

Reaching into my bag. I took out a piece of paper. "I signed up for a post box at school. Here's the number."

He smiled. "Clever little lady."

The young man in charge of the cafeteria had finished with the chairs and circled our table, eager to close. Kyan didn't notice.

"Promise me something," he said.

I smiled. "Haven't I already?"

"No. Not that." There was an alarming gravity in his voice. "I want you to promise you won't do anything foolish while I'm gone." He nodded to University Avenue. "Stay away from all that."

I threw my head back in frustration. "Not you, too!"

"I'm serious, Roya. At this point, *they* have a good grip on the opposition. The prisons are at full capacity." He stared far away. "Trust me, if I thought there was any hope, I'd stay right here and join them myself." He shook his head. "But there isn't."

As I listened, I kept on shredding my paper napkin. Tiny white fragments covered the table like snowflakes on a bare roof.

"When's your flight?" I asked.

"Promise me!"

"Oh, Kyan. Just what do you think I might do?"

"I don't know, something heroic."

"To be a hero takes a lot more than feelings and friendships," I said, sounding as old as my aunt. "Don't you see? I'm not good enough. I'm like a robot, programmed to do as I'm told."

The frustration of a lifetime would not fit into simple words. All these years, I had been like a pebble, rolling down a steep hill without any power of my own.

He reached over and wiped the tears off my cheek. "Just don't let the little robot do anything stupid," he said, and despite the smile that spread on his lips, he sounded as if he, too, could cry.

"So. What time is your flight tomorrow?"

"Early morning," he said. "Long before little ladies wake up."

"I'll be up."

He put his elbows on the table and leaned closer. I could feel his warm breath on my skin – it smelled of fresh tobacco and mint toothpaste. For a second I thought he was going to kiss me and it felt as if the earth were about to move from under me. But he pulled away, leaned back in his chair, and studied me with intent. He joined his hands to form a square and looked at me through it, as if to take a snapshot.

"*This* is how I will remember you."

~

The next morning at dawn, the roar of a plane shook me awake. I opened my window and searched the sky for it, but planes did not pass directly over our house. I watched the daylight grow and listened to the sound of the jet fading away until it became one with the silence around me.

Falling back to sleep, the apple my aunt had spoken of rose in my mind's eye. A large, green apple, tossed into the air, it was now on its way down. Turning, turning...

Fifteen

My entire family went to Tehran to attend the wedding of a cousin. Two days into our trip, on a hot Monday afternoon, while everyone took a nap under the ceiling fan in my uncle's cool basement, I went upstairs to change. Having no idea what one should wear for a prison visit, I chose a simple blue suit. I grabbed my purse and left a note on my aunt's door. "Gone shopping. Will be back soon. R."

Mrs. Payan and Eemon's mother were waiting in a taxi a block away. I climbed in and said hello, without looking at them.

"Roya-joon, I'd like you to meet Mrs. Arfa," Shireen's mother said sweetly, "Eemon's mother, and she is also my second cousin."

I nodded at the slender woman sitting next to Mrs. Payan. She did not have a chador on and her black headscarf gave her pale face an ethereal look. She nodded, but did not smile.

Mrs. Payan turned to the driver. "Hotel Evin, please."

I smiled at her pretense of going to a hotel that used to have the same name as the prison. Most locals had continued to call the existing hotel 'Evin' long after it had changed to a Hilton Hotel. Then again, maybe that was their attempt to avoid embarrassment.

The driver glanced at us in his rearview mirror before zigzagging through the maze of Tehran's traffic. A stranger to this big, busy city, I had no idea where Evin, or any other prison, might be. Since the place housed mostly political prisoners, I had imagined it to be somewhere far away and isolated, maybe out of town. I pictured its tall gates and mysterious watchtowers, something similar to the Nazi prisons I had seen in movies. So when the taxi pulled into a side street in the northern section, and stopped by an ordinary brick wall, I was certain we were in the wrong place.

Mrs. Payan extended her arm out of her chador and offered a crumpled bill to the driver. Her cousin adjusted her scarf before stepping out. I had brought along a scarf and a pair of sunglasses, just in case.

I looked up and saw no towers, just a plain wall with a twisted mesh of barbed wire on top and a solid iron gate where two young soldiers stood guard. Their khaki uniforms were plain, a simple cap covered the top part of their faces, and despite summer heat, the legs of their pants were tucked into heavy boots.

Mrs. Payan presented a paper to one, who motioned us to a window inside the entryway. That was our first checkpoint, but after three further guards had asked for our full name and date of birth, my disguise of a scarf and glasses seemed ridiculous. I continued to remind myself that we weren't doing anything wrong and this was just a casual visit.

"Stay in the waiting area until your names are called," the guard at the last checkpoint said. Contrary to my expectation, the so-called "waiting area" proved to be nothing but an outdoor green with a few bushes and trees. Convinced that invisible eyes were watching, I sat in a shaded area close to Mrs. Payan.

"When they call," she whispered, "we'll be searched before they let us through."

"Searched, how?"

"They have a metal rod they pass around you and it will beep if there's anything suspicious." She thought for a minute. "Of course, people smuggle food and things all the time, but they're looking for weapons." She smiled. "All Shireen ever wants is pen and paper." She motioned to a small notebook in her purse. "They don't mind those."

I noticed Mrs. Arfa was holding a bag of candy and a carton of cigarettes and I felt bad for coming empty-handed.

"Then we'll go to these little visiting cabins, where we are separated from the prisoner only by iron bars."

I smiled sadly. Not just the bars, I thought. I couldn't begin to count the multiple layers that disconnected us from the world of the incarcerated.

A few other visitors also waited, but no one made an effort to communicate. From time to time, a side door at the far end opened, a guard peeked his head out to call someone in, but each time only two names were called. People went in or out; no one spoke, and most faces were blank. I wondered if Pedar had informers in Tehran as well. Each time that squeaky door opened, fear of the unknown made me hesitate to look up.

Mrs. Payan had told me they'd let the prisoner know before calling us in. It had been so long since my last visit with Shireen that I couldn't begin to guess how she might react. With summer at its peak, the tree leaves didn't move and the shade offered no relief. Apart from an occasional cough or muffled footsteps, the only sound was the buzz of bees circling, going in and out of the trees.

The door opened again and a female guard called out. "Payaaan!" To which all three of us jumped.

The woman walked over, and studied me head-to-toe; up, down, and back up again. Her expression lacked respect and she gave me a disdainful look. She turned to Mrs. Payan while wagging a finger at me. "This one can't go."

"She has a permit," Mrs. Payan said.

The woman checked her clipboard. "Permit's been cancelled."

I took a step forward in protest, but like a mechanical gate, Mrs. Payan's arm rose against my chest. "That's okay," she said. "She doesn't mind."

I leaned my back on the tree trunk, too humiliated to feel sad or disappointed. Why would Shireen's mother give up so quickly – why didn't she insist a little? I felt offended, as if their refusal meant that I wasn't good enough, that I was unworthy of admittance.

Before leaving the yard, Mrs. Payan stopped and turned to me. "Please take a taxi home. You shouldn't wait here alone."

I nodded, but sliding my back on the tree, I lowered myself to the ground and watched the people coming in and out of the door.

In their silence, I could sense all kinds of moods in those people. A few seemed pleased, yet the look on most visitors' faces told me what a grim experience it was.

The mere notion that Pedar may be behind this cancellation was enough to make me regret having gone there. I had no idea how long I had been sitting there when I heard Mrs. Payan's voice.

"Dear child, have you been waiting here all this time?" she exclaimed, sounding both sorry and relieved. "I worried so much about you, wondering if you had enough money for a taxi, or if you knew your way around Tehran."

"How is Shireen?" I asked her and stood. My behind was stiff from sitting on the dry, firm ground, and I was very thirsty.

Mrs. Arfa' wiped her misty eyes with the corner of her scarf.

"This visit was a quiet one," Mrs. Payan told me. "Let's go. I'll tell you more on the way."

As the taxi drove us back to Niavaran, she told me the details. "Each time I see Shireen, she seems to have crawled deeper into her own shell." She tried to smile, but her lips only quivered. "She couldn't believe you had come, said to tell you that you are *one sky* crazy?" She shrugged. "Whatever that means."

For a minute we were all silent. Then Mrs. Arfa' spoke for the first time since we had met. She sounded weak, as if just recovering from a sore throat, and the words she said had the sound of an unfinished previous conversation.

"There's just no other way we could come up with that kind of money," she said to us both, as if I too, would understand her meaning.

"I don't know," Mrs. Payan replied. "But now she's made me promise not to borrow for bail."

"What bail?" I asked her.

Mrs. Payan seemed reluctant to tell me as she turned to her side window.

"Shireen's crime isn't exactly political," Mrs. Arfa said. "I mean, there's no evidence of her having done anything besides living in that house. That alone makes it possible for her prison term to be bought."

"Bought? What do you mean, bought?"

"It's done all the time. Not for political prisoners, mind you, but Shireen was only an accessory to a crime. Our lawyer has been working on a deal over her prison term."

Mrs. Payan threw her hands in the air. "Are you joking? This is just another scam to fool the public. The amount they're asking for is ridiculous, they know we don't have it."

The driver glanced back. Mrs. Arfa pushed an elbow into my side, but I wasn't sure Mrs. Payan cared any more. She exhaled in frustration and said to me, "As if that wasn't bad enough, she made me promise we wouldn't borrow what we can't pay back."

I had more questions, but decided to save them for another time. I asked the driver to drop me off a block away from my uncle's.

"I'm sorry it didn't work out," Mrs. Payan said. "You have every right to be disappointed."

"It wasn't meant to be," I said and forced a smile. "Thank you for trying."

The dry afternoon heat felt like an oven. As I passed by a parked car, a man leaning against it eyed me with curiosity, his brown suit too heavy for such weather.

Would everyone at my uncle's still be asleep? And if not, had any of them noticed my absence? I stopped at the corner store and bought a few bunches of green grapes, a pack of gum, and a women's magazine. When I left the shop, the man in the brown suit was still there. As I walked by, he looked at me again and the sun shone on a round scar on his forehead, its pallor contrasting his dark skin, its round shape resembling a large button. I wondered if he was going to follow me.

Turning into the alley, I ducked into a doorway and looked back. The car was still parked where it had been, now less visible through the traffic. The man had gone. I proceeded to my uncle's, taking hurried steps.

The cool air of the basement was welcome on my heat-stricken cheeks. Everyone seemed to be positioned as when I'd left. Pedar lay on a mattress, a white sheet covering half of him. With the back of one hand across his face, I couldn't tell if he was asleep or watching me. The lazy fan turned round and around, blowing a breeze, humming a lullaby.

I put down the bag of fruit, took off my shoes, and grabbed a pillow.

—

On the first day back at school, I rushed to the mailroom to collect my letters. There were three blue envelopes with US stamps on them.

Kyan's first letter had an awkward tone, as if he had made an effort to report every detail of his days. I didn't know what I had expected, but felt disappointed that this first wasn't exactly a love letter. In fact, the only words of affection came at the very end.

"Wisconsin is cold and gloomy, even this time of the year, but thoughts of you help me to feel warm inside."

His second letter was longer, more casual. Number three came in a thick manila envelope that contained his university scarf in shades of purple and navy blue. He wrote on the attached card, *"Some of the boys give their university scarf to the one they love."*

It surprised me to find Kyan could be so shy. Maybe I hadn't noticed that in him because when it came to anatomy or politics, he had done all the talking. That he seemed so lost for words, and struggled to express his emotions, helped me to overlook the shortcomings in his letters.

That afternoon I wrote back and thanked him for the scarf. As for the matters at home, I only hinted, *"Everything here is the same. University Avenue continues to have regular visitors and I haven't done anything out of the ordinary to report."*

I had to admit that my letter had turned out equally inexpressive, but it was hard to break the trend Kyan had set. Responding to his brief letters, I couldn't tell him about my lonely walks, or how school had turned into nothing but heavy volumes of books. His absence reminded me of Shireen's world after Eemon had enlisted in the army. Someone who had been a focal point in my daily life had vanished from sight. It was as though the whole world around me had changed.

In my solitude, I kept on telling myself that, despite Pedar's tough rules and my seemingly restricted lifestyle, the fact that I was not in prison was something. Besides, as long as Kyan went on living somewhere out there, I could hang on to my hopes. How did Shireen endure a world without the prospect of a future?

Sixteen

MITRA RETURNED FROM ENGLAND with an impressive diploma, a glamorous wardrobe, and a job awaiting her at the university. Although she had gained a little weight – which she blamed on the English chocolate – she looked as good as a fashion model. Fine black eyeliner framed her almond-shaped eyes. She had tweezed her eyebrows, an exception among unmarried girls, save for those who had studied abroad.

With both of us now adults, our age difference became insignificant. She enjoyed teaching at the university and seemed to have lost her drive for heated debates. Occasionally, tired of the cafeteria food, we went out for lunch. It was on one of those lunch dates that she brought up Jenab.

"There's something I need to tell you," Mitra said as soon as our server had disappeared. I couldn't remember the last time she had used that tone, and sensed an impending lecture.

"Have you been in touch with your old teacher?" She studied me. "Mr. Elmi?"

I liked the fact that she used his proper name. Somehow the name, "His Excellency" no longer suited Jenab's shattered image.

I shook my head. "Not for some time. Why?"

"Did you ever give him any gifts?"

"Not that I recall." Then I remembered the painting I had given him. "Except that painting," I said and my voice reflected the sentimental girl I used to be. "I gave him one of my works for a keepsake." That entire segment of life, the aspiring artist who idolized her favorite teacher, now seemed unreal.

"And I'll bet you signed it," Mitra said.

"He's not auctioning the masterpiece, is he?" I said, laughing.

Mitra seemed uncomfortable. "He told one of my colleagues at the university that you had a crush on him."

"Ha!" I laughed. The older couple sitting at the next table turned.

Mitra wasn't amused. She went on, "To prove it, he showed him your painting." She looked into my eyes. "Did you?"

"Crush doesn't begin to describe it." I crossed my hands over my chest. "I worshipped that man!"

"You know what I mean."

"That's crazy! Go look at it. It's an old man and a little girl. For Heaven's sake, that's how I loved him. To me, he wasn't a man; I thought he was God."

"Apparently, you still do," she said, and this time I felt the sting.

"Excuse me?"

"He also boasted about your recent visit to the language academy."

"Argh!" It became clear where all this was leading. Oh that pitiful lowlife! Such stories would more than explain my visit to whoever may have seen me there.

"Okay, think what you want. Let's say it was puppy love way back then, but when I went to that damn academy, I was already in love with somebody else," I said in my own defense, before realizing that my secret was now out.

The server came back with more iced coffee. When he left, I went on to tell my sister everything, down to Kyan's marriage proposal.

"Why didn't you tell me this?" She sounded as hurt as I had been when Shireen told me about Eemon.

"I didn't even want to bring it up now. Kyan is far, far away and Auntie thinks I might as well forget about him. So what's the use?"

But Mitra was too excited to drop the subject, and for the rest of our lunchtime she seemed to overlook Jenab, only returning to him before paying the bill.

"Someone should have stopped Mr. Elmi before he could do more damage."

"What damage? Who cares about silly rumors?"

"Not now. I'm talking about back then, when they fired him for messing with his students' minds."

"In my case he did no harm, whereas..." I stopped, but I had already found the dark place that I'd tried so hard to steer clear of.

"So, you've thought about that, too," Mitra said.

I didn't want to say another word.

"Many people suspect that he may actually have had a part in all the..." she hesitated, "... arrests."

"Sometimes I do, too." Jenab's voice rang in my head. *Nothing to explain. Not a thing.* "Maybe it's just a gut feeling, but there was something about him I could never figure out." I didn't tell Mitra the reason I had visited Mr. Elmi, nor would I mention his close association with the Payans. Words seemed to complicate matters and at some point I had decided to keep things to myself.

"I never liked him," Mitra said. "Especially after I heard how he had changed, and whatever it was they did to him to make him change."

"I never quite understood it either."

"I heard his big mouth sent him to SAVAK, and word got to the Ministry of Education."

"I felt bad for him," I said. "He seemed so different after he came back."

"It's his son you should feel bad for, they got him, too."

"His son?" My loud voice made a woman at the next table turn around. Mr. Elmi, being such a legendary figure, I had not thought about his family.

Mitra nodded. "His son was one of *them*."

"SAVAK?" I mouthed the word.

"No, silly." She leaned closer and whispered, "Fadaiyan."

All of a sudden it was as if the curtain had lifted, enabling me to see the stage, with all the players in place.

"How do you know all this?"

"One of my students told me." She tucked a lock of hair behind her ear. "I did some after-class tutoring as a favor and, in return, she filled me in on what I've missed."

"So what happened to him?"

"Who?"

"Jenab's son!"

Mitra took a sip of her iced coffee. "They set him free." She did not sound too happy about that.

"I'm confused," I said. "On one hand you tell me Jenab put ideas in our heads, then you suspect he was an informer. Which is he?"

She hesitated. "What makes you think he couldn't be both? Some people think the switch came when he was going to be fired." She leaned closer and whispered, "But that's false. It appears it was his son's arrest that forced him to join SAVAK."

"No, he didn't!" I said without conviction.

"Despicable as it sounds, I wouldn't put it past him." Mitra's face took on a more severe expression. "To think that he would sacrifice so many lives just so he could save his own snotty son." She shook her head in sorrow.

The spoon fell out of my hand and it clanked against the plate. "What are you trying to tell me?"

Mitra motioned to an approaching waiter. We let the man fill our glasses. When he had gone, Mitra continued, "I don't think he started off that way. He may have even believed most of the garbage he fed to others. In a way, his words encouraged young people to do what a gutless old man could only dream of."

"Okay, I'll accept that he stirred the students, but his own son?"

Mitra nodded again. "Especially his son. Think about it. If a few hours talk could brainwash his students, what would a lifetime of such words do to a young mind?"

I studied Mitra, the rational and calm lady that she had become. "What happened to all your radical views?"

She smiled. "I saw the world, and guess what? It's much bigger than Mashad."

I shrugged. "Anyway, it's over now."

"But is it?" She sat back. "Teachers like Mr. Elmi have done their damage. It may be too late to prevent the seeds they have sown from growing."

~

I was in the library, searching for a text on biochemistry, when Nasrin touched my shoulder. Alarmed to find Shireen's sister looking for me, I thought something dreadful must have happened.

"Can we talk?" she said in a hushed voice.

"What's wrong?" I asked, a little louder than I meant to.

"Shhh!" The librarian shot us an angry look.

Nasrin shook her head. "Nothing's wrong."

We walked out of the library and into the hallway. Taller than I remembered, she seemed otherwise the same as when I'd last seen her – at Ali's memorial service.

"Is Shireen okay?"

"She's fine. It's me who needs a favor. I have something of Shireen's that I can only trust to your care."

Not understanding, I waited for more.

"I've been keeping a diary for her. On each visit, Shireen either tells me things, or gives me the notes she has written." She stopped talking and fearfully glanced behind her. "Our house isn't exactly safe. Besides, Shireen wants you to read them."

Two boys from my class came through the revolving doors. As they gave Nasrin's figure an approving look, I became conscious of her missing scarf.

"Can I bring them to you?"

I thought for a moment. Honored to be trusted with such precious notes, I would have held them safe for Shireen regardless of the risks involved. At my house, no one ever went through my things, much less the boxes of books I kept in the basement.

"Of course. I'll be glad to keep them."

She exhaled hard. "I'll come to your school tomorrow at four. I can leave them on the backseat of the cab and let you take the same taxi home." She thought for a moment and said, "I bring them a little at a time, just in case."

It felt as if I had been asked to play a part in a spy movie.

The next day, when Nasrin's taxi pulled to the curb, I was standing so close to the street that it could have run me over. Nasrin got out and, ignoring me, walked away while I climbed into the backseat and gave my address to the driver. I found the manila envelope on the worn leather, it had a few old stamps and the return address was scratched.

At home, I hid the envelope behind the bookshelf and could not wait for dinnertime to come and go so I could read Shireen's notes.

Late that night, I emptied the contents of the envelope over my desk. At first glance, except for one folded paper, the rest looked like the trash one finds while cleaning a purse: scraps of paper, some wrinkled or torn, matchbook covers, unraveled cigarette boxes. Then I recognized Shireen's handwriting on them.

Mrs. Payan had mentioned how Nasrin sometimes memorized Shireen's words, and wrote her report after each meeting. The typewritten pages had to be those, and I read them first to get a general idea.

"The front door caved in with such a rumble, I thought a crane had hit the building. The heavy wood hit a side window, sending shards of glass everywhere, even over our dinner spread. Two soldiers burst in through the cloud of dust, and they pointed their machine guns at us. Four more followed. I knew who they were even before I looked up.

We all carried our cyanide capsules in our cheeks, but I had removed mine so I could eat. I reached for it sitting next to my plate, but a heavy boot pinned my wrist to the floor. Looking for help, my eyes found Mehdi against the wall. Something was pushed into his mouth to keep it open as the gunman's fingers searched his cheek. The man shouted, 'Give it up, you son-of-a-bitch!' And, when he pulled out his hand, blood ran down Mehdi's chin. The man grabbed him by the hair and slammed his face against the wall. 'You won't get off that easy, you bastard.'

The owner of the boot on my hand brought his face closer. 'We have a plan for naughty little girls,' he whispered, his breath smelling of rotten onions. His other hand clutched my breast, hurting me.

'Tie 'em up,' someone shouted from across the room.

'I'll show you rebellion,' a nasal voice said.

A man in a police uniform stepped on the dinner spread, crushing a plate under his shoes. He spat in my plate. 'I'll make you eat shit.'

The last thing I saw before being blindfolded was Massoud on the floor, his arm bent at an awkward angle, his face colorless, motionless eyes staring at the ceiling. Onion breath whispered, 'We'll have fun, you and I.'"

Here, the typing ended. Mrs. Payan had told me nothing. In Shireen's words, I saw details that no one else could describe and it was more than I was prepared for. Those notes put me at that horrific scene. I saw and felt the heavy boots, the grabbing, and the pushing. I started to shiver violently and had to lower my body to the floor. Still, my hands searched among the pile of paper on my bed, looking for more.

The other notes were all in Shireen's handwriting, some barely legible. She had used a pencil, a pen, and one looked as if she had used a burned matchstick. There were parts where the words went in all directions. As if she had written them with her eyes closed, a few unfinished words indicated her hand had moved beyond the page.

"The interrogators change, but the questions are the same. 'Where are the others?' How stupid is that? Do they think the comrades would stay put?

A girl in the cell across the hall keeps shouting slogans, information for all. She says we are worthless, that the good ones are taken to another location. The rest of us are questioned, even lashed, right here. Sometimes guards get mad and I hear them striking her as she calls them names. Then she's quiet for a while."

I wondered if that's how Shireen heard about Ali or Eemon, someone shouting the news across the hall. How long did it take before she knew they had killed her brother?

The next note was written on the inside of a torn cigarette box.

"My back is on fire, but it can't be half as bad as Meena's. In the middle of the night they brought her a doctor. No one tells me what's happened to the others. I pray they never went back to the house. With blindfolds it's always nighttime around me. Walking, I constantly picture there's a deep well in the next step."

I shut my eyes and covered them with both hands, but it didn't help. I was safe, in my own room, a universe away from how Shireen had felt. The last note was written on a grocery bag, but it read like a continuation of the one on the cigarette box. Her neat print told me her blindfolds must have been removed.

> *"There are no wells here, not even a ditch. The first thing I saw was a barred window high up, framing a patch of light, its glare hurting my eyes. My cell is smaller than I had imagined, and despite the stink, it isn't so messy. There's a dried bloodstain on my mattress and cotton sticks out of the hole on its side.*
> *Two guards took me along the hallway and into a large room. A bright lamp was aimed at my eyes before the questioning began. 'I don't know,' was all I said to each and every question. One of them tore off the back off my gown and when the first lash touched my flesh, it felt like a flexible blade, cutting across my back. A cry escaped my throat, but as more lashes came in regular intervals, the anticipation prepared me. The indignity of it hurt the most.*
> *I came to in the silence of my dark cell, the rough floor against my cheek. I rolled on my back and allowed the cool cement to soothe my pain."*

I turned the manila envelope upside down and shook it. Nothing more came out. So I went back to the beginning and read them again, and again.

I had the urge to climb to the roof and scream for the whole world to hear, "A punishment far greater than the crime!" Jenab should have saved his fancy words for such a time and I wanted to know, just whose crime *was* this? In a just world, those lashes would have come down on his bare back; he and his brilliant philosophy; he and the dead-end roads he illuminated; he and the promises he could not, or would not, keep.

I put the notes safely away, wiped my tears, and turned off my light. "She wants you to read these," Nasrin had said. I could read and re-read every word, I could guard the pages for as long as she wished, but what did Shireen want me to *do* with all the gruesome knowledge she had bestowed?

I closed my eyes and welcomed the night's blanket over me.

~

Three months into her new job, my family received Mitra's good news. Much to everyone's delight, my sister accepted the marriage proposal of a young colleague.

Pedar had started to show signs of aging. He often misplaced his glasses and lost his temper with the slightest irritation. On our occasional walks around the garden, he held my arm and leaned a little heavier than before. Many nights, as I stayed up to study, I saw his light on and heard him cough. His asthma attacks had become more frequent, making him more dependent on his inhaler. Although the smell of opium still lingered around his room, he no longer entertained guests. Once a good player of the *tar,* he wouldn't touch it for months, and rarely listened to any music at all. So the fact that Mitra's news had brought back his smile was something.

One day, when Pedar's doctor stopped by for a house call, I decided to listen to what he had to say. Dr. Ghareeb was among the friends who had enjoyed an "occasional puff" with Pedar – a fact that had surprised me, until I learned about opium's therapeutic effects if, and when, used in moderation.

Standing outside Pedar's room, I could hear Dr. Ghareeb's voice. "Rafi-khan, if you don't stop smoking this stuff, I'll refuse to be your doctor."

Pedar laughed. "It soothes my nerves and you know it."

"I'm not joking," the old doctor said. "This is going to kill you."

I knocked and entered before Pedar could stop me.

My father let go of the pipe he was holding and it fell in the brazier. Seeming annoyed, he said to the doctor, "Let's hear what your novice colleague thinks."

"Come, Roya," Dr. Ghareeb said, "help me to reason with this stubborn man."

"Me?" I laughed. "I'm the last person Pedar would listen to."

He took a serious tone. "Tell him about some of the cases you've seen."

I recalled the black lungs in the anatomy lab. The tar collected over years of cigarette smoking gave those delicate lung tissues the look of a mesh filled with charcoal. I had no idea what opium did to lungs, but imagined it to be the same, if not worse. I wanted to tell Dr. Ghareeb about those horrendous coughs I heard at night, but Pedar's glare prevented me. The 'white' of his eyes was now permanently bloodshot.

"Pedar is a smart man," I said. "I bet he hears you more than he's willing to let on." I turned to Pedar. "I can't play doctor for my own family," I said, "but, if I were you, I'd listen to the best doctor in town." I nodded in Dr. Ghareeb's direction.

That night, as I continued to study, I heard Pedar cough again in long chains. When it turned quiet, I knew he had fallen asleep and went to turn off his light. I noticed he had moved my mother's photograph from the mantle to his nightstand.

~

In a world filled with responsibilities, studies, and miserable news, Kyan's occasional letters were my only glimmer of promise. However, my aunt never asked about him and I knew she didn't expect me to mention his name either.

As my workload increased, so did the frequency of my night shifts. Once in a while patients were brought in who had been savagely beaten. I never dared ask, and the chart most often stated the cause of injury as 'street fight.' Once I saw a gunshot victim, but we were all kept away while the attending doctor treated him. The fact that these victims were invariably admitted around midnight or close to dawn reminded me of what Kyan had said: "They clobber the poor guys." They were mostly boys and all too young to be out at such late hours. When no family members visited and a few disappeared without a formal discharge, it left me no doubt.

Male students in my school outnumbered the girls and the boys took over the residents' room at night with their cigarettes, card games and dirty talk. Sometimes I managed to sneak a nap in the nurses' room. One night, as I lay down, I could overhear two student nurses gossiping.

"I thought they were kept in a separate jail," one girl said.

"Not any more," another replied. "There's no room." She lowered her voice. "I hear the guards rape them, too."

The thought had crossed my mind, but to hear it out loud sounded so much worse. Could Shireen's mind and frail body handle such aggression? Had the Payans really given up on bail, and, how much was it anyway?

The next evening, I was at the movies when I felt an elbow being pushed into my side. In the dark I recognized Nasrin's profile next to me. She reached to the floor and shoved a stack of papers into my purse. The rest of the film could not finish fast enough for me.

By this time, I had become accustomed to reading about people I didn't know, events I could not understand, and a pain that was hard to fathom. All that mattered was to hear more from Shireen and know that she continued to survive. She sounded miraculously sane and nowhere in those notes did I see signs of a breakdown.

"The closest I come to bravery is not to whimper. I tell myself this isn't my body, that the pain I feel isn't mine. I have to remind myself that if I scream, they'll hurt my baby. I'll die before I let them see my tears."

Nowhere in those notes did I read anything that might validate what I had heard in the nurses' room. Or could it be that Shireen found such assaults unmentionable? As I read more, her tone seemed to indicate some form of adjustment. Did prisoners get used to the walls of their cells? In the next pages, for the first time, she mentioned her son.

> *"Sometimes I look at Behrang and think he is somebody else's child. He clings to his grandmother and won't even look at me. It breaks my heart to think of how close we could have been. But, broken heart aside, maybe it's better this way."*

Her last sentence tore at me, and I wanted to reach out and tell her it wasn't so. Behrang would never pick anyone over her. He would want to hold on to whatever was left of his real mother. This I knew.

~

Mitra's modern wedding – with an open bar, candles in the garden and even bridesmaids – went off uneventfully. Auntie let her have her way, though I knew she would have preferred a more traditional ceremony. Following the reception, a line of cars trailed behind the bride and groom's flower-decorated Mercedes, caravanning from our house to their new apartment, and blowing their horns in unison. Auntie, who had worked hard and was tired, stayed home to wrap things up.

Pedar told Akbar he wouldn't need the car. "I'll let my son drive me there," he said and his voice burst with such unforeseen pride, I wished Reza had heard him, too. Pedar sat in front with my brother. "Soon it'll be your turn to find a nice girl and settle down."

"Not too soon, I hope," Reza said and laughed. "I'm much too young."

"Too young? At your age, I was already the father of two!"

Despite the pleasant small talk, I sensed a deep sorrow in Pedar. On the way home, he took the back seat next to me.

"Never mind me," Reza said, "I'll just be the cab driver. Who knows when the practice may come in handy?"

Pedar did not join our laughter. He remained silent all the way home and when I leaned closer, I noticed his tears. "A girl needs her mother to send her away," he said, staring into the dark.

Leaning on Pedar's bony shoulder, I wondered if he had ever regretted having me. Everyone knew that Maman's pregnancy with me had complicated her existing heart condition. But something about the way Pedar hugged me now, said that he had forgotten that long ago.

"Didn't you feel you mother's presence tonight?" he said.

I nodded, kissed his hand and rested it on my cheek.

Reza looked at us in his mirror. "It wasn't just tonight," he said. "I feel her presence all the time."

Pedar gave the mirror a look of surprise. I, too, finally realized how we had all neglected the strong connection between mother and son. The way that full-grown man mentioned his mom made me love him even more.

Pedar reached over and patted Reza's shoulder, but he did not say another word.

The house was dark and Rajab had left for the night. I accompanied Pedar to his room and helped him get ready for bed. I hung his tuxedo in his closet while he changed into pajamas.

"Can you put these in my iron box?" he said, handing me a pair of turquoise cufflinks. Rajab had left the safe under the nightstand, knowing Pedar would need it. I used Pedar's key and opened the box. "Ding!" it rang. Inside, it held the musty odor of old documents mixed with the more subtle scent of opium. Shiny rolls of the stuff in different shades of brown were held together by a rubber band. The rest of the box was full of documents, coins, and stacks of money. When it came to emergencies, Pedar trusted no one to move fast enough, not even the bank. I couldn't help thinking what a world we lived in. My father kept all this money locked up, while the Payans would have sold everything they owned in exchange for Shireen's freedom.

"You want the box back in the big closet?" I asked him.

"No, don't bother. Rajab will do it tomorrow."

I locked the box and pulled the covers up to Pedar's shoulders.

Part Three

The Paint

Seventeen

When I had finished my last exam, I called Shireen's mother to let her know I'd be visiting later. She sounded as if she had a cold and despite her concern that I might catch it, I was there the next afternoon. This time Mr. Payan opened the door. Having lost most of his eyesight, he looked in my general direction and waited for me to introduce myself.

"Miss Afshar! Please come in." He closed the door behind me and led the way. "My wife speaks so fondly of you, I feel as if a part of Shireen is here."

"Thank you, and please call me Roya."

"Yes, Roya *khanoom*."

His warm welcome wasn't the only surprise. Despite his poor eyesight, he seemed to be in charge, or was that only during his wife's recovery?

Mr. Payan opened the door to Shireen's room, where I found a sick Mrs. Payan in bed, propped up against multiple pillows. "Look who I brought you," he said.

"Ahh, Roya-joon," Mrs. Payan said and opened her arms. "Sorry I can't get up. The damn rheumatism has me nailed down, so I spend the daytime in this bed." She gave me a tight hug and motioned to the edge of the bed. "Sit down, dear."

As if time had frozen inside the Payans' home, everything

remained exactly where it had been two years before. As I stared at the pile of science books next to Shireen's bed, Mrs. Payan said, "This is how they'll remember the place. If I keep the same order, their spirits won't have any trouble finding their way around."

I swallowed hard.

Suddenly conscious of having my shoes on, I started to unbuckle them.

"Not to worry, Roya-joon." Mrs. Payan smiled. "Keep them on. None of us are saying our *namaz* any more, and the rugs can take it."

In my mind, I could still see the angelic Shireen in the prayer hall. What had they done to the strong faith of this pious family?

Mr. Payan brought me a wooden chair from the hallway and I was glad to take it and not cramp Mrs. Payan's space. When she beckoned, Mr. Payan bent over and brought his ear closer. She whispered something and he left the room without a word.

"Shireen is still up *there*, you know," Mrs. Payan said, nodding to the ceiling as if Evin prison were upstairs.

An awkward silence followed the mention of my friend's name as we each fell into our own thoughts.

Moments later, Mr. Payan returned with a tray of tea, beaming a curious smile. I saw right away what the smile was about. Next to the cookies was a tiny glass of water and in it, two little flowers. Red poppies.

I gasped, as if he had brought me a lock of his daughter's hair.

Mrs. Payan chuckled and seemed pleased with her surprise. "I asked him to get those," she said, her broad smile revealing a gold tooth in the back. "Shireen made me promise that if you ever came by in spring, I'd show you these."

"But where did you find them?"

"Oh, we have them every year. A long time ago, Shireen spread some seeds in the vacant lot next door. They return every spring."

The memory of the mud roof was so vivid that I could almost taste the rain. *You are not there, and…* She sure wasn't, yet her poetic spirit had brought me "those mirthful gems".

"It's okay," Mrs. Payan said, offering me a tissue. "God knows I've shed my own share of tears. But no more." She motioned to the tray. "Have some tea before it gets cold." She picked up her glass of tea and took a couple of sips. "Ever since my knees make it hard to move, I've learned to enjoy Payan's half-brewed tea." She took another sip. "Though I give him credit for trying."

Mrs. Payan calling her husband by his last name sounded as strange as when Shireen had referred to him as 'Agha-jan.' Did this small man with poor eyesight, who barely knew how to brew tea, possibly expect such formalities?

"I'd love to hear more about Shireen."

A deep sigh escaped Mrs. Payan's throat. "What can I tell you, my dear? How can I even begin to describe what you've neither seen, nor could possibly picture?"

"We're so cut off. Whatever you tell me is better than being in the dark."

A tormented look came into her eyes, as if the remembrance itself gave her physical pain. "The Shireen you knew is gone. Those bastards have ruined her." Watching me look around, she said, "Don't worry, no wires in this room, no phone line either. That's why we like it in here."

I thought of the notes trusted to my care and wondered if there might be more. "Does Nasrin still keep a diary?"

Dead silence. Mr. Payan, who was about to leave the room, stopped halfway and turned around. I didn't like the look they exchanged and the suspense lasted longer than I could bear.

Mr. Payan cleared his throat and after a long, unnatural pause said, "I'm afraid Nasrin is gone." His voice broke with the last word, but he somehow managed to add, "Suicide."

Mrs. Payan covered her face with both hands and began to rock.

I just waited, hoping, willing her to tell me it wasn't so. I had so many images of her that I couldn't just give them up for dead. The horrible news seemed to be delivered faster than my mind could process it. In only seconds, I had been asked to picture that her serene smile and those caring eyes were just ... gone. Funny how, of all the images that came to me, the clearest was one I hadn't actually seen. I had depicted the scene from Shireen's notes with such clarity that by now it was like a personal memory: Shireen alone in her room, the little sister bringing her meals, worried eyes glancing long enough to know she was okay, then leaving without a word. The door was shut. Gone.

"She had no choice," Mr. Payan continued. He sounded so dry that I wondered if the repetition of this phrase had immunized him to the pain. "When they knocked on our door in the dead of night, she knew."

"Why was there no mention of it in the news? Or anywhere, for that matter?"

"I didn't allow it. This time, we wished for our grief to be ours alone."

"Payan!" Shireen's mother protested.

Mr. Payan wrapped and unwrapped his green prayer beads around his wrinkled fingers. "Nasrin wasn't just an accessory to some common crime. She was a leader. Her activities put her in a much more serious position." Reaching under his glasses, he wiped his eyes. "If they'd taken her in..." He finished his sentence with a loud exhale.

Mrs. Payan raised a hand. "Enough! Is it any wonder no one comes around any more? Poor Roya-joon is here to visit, not to listen to your *rowzeh.*" She turned to me. "Would you like another glass of tea?"

At Ali's memorial service, it had been Nasrin offering me tea. Was life nothing but a game of chess – pawns moving forward, changing places, and being taken away? I imagined that the whole family must have been taken in for questioning at some point, but unable to ask about something so personal, I steered the conversation in a different direction.

"How do you get your news of Shireen now?" I asked.

Mrs. Payan, perhaps relieved to change the subject, said, "You remember Behrang's other grandparents are my cousins? They now have custody of Behrang, which in turn gives them rights to unlimited visits."

She beamed a smile. "You should see him. A handsome little devil, and so smart, too."

I recalled Shireen's last note. "How does he interact with Shireen?"

"He likes seeing her, and obviously enjoys the attention. We've told him it's a hospital." She laughed. "What does a toddler know about hospitals?"

"And Shireen?"

"She can be calm, but God forbid Behrang should cry, suddenly she covers her ears and starts to shake violently. Sometimes they have to come and tie her down."

The lump was back in my throat.

"What did they do to her?" I finally got out, knowing full well that I was overstepping my boundaries, as if concern for my friend left no room for good manners. Something told me this time whatever they had done to Shireen was far worse than cigarette burns or sexual assault.

Mrs. Payan wiped her eyes. "They used her love for the baby to make her talk. Clever, no? They played tapes of Behrang down the hall and hearing him cry, even scream, Shireen believed they were torturing her baby." She shook her head. "When they told her that they would cut off the boy's fingers, one by one, she didn't believe them. Then one day, they showed her the bloody content of a crumpled napkin…"

"Beasts!" I screamed and instinctively covered my mouth with one hand.

"It's okay, Roya. She's fine now."

"Fine?" I knew that came out rude, but couldn't find my voice to apologize.

"I mean, she's seen Behrang and knows it was a trick. They moved her to some ward for mental patients and, for a few weeks, none of us could see her. After being discharged, she turned quiet. Not in a good way."

Unable to focus, I did my best to take all this in.

"I was sure we'd lost her," she went on. "Who knew she'd pull through?" Shireen's mother sounded so cold that for a second I had a feeling she would have preferred losing her. "That's human nature for you. Tough as a rock and able to tolerate just about anything." She shook her head. "I bet by now she has adapted to their grisly ways."

She took a tiny cucumber from the fruit bowl, peeled and cut it in sections before putting it on my plate. That used to be Shireen's favorite snack.

"She teaches, you know," Mrs. Payan said.

"Who?"

"You mean, whom does she teach? Other inmates, young prostitutes, whoever's willing to learn. She says it helps her days go by."

That description matched the Shireen I knew, arisen from the ashes of her loved ones, having lost all, yet willing to share what was left. No one but my Shireen would even think of using her empty days to edify a young prostitute.

Mrs. Payan's hospitality went beyond tradition. While she offered me food I received a tender message of affection in the movement of her hands. Each time Shireen's name was mentioned, she'd find something else to offer. I wondered if it was me she fed, or if those loving morsels were in fact meant for her daughter. What went through a mother's mind if her children were never to fill her home again? Would her arms remember the embrace?

How ironic that the more Mrs. Payan tried to reassure me, the more troubled I became. I was not Shireen, never was, and never would be. This country had made a doctor out of me, someone to save lives, but I had yet to touch a life, let alone save one. Some friend I was, sitting on the sideline and watching such a unique soul waste away.

"How much is her bail?" I asked.

"Oh, we have a better word than 'bail' now," Shireen's father responded with bitter sarcasm. "It seems they prefer the term 're-purchasing time' nowadays."

"How much?"

"Who cares, my dear? As they say, 'when you're drowned, the depth of water makes no difference!'"

I did not laugh at his anecdote, and continued to stare at him.

"Fifty-thousand *tumans*," Mrs. Payan answered for him. "More than our house is worth. Payan is set on selling everything, even these rugs." She motioned to the Persian rug under our feet.

A new thought flashed in my mind, though I wasn't sure how practical it might be. I put the glass of tea down. "I'd love to stay, but I can't." I got up to leave.

"You've only just arrived," Mrs. Payan said, disappointed. "Can't you stay a bit longer? Have more tea maybe?"

I shook my head. "I promise I'll come again soon." I bent down and kissed her.

"It was good of you to come, Roya-joon," she said.

On the ride home, I thought about the person I had become. Maybe the hardened clay was not as ugly as I had thought. Maybe what I resented was the color my father had painted me. The time had come to sand away some of that dreadful stain.

~

The hallway phone would not cease ringing and, in a house full of servants, I seemed to be the only one to hear it. I closed my book with fury. Pedar's voice came through the receiver. "Is that you, Roya?"

"Yes, hello."

He was calling from a place near the farms. "I can't find my keys. I must have left them somewhere in my room. I'll hold on while you go and check please."

Pedar never used to forget, but Dr. Ghareeb had cautioned us about a possible loss of memory due to opium. I went to his room and found the keychain on his nightstand.

"Don't worry, Pedar," I said back in the hallway, "I've got them."

"Good girl," he said and I could hear him taking a deep breath. "You'll find my robe hanging in the closet. Just drop the keys in its pocket, I won't be needing them until tomorrow when I return."

"Will do."

He hesitated for a few seconds and then in a self-conscious tone added, "And you don't have to mention this to anyone."

Was my father embarrassed? I smiled at the thought.

~

Maybe if Pedar had not left his keys behind, my far-fetched plan would remain just that. But the opportunity that had presented itself could only be divine intervention. As my grandmother once said, sometimes God puts you to a task.

I had never considered committing theft. Even if I had, the last person I'd steal from would be my father. Now, with those keys in my hand, the temptation was too strong to resist. No doubt I'd be found out, but if I acted fast enough, by the time Pedar realized, Shireen would be free. Pedar could keep his precious opium and his shiny gold coins. But that money waiting there for what he called, "The God-forbid-day," could buy back my friend's life. As far as I was concerned, the God-forbid-day had already arrived.

I lay on my bed, thinking about the stacks of money safely locked in the big storage closet, and the more I thought, the easier my plan seemed. All I needed now was the key to the big closet.

With Rajab gone, the only other key to the big closet was my aunt's. But she had already gone to bed and, judging by the late hour, so had everyone else. I sat up and tried to figure out the best way to execute my plan.

Barefoot, I tiptoed down the hallway and saw a faint light coming from under Auntie's door. So she was up, perhaps reading. I knocked.

"Come in," she called out, sounding drowsy.

"Sorry to disturb you," I said as I entered her room. Holding my belly with both hands, I moaned, "It's that time, Auntie."

Like all other months, I knew she would immediately suggest the one remedy she knew, a drink of hot water and diluted rock candy. But this time, I proceeded to ask, "Could I borrow your key to get some more rock candy?"

Auntie sat up and was about to get out of bed, but I rushed over and put my hands on her shoulders. "Please don't get up. I can do this."

She leaned back and, reaching under her pillow, she mumbled, "I could swear I just filled that jar." She handed me the key. "The maids must be putting it in their tea."

"I'll be right back," I said and left.

Outside the room, I opened my fist and studied the silver key, finding it hard to believe that I really had it. The smooth surface, the oval head and the old-fashioned shape. Cold mosaic against my feet calmed my nerves. I opened the padlock and turned on the bare light bulb dangling from the storage room's ceiling. To my left, large burlap sacks of rice, flour, and sugar leaned against the wall. No wonder Auntie locked up all this food. A dishonest servant could steal a fortune here.

On the white shelves sat rows and rows of bottles: olive oil, lemon juice, rose water, and jars of preserves. The air was saturated with a mix of lavender soap, dried herbs and turmeric. I scanned the room, and all of a sudden, the entire contents of the storage room faded to become a backdrop for Pedar's safe. My vision was consumed with the black box with gold paisley designs, and a fish-shaped keyhole. I stared at it, unable to touch, as if it were a time bomb about to explode. My heart racing, my face felt too hot.

Aware that if I took too long, my aunt would be tempted to help, so I found the big tin marked Rock Candy, took a couple of long sticks, and turned off the light. Closing the narrow doors, I latched them together and passed the padlock through, without locking it.

The lamp on Auntie's nightstand was still on when I returned her key.

"Found what you needed?" she asked, her voice indicating that she was about to doze off.

"Yes, thank you," I said and headed for the kitchen. Might as well complete my little act. Besides, maybe warmed rock candy could settle my nervous stomach.

~

I lay in bed with my eyes fixated on the fluorescent green of my alarm clock. Its arms did not move fast enough. Finally, someone turned off the garden lights and the house submerged into a silence that was only interrupted by a cat's mew in the distance.

I removed my pillowcase and grabbed a flashlight along with my father's keys. As I slid the open lock through the hooks on the door, the palms of my hands were covered in sticky sweat and I feared I might drop it. Feeling my way in the dark to the iron box, I decided not to move it for fear I might hit something and wake everyone up. I turned the key with caution.

Ding!

The wretched bell made me jump. *Damn!* I had forgotten all about that. I waited, listening to my own rapid breathing and the thump-thump in my ears. I don't know how long I paused, afraid to move, but when no sound came from the rooms, I continued.

Using the flashlight, I inspected the inside of the box. Under its circle of light, I saw my father's packs of opium, a stack of documents and under those lay bundles of crisp thousand-tuman bills. I picked one up and felt silly for having brought a pillowcase to carry them. The money looked and felt brand new, and each pack was held together with a brown paper band. I flipped through and figured there must be at least fifty in each, maybe even a hundred. A quick calculation told me all I needed was one pack. The less I took, the longer it might take Pedar to find out.

I placed the other items back in the safe, making sure they were in the order I had found them. I locked the box, and the big closet, and went to put Pedar's keys back in his pocket.

Back in my room, I wrapped the money in a newspaper, tucked it inside a book and placed the book in my large brown handbag. For hours, I stared at the darkness outside my window, and wondered if the night would ever end.

—

The next morning, I snuck into Pedar's room before anyone was up and, using the phone on his bedside, I dialed the Payans' number.

"Mrs. Payan, it's Roya," I whispered.

She sounded half asleep. "Wait a minute," she said and I heard the rustling of bedcovers. "Something wrong, dear?"

"No. I'm coming over in about half an hour. I have the money for Shireen's bail."

She did not respond and I wondered if she had understood me. Maybe she was too overwhelmed to talk.

"Mrs. Payan?"

"Don't!" she said. "I don't want you to come here." And she hung up.

She couldn't mean that. I put the receiver down, baffled at her response and decided I would explain more later on. This wasn't a loan that she had to worry about paying back. There would be no strings. Who else would make her such an offer?

I returned to my room, dressed and then went to find Auntie. She sat by the samovar in the family room, preparing tea for breakfast.

"I'll be going earlier today. I have an important test."

"Eat something," she said and kept working on the samovar.

I assured her I would buy something at school.

There would be no taxis on Golestan Avenue at such an early hour, so I started to walk toward Jaam Street and just then, a cab turned the corner and I saw the taxi light on its roof. I waved at it frantically.

Rushing into its back seat, I gave the Payans' address and we were off.

For the first time since the evening before, I became conscious of my vulnerability. No longer in the safety of my home, I began to doubt my decision. Here I was in a cab, out on the street, taking stolen money to a family the media had called "terrorists."

How did Pedar's obedient daughter get here?

I looked around for something to take my mind off the money in my handbag. Here and there were signs indicating the street had begun to awaken; the greengrocer sweeping his storefront, the policeman getting settled on his platform, the owner of the corner bookstore rolling up the tin shade of his display windows. We stopped at a red light and I had the feeling the cab driver was watching me. I looked up, but all I could see were a pair of oversized sunglasses filling his rearview mirror. My heart dropped.

Looking away, I thought anyone could be wearing those, but just then, the driver made a wrong turn. Now we were headed south, while Shireen's parents lived north.

Come on, Roya. You're being paranoid. Taxis make such detours all the time just to make a bit more money.

"Excuse me," I said in a shaky voice. "Aren't we going in the wrong direction?"

He glanced at me again without a word. When he got off Pahlavi Avenue and turned into a cobblestone street, I knew we were nowhere near the Payan's.

"Where are you going?" I said, this time in a more aggressive tone.

Again, he did not respond, but I heard a click and saw the buttons go down to lock the passenger doors.

"Stop the car!" I said. "I'll get off right here."

The taxi picked up speed.

I reached over to roll down my window and realized the handle had been removed. "I said stop!" I shouted and began to pound the back of his seat. Horrible images of kidnapping and rape ran through my mind.

"Don't worry, miss," he said. "They're probably just going to ask you a few questions." His polite explanation added to my horror. The word *they,* could only mean one thing.

"Put your head on your knees," the driver commanded.

"What?"

"Routine procedure, and I think you'd better comply."

"I need to see your ID," I said.

He chuckled. "You'll just have to take my word for it." When I didn't move, he pulled to the curb in an empty street, turned around, and tapped on something on his chest. "The only proof I have is *this.*" He opened the front of his jacket just enough for me to see. Knowing he carried a gun, I put my head down and he threw a heavy blanket over me. It smelled of old shoes and sweat, making it hard to breathe.

I was finished. SAVAK must have listened in on my phone call. That's why this taxi showed up. Even if this proved to be a routine questioning, once they found all that money on me, I would be making headline news. I could just hear people's disbelief at such theft being committed by little mousey Roya. I saw the veins pop on Pedar's forehead, Auntie beating her chest. And Kyan, I'd never see him again, not after going back on my promise in such a scandalous way. My whole world was going up in flames and I had no means of stopping the fire I had just ignited.

The car finally left the bumpy cobblestone and as I heard gravel hitting the sides, I thought we must either be in another alley, or worse, had left town. Before I had worked my way into total despair, the car stopped and the driver killed the engine. When he opened the door and took the blanket off me, the cloud of dust behind the car made me cough. Squinting against the bright sunlight, I saw we were in front of a nondescript building with whitewashed walls. The driver nodded to the door and motioned me forward. As I left the alley and went up the steps to what looked like a house with no number, I wondered if I would ever climb back down those stairs.

~

There was a long wooden table in the hallway with a policeman standing by, and a rather large woman sitting behind it. When we reached the table, the woman stood and her beady eyes studied me head to toe.

"Put your bag down and spread your arms," she said. Something in her rude tone reminded me of the vice principal of long ago and, closer, I smelled the same body odor. While her clammy hands ran up and down my limbs for a body search, I felt as if she were molesting me. Sweat ran down my back and I knew she could feel me trembling. Meanwhile, the policeman had dumped the contents of my bag onto the table and laid them out for visibility.

The woman went behind her desk and, picking up the bundle of cash, looked at me with a smirk. "A bit more than cab fare, isn't it?" And she flipped the notes as if doing a quick count. She put them in the plastic box on the table and continued her search. Unzipping my wallet, she went through student cards, photos, and every little scrap of paper in its pockets.

"Well, well," she said, holding a piece of paper up to the light and reading, "If I shall rise..."

Damn! That verse must have been there ever since Shireen's mother had given it to me. I prayed the woman wasn't smart enough to make the connection.

The rest of her search went quicker. Finally she gave back my personal effects, all except for the money and the piece of paper with Shireen's handwriting.

A uniformed guard ushered me to a smaller room halfway down a long corridor. He pushed the door open and waited for me to go in. The room's meager furniture consisted of a rickety metal table and three folding chairs. The fluorescent ceiling light buzzed constantly, and the muggy air reminded me of a bathhouse. The guard glanced at me before closing the door. I wanted to call and tell him I needed to use the bathroom, but thought it best to keep quiet. I heard the key turn. *Was this going to be my cell?*

I tried to evaluate my situation and be realistic about it. I pictured men with earphones, listening in, tracing my call. Did Mrs. Payan hang up, or had they cut her off?

Lowering my body onto one of the chairs, I held my head with both hands and tried to estimate the gravity of my crime. Considering that this money was intended for the release of someone they considered "involved in terrorist activities" wouldn't they put my action in the same category? And if so, would my fate be any different from that of Ali, Eemon, or Shireen's? The thought of such possibility tightened my stomach and I needed to throw up, except there was nothing in my stomach.

One minute I saw myself as Alieh, disappearing into a ditch until God knows when someone would find my remains, and the next, I was shipped to Tehran to join the prostitutes and thieves in the women's penitentiary. Would I see Shireen, or were they going to take me where no one was allowed to visit, my only connection to the world a barred window? It was no comfort to realize that my biggest fear was still of Pedar, what my capture might do to him, or worse, what he would do to me.

To be sure, I had broken all of Pedar's rules. One way or another, I had feared him all my life, but I couldn't stretch my imagination enough to picture how he might react to this. I was too old for physical punishment, he would never resort to financial threats, and he honored the family too much to expel me. So how could he possibly treat me worse than SAVAK might?

Every now and then, I heard footsteps in the hallway and my whole body tensed in anticipation. When no one opened the door for what felt like an eternity, I decided they were just going to let me rot there. I didn't know which was worse, the clos ed door, or all the horrible possibilities that might walk through it?

By now, they must have called Pedar. Dear God, maybe it was best if SAVAK just kept me here and I wouldn't have to face my father ever again.

Eighteen

THE SOUND OF A KEY turning in the door gave me such a jolt, it might just as well have been an explosion. I stood erect, like a soldier on guard, pressing my hands to my sides in anticipation of the worst.

Three men walked in, two in civilian clothes, one in police uniform. The heavy-set civilian walked one step ahead. The other, a rather short and skinny man, pulled up a chair and placed it on the other side of the table. The fat man lowered his mass into it. The smaller one also took a seat, before reaching into his pocket for his notepad and pen. The policeman removed a file from several he had under his arm, placed it before the fat man and stood in the corner, half his face hidden beneath his cap.

Looking at me from under droopy eyelids, the fat man motioned to the chair I had been sitting on a moment ago. I took it just as my knees were about to fail.

"State your name, date of birth, and occupation," the small man demanded in a surprisingly strong voice. He didn't seem so short now that he was seated.

I did as told, but noticed he did not write anything down.

The fat man opened the file and on the first page I saw my picture, the one that had been taken for my student identification. The file had many pages and I wondered what they could possibly contain.

To divert my attention, I looked at the policeman. He turned his face my way and suddenly what little strength was left in me vanished. He had removed his hat to fan his flushed face, and when I saw the white scar on his forehead, it didn't take long to recall where I had seen it before. The vision of that man, leaning against the taxi a block away from my uncle's came back as if it had been only days before. I blinked. That was absurd, he couldn't possibly be the same man I saw the day I went to Evin. That man had been a civilian in Tehran, nearly a thousand kilometers away. Besides, SAVAK had no reason to follow me then, much less utilizing a policeman in disguise. Realistically though, there couldn't be too many dark-skinned people who bore such a button-shaped scar on the same spot.

"What is your relation to Shireen Payan?" The fat man's voice returned me to the small room. I hadn't prepared for such a direct remark, but in a way, it was a relief to know they were getting straight to the point.

"She's my friend from high school," I said, my voice emerging as a murmur.

"We know that," he said. "What is your connection with her *at present*?"

"Same," I said, stopping for fear I might cry.

"And that, I presume, was enough reason for you to think you should collaborate with a criminal and provide financial aid to terrorists."

I resented his choice of words, but said nothing. He put his elbows on the table and supported the folds under his chin with both fists.

"How long have you been a member of the Fadaiyan?"

"A member?" I exclaimed. "I am not a member," I said using a softer tone, and I immediately realized that might be my only salvation. Not that they would believe me, but I was not a member, not of them nor of any other opposition group. Considering they knew everything, they had to know that, too.

"In fact, I am not political at all," I stated with newfound courage.

"No?" he said with a sneer that made his flared nostrils seem even bigger. He reached into his pocket and took out the tiny scrap of paper the woman had taken from my purse. "Then what do you call this?"

I glanced at the verse and shrugged. "That's just a poem I like."

He chuckled and turned to the other man. "A poem she *likes*!" He hit the table so hard that even his colleague jumped. "You are not dealing with idiots, Miss Afshar! A lover of poetry, yet all you have on you is the pledge of Fadaiyan?"

That was their pledge?

"You might as well come clean, " he yelled. "I'm going to ask you this. One. Last. Time!" And he continued to hit the table as punctuation to each word, making me blink on every strike. "How. Long. Have. You. Been. Involved?"

I could sense a trap closing around me. If they could pin this on me, having stolen from my father would be the least of my problems.

"I'm not involved," I pleaded. "It's the truth."

The man paged through my file. "Let's see. Frequent visits to Payan residence, attempt to join demonstrations, impersonating a cousin for a visit at Evin," he closed the file with a loud tap. "The list goes on and on, Miss."

"I am just her friend," I said, now sounding as if I was about to cry. My mind raced back and forth in search of a proof, but I didn't know if they even needed one.

There was a knock on the door. The fat man looked up, surprised at the interruption. I felt my heart jump into my throat as the door opened, certain that Pedar would walk in next. Instead, it was a scrawny young man in a soldier's uniform, carrying a black phone in one hand with its long cord in the other.

"You have a call, sir," he said to the fat man. "It's urgent."

"This better be important," he snarled.

The young man nodded several times. "It is, sir. It's General Nazemi," he said and knelt down to plug in the cord.

At the mention of the chief of Mashad's secret police, the room submerged into silence. The fat man grabbed the receiver and sprang out of his chair, as if respecting the arrival of a senior. "Good morning, your Excellency," he said with a small bow.

He listened intently and I might not have paid much attention if it weren't for the fact that he kept glancing at me.

"Yes, sir. We are." He looked at me again. "No, sir, routine procedure."

The call couldn't have anything to do with me. They must be seeing such cases every day. SAVAK had to have more important things to do, especially lately.

"Yes, sir," he said again, his brief replies and stern expression indicating his displeasure. "Of course. It has been an honor, sir." And he put the receiver on its cradle.

A few seconds went by in silence. He did not sit down and would now not look at me. Someone laughed in the hallway and I wondered if I would ever laugh again. I had a bitter taste in my mouth. Was that phone call my death sentence, an order to quietly dispose of me?

The other civilian looked up, as if he too waited for an order, an explanation. The fat man bit his lower lip, thought for a moment, then marched to the door.

"In my office," he said.

The two followed. The policeman was the last one to leave. He put his hat back on and shut the door behind him. I didn't hear the key.

Sitting under the fluorescent light, I listened to the buzz and imagined it to be the cry of all the insects trapped in that long tube of light. Any minute the men would be back for more questions, but maybe this time they'd have torture instruments, too. The level of one's involvement didn't seem to matter. To them, anyone who knew Shireen was a member of Fadaiyan, and I had given them ample reason to see me as a suspect. I had no way to prove my innocence and they must be convinced that I knew more than I admitted to. Gruesome scenes of torture from the movies flashed before me.

Staring at my hands, I thought of the tiny finger Shireen had found in that bloody napkin. I had seen Behrang with all his fingers intact, but what did Shireen know at the time? Reza's words now sounded too close to reality. *They'll get you where it hurts...*

Had Shireen broken down and cried, too? Had she felt as weak and helpless as I did, or would she have been more prepared for such encounters?

Hours later, when the door opened, I had no energy to get out of my chair and was ready to receive the worst.

The same woman who had searched me at the security desk entered the room. Her face now blank, she threw my handbag on my lap. "You can go."

It took me a while to realize she really meant it. What was next? This could not be so simple and I had nothing left in me to figure out their trick.

"How?" I asked, and although that one word could signify any number of things, she took it for its simplest meaning.

"There are taxis out in the alley," she said and pointed to the half-open door.

Like a captive bird that had seen an opening in its cage, I wanted nothing more than to fly out, but by now I could not trust anything to be what it seemed.

"Get going," she said with contempt and nodded to the door.

I clutched my handbag and ran out before she could change her mind. I knew they had kept the money, and at that point I would have given them nearly anything just to be free. The sound of my steps echoed in the hallway and I dashed straight for the rectangle of sunlight at the end of that tunnel of fear.

Outside, the policeman with the scar stood at the door. Would he grab my wrist before I had stepped into the alley? I circled him, trying not to be within reach, and he acted as if he didn't see me.

Two orange taxis were parked in the shade of the brick wall and... oh, God! Behind them was my father's Land Rover, Akbar standing next to it.

Out of the pit and into a well.

Pieces of the whole strange puzzle began to fit together, and I grasped the complete picture. Sometime in the past, maybe a year or two previously, my father had mentioned a poker game with General Nazemi. At the time, the name had meant nothing to me, but now I had to ask myself, just how well *did* my father know the head of SAVAK?

~

From across the room, I could hear Pedar's asthmatic breathing. I tried to look away at the pale sky, but there was no escape from the weight of his stare.

"So you had to put your nose in shit after all, didn't you?"

I didn't need to look at him to see the rage in his eyes.

"I'm talking to you!" His voice came out so loud that everyone in the house must have heard him.

When I looked, he opened both his fists and showed me what was in them. In one, he had his tiny Colt revolver, the one with the mother-of-pearl handle that we jokingly called his ladies' gun, and in the other, half a stick of opium.

"Take your pick," he said and his eyes showed no mercy.

He hurled them at me. The revolver hit my chest before falling to the floor and I was amazed at how heavy it was for such a small object.

"I could kill you with my own two hands and no one would blame me for it!" he spat out the words.

This, I realized in horror, would have been true.

He stepped closer and grabbed my arm. "But you will never understand what your life means to me, or what it cost to let you live!"

Before that day, I had never dared respond to Pedar's anger, but that day had been too much, and now I yelled back, "Cost?" I laughed. "Is money all you ever care about?"

He moved too quickly and his heavy hand came down before I had a chance to even blink. The blow to my mouth sent me staggering back. I tasted blood and heard him growl, "You don't even deserve to live, much less live *her* life!"

I stared at him. Whose life was he talking about?

Pedar turned away and reached over to his nightstand, where he kept my mother's picture. He picked up the frame and thrust his arm forward as if to push the picture into my face, making sure I took a good look at Maman.

"Money?" he said through a foaming mouth. "No amount of money could bring *her* back, you pathetic, worthless piece of shit!" He dropped the frame on his bed and stared at me from behind a shield of tears. "Oh how I pleaded with her, begged her to listen to the doctor's advice and let you go to hell. But no! You had to have an angel for a mother, one who would not harm her unborn child even when it could save her own life." He started to pace the small space between the wall and his bed. "She believed in you. You were meant to have the greatest life, fulfill her dream of being a doctor, enjoy the chances she never had." Pedar's chin quivered and his face was covered with tears he did not bother to wipe. "Look what you've done to me!" he said and slapped his forehead. "She made me swear I'd never tell." His voice became a mere whisper. "There goes my word of honor."

My head spinning, I saw my mother in bed, a pear shaped pendant on her chest, going up and down, up and down ... until it stopped.

"That's not fair, not fair," I heard the scream and knew the shrieking voice couldn't be mine. I ran out with my hands over my ears, but the scream followed. Its horrible sound hit the walls of the garden and came back to me, now the flowers were screaming, the crows, even the trees. And I screamed with them, emptying my lungs, pushing out all my trapped breaths in one long howl. I screamed for all the times Pedar had hushed me, for the losses I had endured, and for the child who had not asked to live a motherless life. And when there was no voice left, I cried for my mother and for the tyranny that, like a black *chador,* covered our souls.

The quiet, obedient child had finally found a voice to shout her buried emotions, and if Pedar wanted to shut her up, he'd better put his ornate revolver to good use.

Nineteen

THE BRASS RINGS OF MY BEDROOM CURTAINS jingled against the rod as someone pushed them open. Warm sun spilled on my closed eyelids and I heard my aunt's soft voice. "Time to get up, Roya-jan. The doctor's here to see you."

I opened my eyes. What was Dr. Ghareeb doing in my room?

My father's doctor smiled and taking his stethoscope from around his neck, he brought it to his ears. "Don't move, dear." He placed the cold metal on my chest, closed his eyes and listened. Then he took my pulse, blood pressure, and finally removed his penlight from his pocket and shone it in my eyes.

As he wrote on his notepad, I tried to figure out why I needed such a thorough health check. Little by little, the events that had put me there started to come back to me. For a brief moment, I hoped they were the remnants of a nightmare, but my swollen lower lip and the sore inside my cheek suggested otherwise.

"Did I have a nervous breakdown?" I asked him, colleague to colleague, as if I referred to a mutual patient.

Auntie prepared to leave. "I'll get some more ice for your lip," she said.

I asked the doctor again, "Did I?"

He nodded. "Close. Very close."

He took a bottle of pills from my nightstand and said, "You won't be needing these any more, I'll give you something milder." Picking up his black leather bag, he added, "But as you know, the medicine only helps a little. The actual healing should come from within, especially where nerves are concerned."

After he had left, I tried to sit up.

"Don't move," Auntie said on her way back in. "Try to relax, dear. You've had a tough night." She walked over with a bag of ice, which she wrapped in a washcloth and placed over my chin. "Hold that on your lip. I'll put on some Vaseline later."

Closing my eyes, I tried to revisit the events of the night before, but the only thing I recalled, was people coming in and out of my room. At one point, I had heard Mitra cry, but it must have been the effect of the sleeping pills. Had my father really hit me? I reached up and touched my mouth and Auntie must have noticed because she said, "This should never have happened." Her voice was filled with remorse.

I looked at her. "Many things shouldn't have happened, Auntie. My mother…" I said and knew that I wasn't strong enough to talk about it yet. Pushing my tears back, I pointed out the window. "That whole mess out there shouldn't have happened, Shireen shouldn't have suffered the way she did," and I started to cry. "The way she still does."

My aunt sat at the edge of my bed. I wasn't sure whose side she was on. Would she back my father, or did she understand me now? Hard to even believe there was such a division among us. Just when did my father and I start being on opposite sides?

She patted the back of my hand. "Hassan is going to send up some soup for you. I want you to eat, and then rest."

Auntie got up to leave.

"Please don't go! Talk to me," I said to her back.

She stopped and pointed her walking cane to the corner where her armchair had been placed. She took her time to reach it, sat down, and gave me a pale smile.

"I'm not going anywhere. Try to rest now. There will be plenty of time to talk."

~

For three days, all I did was sleep, eat, and sleep again. My aunt stayed with me most of the day, and at night Naneh brought her bedroll and slept on the floor. When she locked the door on the first night, I asked her why.

"It's your Aunt's orders, I guess it's so no one will disturb you."

Only once did my aunt mention Pedar. "Your father called earlier to make sure you're safe."

"Safe?" I said and laughed. "That's interesting coming from a man who offered me the choice of death by a bullet over opium poisoning."

"Someday you'll understand a parent's concerns. He has always had your safety in mind." She sighed. "That man lives for his children."

I wondered about that. Here I was, twenty-three years old, about to become a doctor, locked up in my room with no connection to the outside world. Did he plan to keep me "safe" 'til my hair turned as white as my teeth? Or had he made a deal with his poker buddy? *You just give her to me, General Nazemi, and I'll make her wish you'd kept her here!*

I tried to push guilt out of my mind, falling back on every psychological trick I had learned. I would not be victim to Pedar's devious plan. Surely that whole performance – the story he made up about my mother – had to be his idea of unbearable punishment. If that were true, Naneh, Auntie, or somebody would have said something before. Then again, what was the secret Auntie wouldn't reveal? Could that be what she meant by not breaking her promise? Whenever I reached a point where my father's story came close to being believable, I had the urge to start screaming again.

When I asked my aunt if Mitra had come to see me, she shook her head. Neither Reza, nor any of the servants were allowed in my room. During the day, Auntie kept me company, but at night, when Naneh's snoring made it hard to sleep, the reality of my situation confronted me. I didn't ask my aunt for an explanation, and she never offered one.

One night, as I was about to fall asleep, I heard the latch on my door. When it opened, I saw Reza's tall silhouette in the doorway.

"What—?"

"Shhhh," he whispered, pointing to the floor where the old nanny, fast asleep, was warming up to her nightly snoring.

"You're not the only one who can steal a key," Reza said and I heard his soft chuckle before he closed the door behind him.

So, everyone knows.

His presence was a ray of light in my dark cave. I held on to him for a few minutes, afraid that if I let go, he might disappear.

"Okay, sis, time to close the juice factory," his sad voice contrasted the light-hearted comment. "You've got to take these things as they are," he said, wiping my tears with his pajama sleeve. "Pedar has his ways and we have ours. That's how it's been for generations, and that is how it is always going to be."

Afraid that we might wake up the old nanny, we spoke softly for some time. My big brother, who in our childhood would beat up my cousin for making me cry, was there once again to comfort his sister. With that unexpected visit he charged me enough to endure the gloomy days ahead.

Before Reza had gone, I begged, "Please come again soon."

He shook his head. "We mustn't upset Pedar."

Only after Reza left did I realize that at no point had he shamed me for breaking my long-ago promise to him about becoming involved with Shireen and her family. Nor had he criticized me.

~

From time to time I wondered if Kyan had written any new letters, but even if he had, there would be no chance for me to pick up my mail. And even if I read any of his letters, what was I to write back? That I had ignored his one request, and that by doing so I may have ruined our chances?

Three times a day, Rajab brought me a tray of food. He greeted me with a simple hello and took away the previous meal's tray without another word. Sometimes Auntie joined me for lunch, and we seemed to mutually avoid mention of my father. One day, I finally gathered enough courage to ask, "Was Maman's death a choice?"

Auntie looked up in shock. "Whatever gave you that idea?"

Her cheeks lost their peachy tone.

"Come on, Auntie. You know what I'm talking about. Pedar already told me this much. I only want to know if he made it up or not. You know? If he lied."

My aunt glared at me. "I expect you to show more respect for your father."

"Okay, did my Lord and Master speak the truth?"

My joke seemed to make her angrier. "Why don't you ask him that?"

What Auntie didn't say suggested enough. I decided not to probe any deeper. What would stirring such a painful memory serve? Pedar had already said enough and knowing how much he had loved my mother, I wouldn't be surprised if he had resented my existence even before all this.

As the reality of my situation sank in, it became harder to fall asleep at night. I imagined how different my family would have been if she'd decided to do what her doctor had advised. What a happy foursome they would have been! Would my father need the comfort of opium if he had a wife to keep him happy? If it weren't for the help Dr. Ghareeb's medication offered, I doubt I would have slept on any of those nights.

My father did not come to see me for two weeks. By then, my tangle of thoughts had reached a point where I could picture him with savak. A prison was a prison and, lucky me, mine happened to be first class. By the end of the second week, it wouldn't have surprised me if he'd shown up with the executioner.

Finally one day I heard his familiar knock on my door: one-one two-one. I didn't respond, but Pedar entered anyway. He stood at the door, saw me reading in bed, then walked over to Auntie's chair and sat down. I observed all this from the corner of my eye while pretending to be absorbed in my book. Rajab came in with a tray of tea and an ashtray, pulled up a small table and set the tray on it.

"I've decided to spare you," Pedar said, though his harsh tone told me otherwise.

I kept my eyes on the book.

"I am sending you away."

I looked up and opened my mouth, but he raised a hand.

"Nobody's interested in your thoughts. You will listen, and you will do exactly as told, or else I'll have to send you right back to *them*." He pointed to the door, as if SAVAK was waiting behind it. "You've proven yourself unworthy of my trust on all accounts." Reaching for his cigarettes, he shook one out of the package. I heard the click of his silver lighter and I smelled the fresh smoke of that first puff.

"It'll be a shame about your school," he said. "Another year, and you might have become somebody." He shook his head as if to pity the 'nobody' I had turned out to be.

I thought of all the long nights I had stayed up to study, Kyan's lessons on how to tell the dumb nerves from arteries on a stinking cadaver, memorizing thousands of facts I couldn't care less about. Six years. Six whole years of my life.

I shot him a look. "You can't do that," I said, feeling as though he had stabbed me.

He glared back, his dark green eyes overflowing with disappointment. Not even bothering with a response, he got up and left.

When Rajab came back to take the cold tea away, he did not say a word, but I heard his *tsk-tsk* as he picked up the tray and shook his head.

"Tell Auntie we need to talk," I said.

I waited all day for my aunt. Naneh came in with her sewing sack, sat on the floor without a word and worked. I saw she was mending a pair of socks, watching me between stitches. Did I now need a babysitter? Once in a while, I heard voices outside to remind me this was still a family; my aunt in the hallway talking on the phone, the clanking of dishes in the dining room over the hum of a conversation, and finally Pedar calling for his car. I had never been happier to see him leave the house. When my aunt came in at last, my questions poured out before she had a chance to sit down.

"Sending me away? Away to where? Why is he doing this, Auntie? Are you going to let him? Why?"

She watched me pace the floor and talk and talk.

"Are you done?" she said the second I paused.

I just looked at her.

"He made a deal with the secret police. They agreed to let you go, provided they'd never hear from you again."

No matter how many more questions I asked, Auntie's response came back as something along the lines of, 'You need to talk to him,' in all the varieties of the phrase. Three days later, a photographer made a house call and took my passport pictures. Over the following weeks, my aunt and Naneh alternated their shifts, guarding me with diligence.

I had already memorized every corner of my room, arranged and rearranged my bookshelves, and knew there were exactly nineteen pushpins and six holes on my walls. From the muffled sounds in the hallway, I tried to picture what went on; the ringing phone, the chime of the grandfather clock, the sound of Rajab's squeaky shoes taking hurried steps. But after a while I gave up guessing.

As the silence grew, I started to feel lonesome even when someone was present. Auntie mostly read her newspaper or brought in a knitting project that seemed to need all her attention. Neither of us found much to say. Naneh talked incessantly, but hers was mostly the neighborhood gossip and she only stopped when she was about to fall asleep. Just when I was convinced I would die of seclusion, my door opened one evening and the whole family poured in.

Mitra ran to put her arms around me. "You've lost so much weight!" She sounded terrified.

Reza stood to the side and watched us, but the look in his eyes told me he was still on my side, whatever that might be.

Pedar entered the room last. In his elegant navy-blue suit, he looked like an executive about to attend a business meeting. He stood behind Auntie, rested his hands on the back of her chair and surveyed my room as if seeing it for the first time.

When everyone had settled down, Pedar cleared his throat. "I've arranged for you to go to America," he announced in a casual tone, as though suggesting a trip to the farm.

"My lawyer has prepared the necessary documents," he went on, ignoring my stare. "And I have spoken to a good friend, Mr. Farhang, in New York. He and his wife will meet your plane. You'll stay with them until further arrangements are made."

I looked around for a reaction, but everyone's calm told me they already knew. I told myself I'd only be across the globe and could always come back and visit. But the morbid look on their faces indicated Pedar was shipping me to another planet.

"Your ticket is one-way," he said at last. He looked at everyone but me. "And it shall remain that way so long as I'm alive." And, just when I thought he had delivered his hardest blow, he added, "You leave tomorrow."

The heavy silence that followed was interrupted by a distant cry of a street vendor. I'd never know what the man was selling. I'd never be out on those streets again, would never see the man mending china dishes, polishing copper pots or fluffing the cotton stuffing of old pillows and quilts.

Among all the visions that flashed before me, one came so clear, it was as if I were standing at the far corner of the orchard, watching men drag a lamb to be slaughtered. Two village men held the struggling animal while someone pushed a sugar lump into its mouth. That seemed to be a necessity in the gruesome ritual before putting a sharp knife to the throat of sacrifice. Hassan the cook used to call it The Last Treat. "If he dies happy, his meat will taste better," he had reasoned.

This gathering must be my "last treat."

After close to a month of isolation, I had no trouble sitting there in absolute silence. How hard I had tried to picture the worst punishment, but once again Pedar had outsmarted me by coming up with the unimaginable. Bad news didn't kill, after all. Judging by everyone else's faces, they had a much harder time accepting what sounded like my life sentence. Reza looked the worst, and he seemed on the verge of tears.

One by one, they all said good night and left while I continued to stare at the rug. Auntie stayed behind.

"I'll be here tonight to help you pack."

"Thank you," I whispered without looking up.

She sat at the edge of my bed. "This is no longer just about you, sweetheart." She reached for my hand. Her crooked fingers felt ice-cold. "It is breaking all of our hearts."

I said nothing.

"Your father told me what happened with the… authorities," she said. "You were lucky he knew people who could help." She tapped the back of my hand and her loving tone changed to one of warning. "Use your freedom wisely."

"Freedom?" I laughed.

"Look around you, my dear. How many people get a second chance these days?"

"You don't think I know? That's exactly what I wished to give Shireen." I swallowed hard. "A second chance."

"Let's not talk about *that,*" she said. "Life is full of unfairness; it's up to you to find the good when the bad happens."

"So, which is *this*?" I grunted. "The good, or the bad?"

"I see this as your break. Take it and put it to good use." She put one arm around my shoulder and pulled me close. "For those of us who love you, this is far better than the alternative."

In need of a good hug, I put my arms around the woman who had done her best to be mother to me. I held her a long time, sniffing the scent of her hair, memorizing the warmth of her embrace to hold for all the lonely years to come.

I left Mashad on a cloudy Saturday afternoon.

Before I left for the airport, Reza came to me. "I want to say my good-bye right here," he said and handed me a square package, wrapped in blue paper. Noticing my surprise, he added, "Airports depress me."

I unwrapped the gift to find a pocket camera, the new kind I had seen around.

"This is the newest instamatic, the easiest to work with. Just click here." He pointed to a button. "Send me lots of pictures. I want to know all the places you visit."

I broke into a soft sob.

When we hugged, he stood so much taller than me that I had to wrap my arms around his waist and let him hug my head. I felt him trembling, but knew he didn't want me to see his tears.

"Promise you'll come to America," I managed to say.

"Sure," he said, his voice hoarse. "I'll be the next."

The rest of my family saw me off at the airport. Pedar was the last one to say goodbye. I saw him standing a few steps away, his dark suit hanging loosely around his thin body, his fedora pulled down to shade half his face, and I noticed he carried a walking cane, too.

I went to him and extended my hand for a civilized handshake when all of a sudden he pulled me into his arms and held so tight it cut my breath. "I loved you the most," he whispered into my ear.

Taking a deep breath, I did my best to pull in the mild scent of his Aramis cologne, making sure it would stay with me for a long, long time.

~

At Tehran's Mehrabad airport, I checked in for my connecting flight. Only when I was on board Iran Air flight 829 to New York did I think of all the people I had not said goodbye to. Eleven hours later I would be tossed into a country of cowboys and Indians. I imagined a city of skyscrapers where everyone carried a gun. Not a pretty picture, not my choice, but what did choice have to do with my life?

I thought of Kyan, living somewhere in America. In another existence, this could have been the most joyful moment of my life. But now things had changed. He planned to return and work in Tehran, while I was being sent on a trip with no return. Exile.

"Would you please make your dinner selection?" a hostess asked in clear British English.

I shook my head and asked for an extra blanket and some water.

After taking two of Dr. Ghareeb's tablets, I pulled the blanket over my head, had a good cry, and finally fell asleep.

~

In and out of broken nightmares, I knew the night had ended as one by one, window shades went up and hostesses pushed coffee up and down the aisles. When the captain announced the local time, someone behind me said, "We've gained a day." How ironic that I had to lose a life in order to gain a day. When other passengers began to admire the view below, I craned my neck, but all I saw was a vast body of water extending to the horizon. Someone mentioned the Statue of Liberty and all heads were now turned to the left. I smiled bitterly at how quickly the word 'liberty' had lost its significance.

Kennedy airport made Mehrabad seem like a bus stop and I saw no sign of the raggedy porters. Although there were a few uniformed men and women helping the elderly, most people pulled their own carts. Speakers blasted with announcements, but despite my fluent English, I hardly understood any of their rolled words.

An hour passed before I had finished re-packing what the woman at customs had jumbled. The busy hallways smelled of perfumes, tobacco and coffee. People were dressed in the brightest colors and even those who were overweight or elderly didn't seem bothered about being seen in their shorts and mini-skirts.

Out in the lobby, I looked for my father's friends. What if they never showed up? Pedar had been so sure, that he hadn't even bothered to give me their number. With the insecurity of a lost child, I scanned the crowd of mostly tall people and felt a little like Alice in Wonderland. And then I spotted a rather plump woman with highlighted hair, carrying a heavy shoulder bag and waving frantically at me.

The Farhangs had lived in the US for ten years, though I wouldn't have known that from their deep accent and broken English.

"You *vait for verry* much?" Mrs. Farhang asked me.

"Nah, alan residam," I answered in Persian, encouraging her to switch.

So I had finally arrived. This crazy, colorful, and loud place would be my home for the foreseeable future. No matter how optimistic I tried to be, my mind would freeze at the mere thought of it, the uncertainty paralyzing me.

~

My detachment from home proved much harder than I had imagined. The only life I had ever known was in the comfort and safety of my father's house. I was used to having a family, friends, and people who took care of my daily needs. Familiar with every corner of my hometown, I had enjoyed knowing people on the street. Now hurled across the globe, I was at a total loss where no one seemed to know anyone. I sometimes wondered if my isolation was any better than a prison term. After all, prisoners did have visiting hours while I had abandoned hope I'd ever see my loved ones again.

The Farhangs were a nice couple and it surprised me that, despite having lived in America for a decade, their Persian-ness remained intact. In the beginning, especially whenever I spent a day on the busy streets of New York, I welcomed the familiarity of their home. It would put me back in Iran, eating rice and lamb, listening to Googoosh, even reading Iranian magazines. But as time went by, it became clear that in order to adjust, I had to learn more about the American way of life.

To my disappointment, New York had no cowboys and its tall buildings were clustered in the middle of the city, far from where the Farhangs lived. When I had learned how to use public transportation, Manhattan lured me with its impressive vertical dimensions, magnificent parks and museums. Here, the crowd seemed to be in a terrible rush regardless of the time of the day. Two weeks into my arrival, I signed up for an advanced English class, but it took me a good month to make any friends.

Some nights, hours after my hosts had gone to sleep, I stayed up in my room and tried to imagine what went on at home. My night would be their daytime and I pictured life as it had been just a short while ago. At times, I could swear I heard the snip-snip of the gardener's shears trimming the lawn. I wrote long letters to Mitra, Reza, and my aunt, but never mailed them for fear SAVAK would track me down. My sole communication with the family came through our phone calls, but we tried to keep the conversations brief. Pedar sent his messages through Auntie and those were mostly in regard to money matters. Auntie wanted to make sure I ate right and had everything I needed. Reza's message surprised me the most. "I hate phone calls," he had said. And I knew that meant he missed me the most. I kept my promise and sent him stacks of pictures via travelers to Iran. Mitra was the most talkative and my news of Reza came solely through her.

Wan-Fong, a girl from Malaysia, was the only classmate whose conservative demeanor indicated we had grown up with similar standards. I think I was also drawn to her because something about her reminded me of Shireen, though I couldn't decide what. One day, while we had gone for coffee after class, our conversation shifted to world politics. How strange it felt to learn that she had never heard of the recent riots in Iran. In fact, most people had not. The West associated Iran with rugs, oil, caviar and a few had heard of the Shah, but as far as I could tell, no one knew more. Then again, considering how little I had known of this country, I couldn't blame them. The world seemed to be divided by more than mere distances.

Thoughts of Shireen rarely left me and I prayed she'd never hear of my foolish act. The last thing she needed was more guilt. I also prayed that the Payans had found a way to buy her prison term. I searched my limited sources of international news for a topic even remotely related to Shireen's party, but found nothing about Iran, let alone its opposition groups. If my family had any news of her, they never mentioned it.

When I told Wan Fong that I wished to move closer to school, she told me about a vacancy in her building. The next day, I went to see the room. Small and dark as it felt, the rent seemed reasonable and it was conveniently located near my bus stop. I decided to take it. Hospitable as the Farhangs had been, they seemed relieved to see me go.

Wan Fong helped me to buy what the room needed: bed sheets, a lamp, a trashcan and such, but deep down I knew what I needed most was not sold in stores. I decorated in familiar patterns and warm shades of autumn. I even hung a strand of glass beads on my mirror that resembled Persian turquoise. But still, somewhere inside I held on to the hope that one day my father would arrange for my return, that this lonely life was not going to last for long.

Two months after I had left, Mitra finally emptied my mailbox at school and sent me Kyan's address. *Wisconsin?* Now for the first time since his move, I had some idea where that was. I held on to the address for a few days before I could will myself to write him. My letter was brief and while I tried to explain what had become of me, I gave no details. By now an expert in letting go, I had come to terms with the fact that we had no future together. An attempt to contact him, knowing he would not respond, might give me the closure I needed to move on.

Kyan called the minute he received my letter.

"Welcome to America, little lady," he said, his voice happy, full of energy and pumping life back into my soul. At first, our conversation was awkward, but the more I braced myself for his questions the less he asked and soon he had managed to bring me into a comfort zone where I could talk without fear. I told him all about my school, New York, and the few concerts, plays, and museums that I had enjoyed.

"Wow!" he said and chuckled, "Bragging like a true New Yorker already?"

I laughed, really laughed.

How long had it been since I felt this way? It was as though I had just found a treasure that I had given up for lost. We spoke for some time and it wasn't until he had made me promise to stay in touch and hung up that I remembered my situation. How could I overlook my "one-way ticket," as Pedar had put it? Kyan's family expected him back in a year or so, not to mention the job already awaiting him at Tehran Clinic. And me? I was no longer his colleague. At this point, exile had knocked all the enthusiasm for a future out of me. Soon he would realize this, and then what?

Still, alone and in love, I could not deny myself the pleasure of our conversations. Kyan planned to move to Chicago where he was to do his residency at University of Illinois. We spoke on the phone on a regular basis and, when I relocated to Chicago that November, my main reason was to be near him. Once again, Wan Fong helped me find a place. She connected me to her friend in Chicago, who would soon return to Malaysia and her landlady agreed to let me take her apartment.

Aware that he had not committed to any permanent relationship, I didn't tell him when I would arrive. Chicago weather put all of Mashad's snow and ice to shame. I thought the city had a lot of charm, but it was cold, not just the weather, everything about it felt cold and distant. It was after I had settled into my small apartment on Oak Street that I called and let Kyan know. We had planned to meet at a coffee shop on Rush Street. Living close by, I decided to walk and still arrived ahead of schedule. I sat near the window and watched the early Christmas shoppers go by with their colorful packages.

As the traffic light changed, I spotted Kyan, crossing the street among other pedestrians. Unable to remain calm another second, I rushed out of the café and met him halfway down the sidewalk. People stopped to stare as I wrapped my arms around him in his big-fat-down-jacket and shamelessly cried tears of joy. He held my shoulders tight and buried his face in my hair, his warm embrace more than making up for the coat I had left in the café. For hours to come we sat at a corner table, ordered coffee, and talked.

Kyan stirred his coffee and said, "My friends in med school told me you had left."

Maybe that was his way of telling me I could talk about what had happened but I still could not bring myself to discussing it. I nodded. "Call it a turning point!" I said and tried to smile.

"So what's your plan now?"

"I think I'd like to be a teacher, maybe biology?"

I wasn't sure why I said that. I hated biology. If a teacher, I would rather share my love of literature with young people without messing up their minds. Kyan nodded several times, his calm demeanor unchanged. From then on, he let me talk about whatever I wanted to. He, in turn, told me about life in Wisconsin. With all that had passed, I saw how perfectly he fit into my life, as if it had been just the other day when we were together in the medical school's cafeteria.

Later Kyan walked me to my new place on Oak Street, holding my hand, hovering over me and making sure I did not slide on the shield of ice that covered the sidewalk. For the first time since my arrival, I appreciated my newfound liberty. So far, America's comfort and glamour had failed to impress me, but the freedom in that simple walk spoke volumes. I thought of Shireen and how she had been locked up in her room for such an act, how her father had repeatedly called her "A bad girl." Now a universe away, the unfair punishments for such innocence seemed beyond unfair. I tried hard to remain happy, focus on the beauty of the moment, and I held on tighter to Kyan's hand.

At the front steps of number 160 Kyan held my face between his hands and kissed me for the first time. "Don't be so nervous, Roya," he said and adjusted my wool scarf around my neck. "I'm not your father, and I won't judge you. If there's one thing you can be sure of, it's the fact that I'd never do anything to hurt you."

It took me months before I truly believed that. Then one day, I caught myself telling a joke and realized I had healed enough to chat, laugh, and enjoy being alive.

~

Having failed to please Pedar, I realized the 'doctor dream' had never been mine. With my passion for poetry and literature, the choice was clear; still it took me a while before I decided to become a teacher. Kyan encouraged me to enroll in a teacher's training course. I began the program alongside my studies of American literature.

Auntie called on a regular basis and filled me in on the family news. Mitra had been promoted to head of her department, Reza was out so much she couldn't tell me what he was up to, and Pedar stayed home more than Auntie wanted him to. She sounded distant, or perhaps just tired or sad.

A month later, Kyan asked me to marry him. When he presented me with the lovely ring he had bought, I took that to mean he had either known what my answer would be or had become too American. I said yes before he was finished with his clumsy speech. That day, we called home to ask for both families' blessings. Auntie did not sound surprised as I had already mentioned meeting Kyan and she sounded happy to hear this. I told her, "I'm also holding you to your old promise for obtaining Pedar's permission." This gave her a chuckle and she said she would. But neither of them called back in the days to come. At this point I had learned not to expect much.

Kyan and I were married in a civil ceremony at the Town Hall. Two of our American friends stood witness and that evening we would go out to dinner with a few others. Before the Justice of Peace had arrived, I looked around the cold hall and its meager furnishing. Visions of Mitra's elaborate wedding came to me. Oh, how Auntie had resented not being able to do things her way. *What would Auntie say to this?*

I studied my reflection in the hall window: my simple yellow suit, the tiny hat, and the bouquet of white roses that Kyan had bought from the corner florist. Shireen's voice rang in my ears, *"All that frill is nothing but an imitation of the western fashion."* Secretly, I couldn't help but wish for some of that "imitation". I tried to push such thoughts away. After all, I was about to marry the best guy I had ever known.

A few days later, I sent a brief report and a few photographs to my aunt. She didn't call, but the following week I received her card, congratulating us on behalf of the entire family. "Doctor Kyan seems really nice," she wrote, "everyone here approves of your choice." I had to assume that "everyone" also included Pedar.

A few months into my marriage, a large package arrived from home with another letter from Auntie.

"Tradition is for the bride to furnish her new home," she wrote, "But what could we send you that America doesn't have better? Your father wants you to have this silk Persian rug, which belonged to your grandmother – may she rest in peace. He has also forwarded money to your account for whatever else your new home may need. A smaller package is tucked inside the rug. The pearls are your mom's, with matching earrings from me. Wear them in good health. The box of baklava is to be enjoyed by both of you as well as your friends. May life always offer you something sweet."

I pictured Auntie's hands and could almost see her crooked fingers as she put all that together, perhaps shedding tears for not seeing her pet niece. God I missed her.

There was also a card from Mitra attached to a package containing a silver platter from Isfahan. I searched among the wrappings for a note from Pedar, or from Reza, but there was none. Pedar had long made himself clear, but Reza? His roundabout messages were bad enough, but this time I expected more. The Reza I knew would be too excited to keep quiet, especially when I had mentioned that wedding photographs were the products of his handy camera. Where was he?

Twenty

"THIS IS THE THIRD TIME I've tried and I demand to know what's going on," I yelled at Rajab over the phone. "I'm not going to hang up until I've spoken to one of them."

"Sorry, Miss Roya, but they're out. Your aunt is at a luncheon and the Master has gone to the farm."

"Then go and get *agha* Reza. Tell him it's urgent."

I heard a muffled cough.

"Rajaaab!"

He sniffed. No, this wasn't a sniff, he was crying. Sobbing.

"What has happened, Rajab?" My voice was shaking and I felt a knot in my stomach. "Answer me!" I must have said that loud enough to pull Kyan out of his study.

"What is it, Roya?"

I looked at him and shook my head violently.

"Give me that." And he took the phone. "*Allo*?"

I thought I heard more crying on the other end, but Kyan walked away as far as the squiggly cord would let him.

"I see..." he said, but sounded confused.

I followed him and pulled at his sleeve.

He raised a hand in the air to hush me. "When did this happen?"

"Is my father okay?" I begged.

He nodded absent-mindedly and continued to listen. Another long pause and now his face had lost color and he took another step away. Whatever Rajab was telling my husband he didn't want me to hear it. Unable to stand the suspense I lunged forward and grabbed the receiver. Rajab was going on and on, his words minced amid sobs.

"*Ay* doctor-*jan*, we are ruined. Master's son was like my own..."

Kyan took the phone away but I could still hear Rajab wailing.

My knees had turned awfully soft. Aware that I was about to lose my balance, I welcomed being pulled into a deep black hole.

~

Reza, who had never been sick more than a day, the boy whose aim in life was to make everyone laugh, the young man who worshipped his father enough to stay away from trouble, my Reza was gone. Here I was, lying on some hospital bed in the suburbs of Chicago knowing more with each passing day that I'd never see him again.

How long had I been there? Two days? Three? "He wasn't even involved in anything," I kept on saying more to myself, still hoping for this to be a huge misunderstanding. The sedatives made me drowsy, but there was no cure for the stab wound I felt inside.

"An innocent victim of the recent riots," was how Kyan had described Reza's tragic fate. He tried in so many words to help me understand how innocent bystanders could be harmed in crossfire. "Reza was not involved in the actual demonstration," he assured me, "but as the crowd gathered behind the line of armed officers, he stepped in to help a victim..." This was where I would invariably stop listening. That was my Reza, stepping in to help. I pictured his body soaked in a pool of blood and could not bring myself to ask if anyone had been brave enough to try and help *him*. As if losing his life wasn't bad enough, my only brother had to lose it for no reason.

"No reason!" I said out loud, my voice now unfamiliar and hoarse.

Kyan took a tissue and wiped my cheeks. "You can't go on like this, honey."

"No reason," I said, this time in a whisper, and let more tears flow. My Reza would never see Chicago's magnificent highways; we would not go to the top of John Hancock's to peek at the city through those telescopes. He'd never be a guest at my home, an uncle to my unborn child. Everyone had said I should be happy the shock did not end my pregnancy, but happiness had never seemed so inaccessible before.

For months, I had pictured Reza on the other side of the planet, living, laughing, and bringing joy to those around him. I used the camera he had given me and took odd pictures of what I thought he'd find funny. That was my way to let him know how I missed him. What now?

"There's no one to send silly pictures to," I said amid tears.

"Think about your condition." Kyan gave my belly a gentle stroke.

"My condition? Who cares about *my* condition?" And I cried like a child crying over a broken toy. "I want my brother!"

"Don't do this to yourself," he said and as he hugged my head, I felt him trembling.

Six whole months and they had managed to keep it a secret from me. *"Reza says he hates phone calls."* Why did I believe such a ridiculous excuse? Then again, what made me believe them now? Somehow, Reza's zest for life made it impossible to believe his would ever end. I had assumed Pedar's refusal to come to the phone meant he was still upset with me. Now I wondered what was left of my poor father.

My mind flew back to that day in Golsara and Reza's words hit me harder than when he had first spoken them. *They'll get you where it hurts.* I ran the figures in my head. They must have taken him shortly after I had left. Hit-and-run, that's what I'd done to him, causing trouble for the family just to be tucked away safely in another world.

"They took him in retaliation for my escape," I said out loud, as if to test that grim possibility.

"Don't be silly," Kyan said. "You hadn't done anything and your departure wasn't exactly an *escape,* either. We aren't even sure if he really stayed uninvolved."

"You don't know Reza. He doesn't..." I stopped and it took me a while to realize I could no longer speak of my brother in present terms. "He never *did* anything that might upset Pedar. He worshipped the man."

My father's image filled my mind. I couldn't begin to imagine how he dealt with the loss of his only son. Did he ever wish it had been me, instead? Dumbstruck, I realized nothing could ease my pain. Reza and I were supposed to grow old together, have families, watch our children play, fight, and be friends. His loss was nowhere in that plan. Unable to deal with my grief, I now had a remote understanding of how Shireen's family had felt for their multiple losses. If all the love, comfort, and modern medicines failed to help me, how did Shireen survive from one day to the next?

After I had returned to our apartment, Mitra phoned, but I could not take her call. I was done talking, done crying, done understanding. How strange it felt to know, to be certain, that I was losing my mind. From that day on, Kyan took the calls. I didn't even care what kind of excuses he came up with. He stayed home for a week, and judging from the way he never left my side, I had a feeling he feared for my life. Sometimes I heard him on the phone, talking to my aunt, and sounding as if he had known her all his life.

"Yes, Auntie, she's going to be okay, at least, I hope she is." He also told her about my pregnancy. "Due in four months, yes, that was very lucky and now it looks as if she'll carry full-term."

Pedar never called, though I received messages through Kyan, who had received them from either my aunt or Mitra. "I don't blame her any more," he had said. "She was too young to know and too caring to stay away." Oh, they could bring as many of those pathetic messages as they wanted to, but as long as my father refused to talk to me, none of it meant a thing.

As my doctor discontinued some of my medications, I adjusted to a sleep disorder. After Kyan had gone to sleep, I would roam around the house with my painful thoughts, the worst of which were of Pedar and his loneliness. Was Mitra's presence enough to make up for the absence of his other kids? It was with such thoughts that one night an old poem came back to me.

"There is so much pain gathered in my heart,
That if from this maze I should survive
I'll limp my way to the portal of existence
And not allow one soul to come alive."

That night, hard as I tried, I didn't sleep at all. *What was I doing?* I tossed and turned and stared into the darkness, listening to Kyan's soft snores. By breakfast, I had made up my mind.

"We should never have children," I said.

Motioning to my bulging middle, he chuckled. "Isn't it a bit late for that?" But when I didn't laugh and repeated it in my firm tone, he suggested I needed to seek professional help. Later on my doctor agreed with him.

After numerous sessions with a psychiatrist I reached a semblance of recovery, but following another sleepless night, I announced my decision to go home for a visit.

"Bad idea," Kyan said and this time he sounded furious. "What purpose would that serve?" he asked and gave a sigh of resignation. "Suppose SAVAK takes you, too. What then?" He pointed to my belly. "In case you've forgotten, that is *my* baby, too."

"I want to see my father before he dies." There, I had finally said what was bothering me the most.

Kyan lowered his voice and wrapped an arm around my shoulders. "He's not dying, honey. Your aunt assured me he's okay. He has retired and is well cared for." He thought for a moment. "Besides, from what I hear, a lot is happening over there. Soon the Shah may be leaving. There could even be a revolution. This is hardly the time to even think about going back." He sounded so firm that I had a feeling he spoke on everyone's behalf. I could almost hear my aunt's voice, *"Promise me you won't let her do such a foolish thing."*

I did not have the energy to argue and decided to drop the subject for the time being.

I thought and thought, feeling responsible, taking the blame, until I had convinced myself that I had been the cause of this disaster. SAVAK must have hoped I'd go back. They must have found more reason to want me back, maybe they thought I had information on Shireen, knew things they didn't know. Maybe they were just maniacs torturing innocent people. But who cared when nothing could bring back Reza?

My defeat went beyond the loss of an only brother. *"Reza is lucky to have you,"* Pedar had said a lifetime ago. What did he think of me now? Feeling increasingly distanced from my father, I knew I had lost my last chance for returning to him.

~

Over the next year, the whole world seemed to change, but the changes in my country were too quick to grasp. Following the news, I pictured a book of history sitting in the wind, its pages flipping so quickly that not a word could be read. As much as we had dismissed the reports about the Shah's imminent defeat, it was now a reality. Iran had been ruled by monarchs for twenty-five centuries, but was now at the brink of a revolution to become an Islamic Republic. I wasn't sure what that entailed, except that the clergy would rule.

How quickly the world seemed to forget the glorious history of Persia! The clips of Iran on the evening news bore no resemblance to the place I had known and loved. There were more street demonstrations, except now they seemed to be more of a peaceful march in support of the revolution. On the other hand, those who had been pro-Shah and had not managed to get out of the country, faced imprisonment, torture and even execution. This included people in the religious minorities, who had enjoyed safety and a semblance of peace during the reign of the Shah. As if mourning for Reza wasn't bad enough, now I had a whole nation to grieve for.

It took me months to cope with my huge grief. The fact that I had not been there to witness any of the events that led to my brother's loss, and especially not having seen his funeral, made it hard to believe he was no longer there. "We buried him next to Maman," Mitra had said to Kyan. I tried hard to picture that, but somehow could not. What did they write on his stone? Which picture was now hanging on the wall of that tomb?

Just when I thought I had adjusted, Kyan advised I should re-establish regular contact with my family.

"What do we have to say to each other?" I asked bitterly, as if they were responsible for Reza's loss.

"You don't have to say very much, but it might help you to talk to them, hear their voices."

He dialed Mitra's number and gave me the phone.

At first, Mitra and I both cried. When we spoke of our grief, my sister sounded distant and unfeeling toward my share of it.

Auntie sounded more understanding. In fact, it was she who from that day on called me on a regular basis. In her soothing tone, she continued to deliver indirect messages from Pedar. "It's a relief to your father just to know you're safe." But I hung on to my deep guilt and deciphered Pedar's brief messages for their worst meaning. *What does she care? She's safe! That's what he means.* Neither my aunt nor I mentioned Reza.

Americans had changed, too. Neighbors and friends, who barely knew Iran, developed a sudden interest in what was happening to it. Having buried my head in textbooks, I'd never even heard of Khomeini before. But now even Americans knew who he was and they spoke of "The Shah" as if the word was his real name.

When I asked Mitra who he was or what changes he might bring to the country, her response was full of enthusiasm.

"We shall be the first Muslim nation to practice a modern Islam."

I chuckled. "Come on, those two words don't even belong together."

"And why not?" she said as if to shame me. "All religions were once old-fashioned and fanatic, except many of them have changed with times. Look at the European lifestyle of today. They're still Christians, but are they the same people as the crusaders? Or the ones portrayed in The Scarlet Letter?"

There was no point in arguing with my sister, so I switched the subject.

I wondered about the whereabouts of all those oppositionists now that the Shah had left. As much as I had detested his SAVAK, to watch the fall of a king was to see a monument demolished. Mobs filled the streets and I couldn't help thinking of all the sacrifice, just to reach such pandemonium. With each item of news concerning Iran I thought about Shireen. Would she be free once the regime had changed? Would she be happier in a country that no longer had a Shah, and where saying the daily prayers was now mandatory?

The media broadcast mainly the Islamic revolution's victory, but I also learned of the chaos and the hardship people, especially the women, faced on a daily basis.

"These guys just kill and kill. No court, no trials," a university professor, who had smuggled his family to Turkey under a shipment of pistachios, told us. "There's nothing in the stores. You're lucky to find any eggs, sugar or milk. Women suffer the most. It's boiling hot and they arrest them for not being covered head to toe." Or worse, "Guards raid homes in search of bottles of liquor and arrest anyone who has them. The damn Islamic 'sisters' wipe women's lipstick with a razorblade. And if you dare to paint your nails, they'll pull them out!"

After a few more such stories, I had a clear picture of the "Sisters" in my mind: Fundamentalist women, armed with rifles and hearts as dark as the shroud they called *hejab,* policing the area alongside their bearded "Brothers." Rising from deprived families, their cruelty toward ordinary people might have helped them vent their hatred, but I was certain it did nothing for their deep-seeded resentments.

Each day, Kyan relayed more news he had heard at work. "The new Islamic secret police, SAVAMA, acts with such cruelty that they make SAVAK seem human," he said.

I just listened and felt numb, cared and didn't care, remembered and tried to forget. My past would remain a hidden pride, yet I wished to leave it behind.

My father had always said that his biggest dream was to hold his grandchild in his arms. Mitra did not plan on having children. So when my son was born two weeks after the Islamic Revolution, certain that Pedar would never have a chance to hold him, I insisted we name him Arman, "implausible dream."

Arman had Reza's eyes, a fact that pleased me, and a gift that I did not deserve.

Twenty-one

I FINISHED SPRINKLING THE BAG OF SALT over our frozen driveway just as the mailman greeted me with a stack of mail. My disbelieving eyes found a blue airmail letter sitting on top. No longer the familiar stamps of the Shah, the new ones featured one ayatollah after another. A neat print, all in capitals, spelled my address and under it was written in Persian, *To Roya*. I would know that handwriting anywhere. My heart overflowing with excitement, I sat on the icy front steps and tore Shireen's letter open.

Dear Roya,

I saw Mitra in town and she gave me your address and told me all about your relocation, marriage, and baby. Glad to know you're safe. Mitra said you still think about the past. I do too, but for me that's all there is to think about. I leave the future to my son, and yours. Behrang is my single excuse for life. I take each day for what it is: sunrise to sunset. No more, and no less. One could say, I no longer live in The Lagoon – I have now become it.

How we both had loved that poem without realizing that at some point, we too, would experience such a life. Shireen went on to thank me for visiting her parents. If I had not known about her life in prison, the letter would have told me nothing.

Mitra seems to think you're oblivious to what goes on here. But she's wrong. Maybe the big tides would come if we all made a tiny wave as you did. We chose the wrong stage, one that collapsed under so much weight. But there you stood, always with both feet on firm ground.

Here she goes again, I thought. Leave it to Shireen to provide the boost I so desperately need, helping me to live with myself.

Do you remember Tahereh Ahmadi? She is now the head-nurse at Central Hospital (Now called Imam's Hospital). I doubt she'd be there if it weren't for your help along the way. I'm also convinced that my quick recovery is owed to the special care she gave me during my hospitalization. So, you see? You've helped us both.

The name, Tahereh Ahmadi, belonged to another life. I remembered my classmate with a face full of pimples and socks sewn in several places. I could still see her sitting at the edge of my bed, running her fingers along the satin cover.

What do you know? Tahereh Ahmadi is a head-nurse.

From her letter, it was clear Shireen had no knowledge of what I had attempted to do. Did Mitra also tell her about Reza? I prayed she hadn't. The last thing Shireen needed was more grief, guilt, and regrets. She ended her letter with:

Dearest Roya, The world is small and round. Wouldn't it be something if our paths crossed again?

I closed my eyes. *Wouldn't it?*

I don't know how many times I read that letter, but each time it made me feel better than the last. Shireen had forgiven me for who I had become.

I put a package of frozen chicken under running water to start dinner before Arman woke up. The phone rang and when I picked it up, the crackle on the line indicated a long-distance call.

"You'd better sit down," Pedar's voice tugged at my heart. This being the first time he had rung me himself, I had already reached for the nearest chair to support my shaking knees. Feeling short of breath with excitement, I said, "How are you, Pedar-*jan*?" The chirp in my voice reminded me of a time when I used that tone to ask for a favor.

"I'm all right," he said. "Considering..." He took a deep breath and it sounded as though he was beginning to wheeze. Then it sounded as if he had covered the mouthpiece and for a few seconds I wasn't sure if he was still there.

"Considering what?"

He cleared his throat. "I thought this might be easier if it came from me."

I braced myself for the grim news he was delivering bit by bit.

"We've lost your good aunt," he said at last and the feeling of numbness told me I had known it from the minute I heard his voice.

Did it really make a difference how or from whom I would hear this? Nothing in the world could have prepared me enough. Auntie was years younger than Pedar, and except for her rheumatism, I didn't remember her having any medical problems. Oh, how I had dreamed of the day Pedar would finally call, but not this, dear God, not this! Like leaves in an autumn from hell, I saw the people I loved fall off the tree of life one by one.

I don't know how long I sat there after our sad conversation. Arman had sleepily toddled out of his room and now found me crouched on the kitchen floor. Startled, he began to cry. That was just what I needed for I now joined in his loud infant-like bawling.

When, hours later, Kyan stepped into the semi dark house, Arman and I were still crying and water from the tap had flooded the counter. I don't know what words I used, but I somehow managed to tell him what had happened.

For the next days, nothing Kyan did or said could help my devastated mind. The bizarre chain of events had left too many gaps, making it impossible to grieve in the normal fashion. Just as I had counted on Reza to live his full life, in secret I had pictured Auntie growing old, needing me to give back some of the care I had received. Sometimes in the middle of the night Kyan would find me weeping silent tears. Other times he had to wake me amid a nightmare. In the end, he suggested it was time to go to Iran for a visit.

"Aren't you forgetting my one-way ticket?"

"Honey, that was back then, I'm talking about *now*."

"I still have a record with the secret police."

"Oh, that," he said. "Times have changed. Not only is there no SAVAK, I'll bet the Islamic secret police loves those who rebelled against the old regime."

"There's more," I said, and my voice dropped. "Pedar doesn't want me."

"Sure, he does. He called, didn't he?" He smiled a sad smile. "From what your aunt told me, that man misses you more than you can imagine. Besides, it'll be good for him to see you, see Arman and have his family around him." He placed a hand on my back as if to give me the push I needed. "Anyway, don't you think it's about time our families met?"

All that night I thought about his suggestion and by morning, I let myself be excited over the idea.

Kyan requested a leave of absence from the university and, knowing our old passports with the Royal emblem were no longer valid, he applied for new Islamic passports. I felt ridiculous covering my hair for a passport photo. Iran no longer a US ally, we had to send our documents to the one room rented by the Islamic Republic of Iran in the Algerian embassy.

While we waited for our documents, a friend who had recently gone back helped me to buy black clothes and items that would be appropriate to wear in the new Iran. Despite the heat, she recommended buying a long raincoat for everyday wear.

I had mixed emotions about this reunion. For years, my father had deprived me from being with my aunt or seeing more of my brother. Neither of them had seen my Arman. Now it was I who found it hard to forgive Pedar. Four years had passed since I last had seen him. How ridiculous it seemed to realize I feared facing my father. Oh, what I wouldn't do to have the good days back.

With all the news articles and the books that I had read, I knew enough about recent changes. Still, as we neared Tehran, it shocked me to see the German hostesses of Lufthansa put on their version of *hejab*, covering their hair under a scarf.

"We will have to clear customs here," Kyan told me as we joined the passport line. "There are a couple of days before our flight to Mashad."

As if the entire nation also mourned Auntie's loss, there were many people in black, men unshaven, and women wearing no makeup. A man, too young to hold a job, asked why my passport had never been stamped. I told him I lived in the United States.

"Welcome home, *sister.*"

The strange new way they addressed women shocked me the first time, but in a matter of days, I grew accustomed to being everyone's sister and a few vendors' mother.

~

Two days later, we were on a plane to Mashad. Looking down from the plane I realized I had never looked at my hometown with such interest before, oh how green it looked, with all the orchards and the tree-lined streets.

The small airport seemed unchanged, but the flag above the roof had lost its crest of a golden lion and sun.

Pedar's embrace felt weightless, just a gentle touch of fragile arms.

He let his tears run down the side of my face and, as we walked, he held my arm and leaned on me.

"I'm so sorry," he said.

Too late for regrets, I cried along and knew all was forgiven.

On the drive home, I sat in the back seat next to my father, with Arman on my lap. Pedar couldn't take his eyes off him. Arman grabbed his silk tie and tugged at it. The city had not awakened yet and most shops were closed. An iron barricade guarded most windows. Except for a few other cars, or a stray dog here and there, the streets were empty. At one of the main intersections, I noticed a Toyota truck, a gun barrel sticking out its window.

"Islamic guards," Pedar explained.

"I know," I said. "The *Kommiteh.*"

"Hmm, you've kept up with our hideous changes."

I smiled sadly. Reza would have been sure to crack a joke at that.

Most streets had new names and that made me wonder if I'd be able to find my way around. Huge banners across the road showing pictures of clergymen seemed out of place. Most stores displayed black flags with Arabic prayers written on them. The few cars we passed seemed beat-up and in need of repair and I saw no sign of the fancy sedans or even yellow taxis. It felt creepy to find my town so unfamiliar.

I slid one arm behind Pedar. "How *are* you?"

"*Ay,*" he exhaled his sorrow and stared into the dark without a word. We passed a few more streets before he spoke, still facing the window. "The last thing I imagined was for that fine woman to go before I would." His breathing sounded painful. "Where she got her strength from, I'll never know." He rocked gently, as if to calm himself. "That crippled leg of hers never slowed her down. May her grave be showered with light." Then rolling his prayer beads, he whispered a few Arabic verses.

I pressed my cheek against his back.

He turned around and held me tight.

~

I woke up to Naneh's voice, "How's my girl?" My old nanny seemed busy, tying the curtain to its hook on the wall, sounding pleased to have me back in my room.

I surveyed the pink walls, the curtains with tiny daisies, my bookshelf and the Monet poster next to it. For a few sleepy seconds, I was living my old life. Naneh gave me a hearty embrace and kissed me on both cheeks, leaving spit marks as always. "My little girl is worth a hundred-thousand *tumans!*" she chanted. As a child, that amount had impressed me. Now, with the decline of the new *tuman,* I smiled at my current value of a hundred dollars.

"Everyone else has had their breakfast, but Master said not to disturb you. Mr. Kyan took the baby and said to let you sleep."

Sad at being reminded my reason for being there, I buried my head under the pillows and mumbled, "Good idea."

"Ay, Miss Roya, it's almost lunchtime. If you sleep any more, you'll be up all night." She took the pillows away and pulled a small table close to my bed. Picking up a tray from the floor, she placed it on the table within my reach.

The smell of hot bread made me realize how hungry I was. While I ate, Naneh started her report. "Everybody is here: your uncles, cousins, even a few friends." She sat on the bench by my dresser. "But this household isn't the same without that lady."

"This household isn't the same without my Reza, either," I said and thought of how people had already put his loss behind them.

Naneh gave a deep sigh. "God sure picks the finest flowers." A distant look fell on her wrinkled face, as if she could see God's garden.

"How was it, Naneh?" I asked, "I mean, how did Auntie go?"

"Like an angel," she said. "One morning, she wasn't by the samovar and when I went to her room, there she was, lying on her bed, eyes closed and with an angelic smile." She wiped her tears with a corner of her white scarf and went to get my clothes.

The next hours were no different than a funeral. People greeted me with tears and expressed their sympathy for the loss of my aunt. No one even mentioned Reza's name. When the last of the callers had left, Kyan stayed with Pedar and Naneh took Arman so I could go to the shrine.

"At least Reza is with Maman," Mitra said as she drove us, and I had a feeling her meaning went beyond the location of his burial. "Auntie's place is in the courtyard."

I followed Mitra. Pilgrims stepped over stones without paying attention that these were also graves. Mitra had no trouble finding Auntie's burial. Having been only a month since her passing, a servant sat there, guarding the flowers, platters of fruit and dates, and a candleholder. Pedar must have pulled a few strings to get that beautiful marble slab with a verse from Hafez:

"Immortal is the one whose heart comes to life with love."

It felt awkward to imagine my aunt under that slab of marble. On all my previous visits, I had never been conscious of my mother's body actually lying under the ground. I had seen Maman's name on the wall of the private chamber, but had never connected it to the grave on its floor. To her youngest child, she had remained a mysterious fairy, flying about, watching over her. But my aunt's name on the open courtyard's stone was bitter proof that her body lay underneath. Did she know we were there? Oh, how I would have loved to see her one last time.

I squatted down and said the only prayer I knew by heart, but had no doubt she didn't need my help to reach eternal peace. We bought some candles and while I lit them, Mitra paid a clergyman to recite the Quran for Auntie's soul. In my heart, she'd be my 'immortal' mother, now in a safer place, a rose for God's garden.

"I never realized her strength," I said to Mitra. "In her own gentle way, Auntie was quite the ruler, wasn't she?"

Mitra gave me a pitiful look. "Not that it was ever hard to rule *you*!" She shook her head. "Don't get me wrong. I mean this in a nice way, you *were* the lamb among us."

The lamb?

"I only obeyed out of desperation."

"No, honey. You obeyed because you never knew how to defy."

That comment reminded me of a question I had meant to ask my sister years earlier. "Speaking of defying, what did *you* do that made Pedar send you away?"

"Oh, that," she said and smiled slyly. "When he threatened that if I got involved he'd send me away, I did just that. Not only did I sign the students' petition to free political prisoners, I also marched with the demonstrators. That was enough to win me the trip abroad."

"How devious!"

"Honey, when the opposition is that strong, deception is the only way to win."

We must have sat in the courtyard for a good hour. I finally stood, feeling achy all over from crouching down on the cold stone. I glanced at the room where my mother would now guard my brother's remains and started to walk in the opposite direction.

"Aren't you going in *there*?" Mitra called after me, pointing to the corner now that it was no longer just Maman's place.

I shook my head. "Not today," I said, unsure if I wasn't a coward, making excuses. "I'll come back for that another day. I want this one to be my special visit to Auntie alone."

~

I spent most of my time helping with the preparations for a Fortieth Day memorial service for my aunt. Around four in the afternoon, women began to trickle in, leaving their shoes out in the hallway before entering. Rows of shoes of all shapes and sizes lined up against the wall brought back the distant memory of when I had counted them at my mother's funeral. How familiar this aroma of rose water, Turkish coffee, and tobacco had become. As the adult me looked back, it seemed as if that child had risen from the rubble of a destroyed castle.

I also saw the contrast between this elaborate gathering and the simplicity of the Payans' memorial ceremony. At Ali's, no *halva* had been served, no flowers were displayed and no one, not even his mother, had cried. A clergy gave a long and formal sermon, but it offered no solace. I could hardly wait for the monotonous ritual to end. Had I been away too long?

The next day, I told Kyan I was going back to the shrine. He offered to accompany me, but I needed to do this alone. Part of me wanted to feel closer to God, and part wished to sit down with Reza and say the goodbye I never had a chance for. I also wanted to pay respect to my mother. But above all, I needed to have a good cry without being patronized.

Akbar dropped me off close to the gilded gates. I bowed to the shrine out of habit, but did not kiss the gates as everyone else did. This time, there were no favors to ask for and no hope of receiving any. Now calmer, I surveyed the area. Rows and rows of pilgrims sat in the courtyard. Some prayed, others talked to each other, and a few lay by the wall and napped. The gray stones of the courtyard were covered in names, making it impossible not to step on someone's grave.

At my mother's tomb, the wooden door to the chamber was ajar. It opened with a squeak and I entered the dimly lit room we shared with another family. According to Naneh, Pedar had bought three plots. With Maman and now Reza resting there, I refused to contemplate for whom the remaining plot was saved. My eyes searched the walls. Next to the black and white portraits of strangers, I found one whose eyes were the same as my son's. The life-size photograph had captured

Reza's mischievous smile, and his neat haircut indicated he must have had it trimmed that day.

And I had thought I was over this! I barely managed to kneel before I would collapse. Only then did I realize I was not alone and saw another woman sitting in the corner, praying. My stagger must have startled the woman because she turned to look. Heavy set, she rose from the rug with some difficulty and suddenly opened her arms. "Roya-*jan*!" the husky voice cried out, the light coming through the open door illuminating her pale face.

"Shireen!" I screamed.

She bent down and we embraced for what seemed like an eternity. I put my head on her chest and cried until no tears were left in me. She held me tight, but did not cry. Finally, I let go, wiped my face, and took a good look at my old friend.

No longer the slender girl, the extra weight gave Shireen the look of an ailing, middle-aged woman. Her scarf slipped back, revealing graying hair, now cut short and uneven. Her eyes had exchanged their old sparkle for a haunted expression. It made my heart ache to realize I would not have recognized her in a crowd.

"What are you doing here?" I asked, not knowing where else to begin.

"Ah," she said, and gave me the smile I had missed so. "Waiting for you, of course."

"How did you know I'd be here today?"

"I didn't," she said. "But I would have come back tomorrow, and the next day, and as many more days as it took you to show up."

"Crazy as ever!" I said, and laughed.

She looked away. "Am I?" Her voice lacked humor. "I'm so sorry about your dear aunt." She looked around. "Which one is hers?"

"None of these," I said. "Hers is in the courtyard. I'm here for my brother." Then remembered. "And my real mom."

We both fell silent. Shireen looked at Reza's picture and forced a smile. "Your aunt was a true mother, too," she said trying to distract me.

I shrugged. "True mother, fake mother. I've lost them both, haven't I?" The truth in those words sent a cold sensation through me. Shireen's unexpected presence had helped me to see my sorrow in its actual form. Now I cried for both my mothers, and I yet had to come to terms with the loss of my brother.

Eventually, we sat against the wall with our legs stretched out over the worn rug. In such a holy place, God's eyes must have seen us as the same two girls who had snuck into the school's prayer hall.

Outside, the minaret echoed the call for prayers and a group of pilgrims chanted, *"Allah-o Akbar!"* Having crossed continents to get here, it was as though I had bypassed decades, as well.

"You're still the same," Shireen said. "I mean, older, but the same person."

"I don't know if that's all good."

"It is. I'd hate to see you change, becoming the kind of adult that Jenab cautioned us against."

I frowned. "I loathe that man!"

"How could you hate someone you don't know well enough?"

"I can't believe you still defend that slime."

"I'm just being fair," she said in her patient tone. "At least give him some credit for his wisdom."

"Never mind him. I can't believe we're both here," I said. "If you knew I was back, then why didn't you come to the house?"

"I didn't want to take a chance, or mess up your return to America." She lowered her voice. "The new SAVAMA isn't any better than SAVAK."

"Why mess up? Kyan says association with someone who had opposed the Shah would gain me points."

"No, not if she's not exactly a great fan of the new regime."

"You're not?" This was news to me. "But aren't they devout Muslims?"

"Are they?" she said looking troubled.

The stories I had heard about political prisoners were too disturbing and I had no right to stir her memory. So I told her about Arman and showed her the little picture I carried in my purse. "How is our little Behrang?" I said.

The mention of her son's name softened Shireen's expression. "He is a fine boy, and the best thing to come out of all *that*." She laughed, but seemed nervous. "I don't think Eemon and I could have been as good a set of parents as my in-laws are. He knows we're his parents, but treats us like relatives"

She mentioned Eemon's name with serenity and in a casual manner as if he were still alive.

"Behrang must be about eight, right?" I said, adding the years in my head. "Who does he look like the most?"

"No one I know." She laughed. "Thin, tall, dark and awfully handsome." Each time she laughed, the lack of joy in her voice combined with the lost look of her eyes, took me off-guard.

For a while we talked about school days, a couple of teachers who had passed away, my giving up medicine to study literature. Shireen took care not to mention my brother. Each time I looked at his picture, she would ask me an unrelated question right away. The simplicity of my life in the States seemed to surprise her the most.

"That's so hard to believe."

"But it's true. Most Americans have strong morals and live a decent life."

She laughed. "You're just saying that so I'll respect you."

I hit her with my elbow. "You never did before, so why start now?"

There was that nervous laughter again, cautioning me about the fine line in our conversation. While her voice rose and her face flushed, her eyes were unchanged, cold even. Had the tortures driven my friend insane?

Mrs. Payan's recounts were hard to forget: the tapes of Shireen's baby crying, the threats, and the possibility of other gruesome acts, even of rape. I had so many questions, but was it fair to ask them?

"I never thanked you for protecting me," I said at last. "Giving back my letters, our notes, the Phillips – "

With her eyes closed and leaning against the wall she cut me off. "You always made too much out of nothing."

"Did I?"

She changed the subject with such skill that before I realized it, we were talking about me again.

I held her hand and wondered about her middle finger, now bent out of shape as if from an old injury. The confusion in her eyes averted my questioning. One moment she showed great strength, but by the next I was sure she would fall into pieces. I prayed that my old Shireen was still somewhere inside that unrecognizable body.

Mindful of her condition, I would not pressure her, but I couldn't deny the reality that soon I'd be back on the other side of the Earth. God only knew when we might see each other again. I couldn't afford to let the moment slip away.

"Shireen, I don't know where to begin my questions. Or, if I should begin at all."

"Ask away." She sounded calm. "I'm used to questions. People ask them all the time. At least with you, I don't have to pretend."

"I don't want to bring up what's behind you, but..."

"Nothing is behind me."

"Did Jenab have anything to do with your capture?"

She glared at me. "Leave him alone. I can't believe you'd even think that!" She sounded rational, but I noticed her hands had started to shake a little. "He just knew beautiful words," Shireen said.

"Damn him and his fancy words. He was the teacher, for Heaven's sake. Did he know what he was doing?"

"He wasn't *doing* anything," she said and I could tell from the look in her eyes that she was holding back.

"I don't care what you say. I saw how he planted ideas in your head."

"That's not fair," she said, and I noticed she had gone back to her old tone: she the adult, telling me, the child.

"What are you trying to cover up, Shireen?"

"Nothing. It's just that Jenab, his son, the whole unfortunate lot of them suffered enough." She looked even sadder than before.

"So, you heard about that, too?" I said.

"The whole nation heard about that poor boy. He had only attended a couple of meetings. They took him in along with a group of street demonstrators, but he didn't have a record, so they let him go."

"That's not what I heard," I said.

She gave me a look as if to shame me. "I can imagine what you heard," she said angrily. "Jenab's son must have heard the same nonsense, that his father had made a plea bargain with SAVAK: *us* in exchange for his freedom." She shook her head in utter despair. "The week after Ecmon's assassination, Bijan Elmi went to the courthouse with a bomb taped to his chest." Her hand now shook violently.

Someone had to change the subject or we would both break down.

"I heard you taught in prison. Tell me about that."

But Shireen continued. "That didn't even make the national news. The local radio called it a random explosion. His name wasn't even mentioned, his voice was never heard."

Shireen's pallor now gave her a ghostly look.

I held on to her shoulders. "Enough of Mr. Elmi," I said, my worry bringing tears to my eyes.

"Oh, look what I've done," Shireen said, " and I'm supposed to comfort you at this time of sorrow!"

Where had Shireen learned to take blame?

She opened her purse and took out a box of cigarettes and I remembered a carton of the same brand that Mrs. Arfa' had brought to Evin prison.

"Since when are you a smoker?" I asked her.

"What's a prison good for if you can't smoke?" She took out two, lit both, and offered one to me.

A non-smoker, I held the cigarette and watched the smoke twirl. I wished Shireen could tell me her story, picking up where we had left off, without my having to push her. In another life, she would have filled in the blanks, but the fragile soul of this traumatized woman sitting before me had already endured enough. I saw the ash fall off the cigarette in my hand and waited for Shireen to talk at her own pace.

Outside, a baby cried, and the humming of a crowd told me people had gathered for group prayer.

"I used to pray," she said, as if I didn't know. "But once you've been through that damn place, you're lucky if you can still believe there's a God."

That was her first direct reference to being mistreated.

Shireen took the last drag from her cigarette and crushed it in the corner of the room. "As for teaching," she said, "the monotony of jail can drive you insane. I had to find something to do, but what else am I good for except teaching? The problem was, most prisoners at Evin were more educated than me!" She smiled sadly. "After a year, they needed more room at Evin, so they moved some of us to Qasr prison, where we had to room with what they called common criminals. There at last I found friends who also needed to learn."

"Among thieves and prostitutes?"

She glared at me. "In prison, one's perspectives change, as does the meaning of words such as respect, crime, and even decency." She closed her eyes and I tried to imagine the faces that must have appeared before her. "Some of those women had more honor than you and me. When you reach bottom, you find a whole new criteria."

She looked in my direction, her eyes glazed over and I knew she had slipped into a place I knew nothing of.

"In a way, prison felt more like home than the team-house had." She lowered her voice and explained, "That's what we called the apartment, you know."

I nodded and realized she talked more freely when I didn't ask questions.

"The house was meant for meetings." Forgetting the prison story, Shireen had now gone further back in time. "Every few months, we moved to a different building. SAVAK was everywhere. Eemon and I took care of food and supplies for the comrades. The landlord thought we were just being good neighbors." She laughed again and now it sounded normal. "Ali and Eemon never told me much. Kept me out of plans to protect me."

She sounded well rehearsed. I wasn't sure if her words were the truth, or if the lies had become her truth through repetition. Nothing she told me came close to what I had heard. According to Mitra, Shireen had not said much, not even under torture. That fit her character, as I knew it. But I wondered if in her state Shireen was even able to distinguish between reality and what her mind had designed as a ticket to freedom.

She clasped her hands behind her head and leaned back, staring at the ceiling. "At first, the walls of my cell seemed to be plain white." Her jagged laughter alarmed me. "But after many days of staring at it, I began to see patterns on the white-wash. Some of them looked like math problems."

Sitting up, she moved the palm of her hand in the air, left to right, as if tracing a formula. "It was all there, underneath the paint. And all through the lashing I thought of ways to solve those."

"You don't have to—"

"But I do." She looked at me, the untamed expression back in her eyes. "Who else will understand me? Who's left without problems of their own?" She then reached into her purse for her pills. "Twelve of these a day." She laughed her nervous laughter. "Funny, when you consider they're not sure what's wrong with me."

"I didn't mean to upset you."

"You couldn't upset me if you tried. In fact, you're the only one I feel I can talk to without being judged, or pitied. No one knows how much I've needed to say all this." She shivered more as she opened her arms. "Ask me anything you want. Anything."

Frightened, I held her. "Let's take a walk, get some fresh air. You'll feel better."

"I *am* better," she said in her reassuring tone. "Should've seen me at the hospital."

"Why were you in a hospital?"

"They thought it was serious, something I picked up in prison."

"Like what?"

"Oh, who knows?" She raised her eyebrows, acting arrogant, and smiled. "It's my heart, but something unique, all my own."

"What are you doing about it?"

"Doctors tell me I have the worst case of they-don't-know-what and are making me take shit pills." She laughed and when I didn't she added, "What do doctors know? They've recommended rest. So I rest."

I smiled at the realization that even after what she had been through, Shireen had not changed her opinion about the field of medicine.

"And, you know what?" She smiled again. "For the first time in my life I love being lazy. Who cares if the *Devotees* are still active or not?"

Her voice regained its playful tone, her color improved and when she laughed, despite the fine wrinkles, I caught a glimpse of the young girl I used to know.

"What did I just say?" she asked.

"You said if they're still active."

"Active? I guess you could call it that. But it's no longer the same. There will always be active parties. As long as there's injustice in the world, there will be crazy young minds thinking their party can fight it." She now sounded as if she had seen the world inside and out.

I had one last question we had not even come close to and now it escaped my lips. "Did you ever see Eemon again?"

When she closed her eyes again, I had a feeling she kept on doing that so she could take a good look at the pictures stored in her mind, each answer extracted from in a different file. After about a minute she whispered, "Just once."

I waited.

"Right after the trials, they gathered us all, men and women, in the meeting room: an empty space with cement floors and no windows."

She fell silent and I could hear the humming of a prayer out in the shrine.

"His hands were tied behind his back. He walked with a limp, which I thought was due to the surgery. Until I saw those feet." Her voice broke.

I swallowed hard and, despite the knot in my stomach, I wasn't sure if I had come close to understanding the depth of her pain. "You don't have to tell me more," I pleaded.

She lit another cigarette and fell silent.

I could see that empty room. Someone had told me they lashed men's feet with barbed wire. Shireen had watched her husband as he struggled to steady himself on swollen feet. Eemon stood across the room from Shireen, unable to look at her. Once the shuffling of feet and the clanking of handcuffs and chains stopped, a deadly silence set in. The prisoners lined up against the wall, all of them faceless, except for Eemon with his sunken cheeks and those kind eyes that spoke to Shireen.

"All I could hear was the blood pumping in my ears," Shireen said. When she paused, I heard that powerful sound in my own head.

"I wondered why they wanted us there. To see how we interacted, I guess. He did look at me." She took a long drag from her cigarette, inhaled, and sent the smoke out with the next words, "Only once."

"Oh, Shireen."

"In that one look he said more than I could bear to hear, the hopelessness of what was to come. He told me he remembered the good days, that he missed me, and that he worried about Behrang and I. He asked me to be strong." She did not bother to wipe her tears. "And, to forgive him."

As she rested her head against the wall, tears found their way down her neck, into her shirt. "And I looked back," she said, "to tell him that I did."

For some time, we both wept in silence.

"If time went back," I finally said, "do you think you would have done anything differently?"

"You mean, do I feel remorse?" She shook her head. "Things look different when you look back through old eyes. The best part is that we learn to forgive our mistakes."

She stopped and rested her head on her knees. For a while I thought she was so exhausted that she might fall asleep. But after a few minutes, she sat up. "Perhaps if I were young again, I'd do exactly as I had done, make the same mistakes. Only now, I see the resolution lay elsewhere. None of our passionate rage could have opened those locked doors; the key was in our teaching. It was there all along. We just didn't see it."

She reached under her scarf for a lock of hair. As she twisted it, I smiled at the fact that despite the drastic changes in her, some old habits had remained.

"As school teachers, we could have enlightened generations to come," she said and shook her head in sorrow. "For a democracy, one must first understand its meaning and that, my dear friend, requires a lot of education." She looked at me with the wisdom of a teacher.

"Martyrdom is not a beginning, it is an end. The last thing this world needs is more martyrs." She sighed. "I feel as if my life has been a whirlwind, spinning, and destroying everything in its path."

"Demolition is an essential part of good construction." I said. "Remember that law of physics you used to recite? *'One must take away from something, in order to add to another.'* That's what a whirlwind does."

She looked at me with a smile. "Well, well. We *have* grown up!"

~

If it weren't for the echo of the last *Azan* announcing the evening prayers, I think Shireen and I would have stayed there all night. The melodic chant from the Minaret brought me deep sorrow in the name of Allah. *"La elaha illalah..."*

Heartbreaking as the visit had been, I felt magically better. To know Shireen was alive and to have her by my side had eased some of my pain. I asked her to wait outside and give me a moment alone. After she had closed the door, I knelt down by my brother's grave. I wanted to talk to him, but found nothing to say. I tried to imagine him in a better place, but could not get rid of the horrible images in my head. So I turned to my mother.

"Thank you, Maman. I *did* have a good life waiting for me, and I love you more for letting me see it through." I kissed the cold stone mounted on the wall. Running my hand across the marble, I traced her name. "I hear you and Reza have another guest." The thought, peaceful as it was, brought tears to my eyes. "Take care of each other."

Outside, the gray pigeons were gathering over the gold dome for their night's rest. Shireen stood in the middle of the courtyard and extended her hand, inviting them. None came to her. She smiled at me and shrugged.

Pilgrims had formed their lines, facing the shrine in preparation for another group prayer. The sky had turned dark and I felt the weight of Mashad's gloomy sunset.

Soon we reached the street. I called a taxi and offered to share the ride.

Shireen shook her head and said she had things to do around the bazaar.

"Do you think you'll ever visit me in America?"

"America? It's at the top of my list." She laughed and that fleeting happiness made her look years younger. "I bet your doctors in America can cure my unnamable, incurable disease." The sound that came out of her throat was somewhere between a cry and a chuckle. "I hear they can make us younger, too." She smiled. "Imagine that!"

Even in the dimmed light of dusk I could see her resigned expression. I wrapped my arms around the best friend I had ever known and held her tight, and for a fleeting second wished we could stay in that moment for eternity. When I finally let go, we looked at each other, knowing this would be our last time together. My voice sounded distant and strange. "Good-bye, my Shireen."

And she smiled a crooked smile. "See you later, my friend."

~

The day I left Iran, my father insisted on coming to Tehran to see me off. Before my departure, he held me by my shoulders and said, "Promise me you won't come back when it's *my* turn."

"Pedar! What kind of talk is this?"

He tightened his grip and shook me. "Promise!"

I pushed the tears back and nodded.

"Had a talk with your good husband, too," he said, then lowered his voice to a near whisper. "This land is doomed. Stay where you are and build yourself a new life."

Perhaps that would be best. The country I had just re-visited bore no resemblance to the land I used to know and love. Regardless of the media reports or the tales told by frequent travelers, I had hung on to memories and hoped to find my home intact. But the entire trip had been a forced pilgrimage, a religious procession, and a never-ending funeral.

The last image I took with me was that of Pedar, standing among the crowd on the balcony of Mehrabad airport, waving his fedora as my plane taxied for takeoff.

~

Six months later, my father died of what his doctors believed to be complications of asthma.

"He wouldn't give up his opium, not for a day, not even when the doctor said it was killing him," Mitra reported amid sobs.

That's science for you, never giving grief its full credit.

Holding on tight to the receiver as if it would help me keep my balance, I felt silly asking, "Why would he do that?"

"He said it was the only thing that helped him to forget."

I looked out the window and into Chicago's heavy rain. Somewhere in the distance I could see Pedar across the veranda. He blew a cloud of gray smoke my way and let it slowly spread between us, dissolving his features.

For all I cared, the entire country might as well have died. With Pedar gone, the cord connecting me to the motherland was severed, leaving no magnetism to pull me back. Too old to admit it, deep down the fact that I was no longer anyone's "little girl" hurt the most.

From time to time over the years, I did dream of a return. In my dreams I saw the plane over Mount Damavand with its shades of purple and blue, its snow-covered peak. When the plane had landed and as soon as the door opened, I stood at the top of the stairs and spotted the tall figure standing on the balcony. Taking his felt hat off, he waved it at me. I ran to him, a child full of trust for the mountain of a man who forever protected her.

But I always woke up just before reaching his arms.

Epilogue

Years later, I took Arman, then fifteen, back to Iran for a visit. My signature was required on the sale documents of my father's house, and since Kyan's job would not allow him to accompany me, Arman and I decided to make a vacation out of it.

At this point, I considered Mashad nothing but a discarded oyster-shell that once had held my precious pearls. Unable to come to terms with so much loss, I hung on to the memories of our home and envisioned my family just as it had been. I would not visit Mashad and change that lovely image.

Within a week, we finalized the sale of our father's house with what must have resembled the emotions of an organ-donor. While Mitra used the remaining time to take Arman around Tehran's museums, palaces and parks, I spent my days in bookstores and libraries. Having been deprived of such literary sources, especially where it concerned Persian poetry, I tried to absorb what I could. It was in Tehran's Central library that I finally came across the poppy poem. Longer than I remembered it, the words now meant so much more. Some verses were all new to me and I wasn't sure if I had ever read them before. Their meaning and how it tied to her fate gave me goose bumps:

Rejoice oh ye thirsty, in the arid domain
Dark clouds above bring tidings of rain
See the blossoms of hope we grew in our hearts?
Times crushed their frail stems in vain!

I read the poem over and over, wondering if Shireen ever had another chance to read them later and if so, did she feel as eerie as I did about their prophecy?

For days to come, I went around town unable to get rid of the image of many poppies on the ground, their petals scattered, their stems crushed, and their blood painting every sidewalk in Tehran.

~

"How about a day trip north?" Mitra suggested a few days before our departure. "What's a visit to Iran without seeing the Caspian?"

I agreed. This would give Arman a glimpse of those plush forests and green mountains he'd never see on American television.

Two days later, we rented a car and headed north. As though visiting a friend in a foreign land, I let Mitra lead the way and show us her country.

Along the way, we stopped at a cozy teahouse for breakfast. Wooden platforms were placed at the riverbank, with Persian rugs spread over them and colorful cushions provided to lean on. Arman kept taking pictures of the clear river, shining gravel, and the pale green moss.

A young man in a shabby coat approached us. He carried a cage in one hand and a box of cards in the other. "Let the canary tell your fortune," he said.

Years ago, I had seen these trained birds. Once, the day before an exam, Shireen and I had stopped by such a man on the street and the canary had picked me a card. It read, "Your troubles will soon be over." When the man asked Shireen if she'd like to have her fortune told, she had laughed and said, "No, thank you. But if you want, I could tell you about the poor bird's destiny." Receiving great scores the next day made me a believer of the bird's divine connections, which in turn gave my friend another excuse to tease me.

I paid the man a little money and waved him away. "Shireen would know the bird's future," I said under my breath. Overcome with memories of another life, I could feel my friend's presence as if she stood there by me. I realized Shireen had never left me, not even after I heard that she had left this world. I would always remember our laughter and tears on that last good-bye. But at that moment, I was convinced that if I looked up, there she'd be. Over the gurgling sound of the river, I heard her laughter with its hint of sorrow. Unable to resist the temptation, I turned and looked, but all I saw was the willow under whose shade we sat, the branch closest to me bobbing, as if to nod.

On the way back, we drove faster to beat the evening rush. The bright sunlight had become milder in preparation for sunset. Mountains reflected all shades of green, and the river parallel to the road assumed orange shades of the darkening sky.

"Do you ever see Behrang?" I asked Mitra, trying to sound calm. I had avoided talking about my friend this entire time, so I added, "Shireen's son."

"I know who you mean. I've seen him here and there. He's a professional photographer." She smiled. "I've seen his exhibits, and he's quite remarkable."

Remarkable! Shireen would have loved to hear that.

Sitting in front, Arman continued to click his camera. He would need pictures to remember this, unlike me, the living camera, holding millions of pictures inside.

The driver glanced in his mirror. "Ladies, don't miss that sunset," he said, and nodded to the view behind.

Mitra and I both turned to look out the back window. In the distance, a copper sun made its way into the heart of the purple mountains. Rice patties reflected the darkening sky in their standing water.

As Arman aimed for a last picture, the driver slowed the car down to a near stop.

That was when I saw it: One bright red dot among all the roadside green. With the light now fading and the car taking us farther away, I wasn't sure of what I had seen. This was deep into the summer. There were no poppies left, just as there could never be another Shireen. That was a fact I had to accept.

Then again, stranger things had happened. In a world full of mysteries and divine connections, and as long as one could dream, anything was possible. Anything. Even the endurance of a single, fragile, red poppy.

A Note About Poetry

Iranians' love of poetry develops throughout childhood; it begins with the poetic lullabies and verses sung to us in our youth and evolves in the classroom, where memorizing poems is mandatory. Therefore, poetry is a common denominator for us, an integral part of our culture. In conversation, all Iranians make poetic references, even the illiterate.

This novel begins in the setting of a literature classroom. As such, the references throughout the story to existing poetry are intended as a commentary on its uniquely powerful role in Iranian life and as a reference point for the passions budding within the central characters of this tale. I would like to take a moment to raise your awareness of the poets who have touched my life as well as the destiny of our heroines. Here are the names of a few masters whose beautiful poetry enhances the emotions in this story. Please know that all descriptions, analysis, or translations into English are mine; any mistakes are my fault alone. Only those who have attempted to translate – literally or critically – the magnificence of Persian poetry into another language would know what a challenging task this is.

≈

It is with gratitude that I acknowledge the following poems in the order they are mentioned in my novel:

Manouchehr Neyestani: "Coins In The Fountain", *sekkeh-ha dar cheshmeh*. Courtesy of Mana Neyestani.

Sohrab Sepehri: "The Lagoon", *Mordab*.

Rumi: "One Heart", *Hamdeli*.

Massih Kashi: Untitled – in reference to "Portals of Being", *Darvazeh hasti*.

Hakim Nezami: From *Makhzan al Asrar*.

Hamid Mosaddegh: "Blue, Gray, Black", *Abee, khakestari, siah*.

Hafez: Untitled, *ghazal*.

CPSIA information can be obtained at www.ICGtesting.com
Printed in the USA
LVOW070912301011

252693LV00002B/3/P